'Our paths ... ... they?'

'There is such a lot going on. It is not so very strange.'

'Of course it is not strange,' he said impatiently. 'You have been warned against me.' He gave her a challenging look which annoyed Olivia all the more because she did find him dangerously attractive.

'No,' she said, staring him straight in the eye. 'I was not warned against you, Mr Brooke. I was simply told about you. That was quite enough.'

Dear Reader

Welcome back to both Sheila Bishop and Helen Dickson! FAIR GAME is an interesting exploration of how lives can be seriously ruffled, and obvious to all, in a small seaside community, while MASTER OF TAMASEE takes us from London to Charleston in America, where we see the early beginnings of the move against the slave trade which led later to the American Civil War. The love stories twined into these themes should delight you. Enjoy!

The Editor

Sheila Bishop was born in London, but spent a wandering childhood while her father was in the regular army. Later she returned to England, and worked as a shorthand typist with the Foreign Office. During the war she did secretarial and welfare work with the British Red Cross Society, spending time in North Africa and Italy, where she met her husband. They live in Bath, and have one daughter.

Recent titles by the same author:

A MARRIAGE MADE ON EARTH

FAIR GAME

Sheila Bishop

*First published in Great Britain 1992
by Mills & Boon Limited*

© Sheila Bishop 1992

*Australian copyright 1992
Philippine copyright 1992
This edition 1992*

ISBN 0 263 77888 6

*Masquerade is a trademark published by
Mills & Boon Limited, Eton House,
18–24 Paradise Road, Richmond, Surrey, TW9 1SR.*

*Set in 10 on 12 pt Linotron Times
04-9210-72805*

*Typeset in Great Britain by Centracet, Cambridge
Made and printed in Great Britain*

CHAPTER ONE

A GOOD many people had told Olivia Fenimore that she ought not to go about the country unaccompanied, even if she was travelling post. A young unmarried woman, if she had no convenient father or brother to escort her, should seek the protection of an older lady or, failing this, could satisfy propriety by taking with her a respectable maid.

'I haven't got a maid at present, respectable or otherwise,' Olivia had cheerfully told her critics. 'My dear Katy Murphy flatly refused to cross the Irish sea with me. Not that I ever thought of her as a guardian. And if I could move about safely in wild, rebellious Ireland, surely I shall come to no harm in this law-abiding kingdom.'

Olivia herself came from a line of impecunious Suffolk gentry, but she had lived in the neighbourhood of Dublin long enough to feel herself a little Irish, and was apt to consider the English rather stuffy.

Of course the long journey from London had passed without incident. She had been perfectly comfortable, even spending the night at a posting inn, with a private parlour and an attentive chambermaid. Now she was nearing the end of her journey, about to change carriages for the very last time on the final stage of her drive to Parmouth.

The post-chaise was jingling into Brantisford, yet another grey West Country town, drawing into yet another inn yard, very like all the Red Lions, Green

Men, White Stags and other heraldic houses where she
had stopped on her way.

The chaise came to a halt, and the two postillions
were out of their saddles in a matter of seconds, each
releasing his own pair of horses from the shafts and
leading them away towards the stables. Olivia had
begun to collect her small pieces of baggage. She would
have to change into a different chaise with a fresh
team. The constant transfer of all her small belongings
was the most tiresome part of the journey. A servant
from the inn came out to open her door. His offer of
refreshment was drowned by the clatter of one more
new arrival swinging into the yard at top speed. This
was a very dashing curricle drawn by four steaming
horses and driven by a man in a green cut-away coat
and top boots and a tall hat tilted over a patrician
profile, and an air of commanding assurance.

'Why, Master Tom!' exclaimed the inn servant,
turning away from Olivia's carriage to gape at the
gentleman in the curricle. 'So you've come back to us
once more. What can I do for you, sir?'

'You can draw me a pint of home-brewed, Jos, while
they put the horses to. I've got the devil of a thirst,'
said the man in the green coat.

And Jos, apparently forgetting Olivia, trotted obediently back into the inn. She was left seething with
indignation, stranded in the horseless chaise, while
various minions converged on the curricle.

What was she supposed to do? Stand in the window
and shout 'Help'? The wretched Jos had not even
lowered the steps for her to get out. This added to her
annoyance but it was not going to prevent her marching
into the inn and making her presence felt. Some women
might need to beg for male assistance; she simply

wanted her rights. Firmly grasping her yellow muslin skirt and raising it a little above her ankles, she leant on the open door of the carriage and jumped neatly down. Her fashionable skirt was so narrow that she was obliged to land with her feet very close together and nearly lost her balance, but she was a graceful girl, used to riding and walking a great deal, and she made a quick recovery.

'Bravo,' said an amused voice. 'Very few females know how to get out of a carriage. I never saw a prettier descent.'

It was the man in the green coat. A moment earlier, when she'd decided to jump, he had been giving instructions to his own groom and several horsey men from the stables. Now he was advancing towards her, carrying the tankard of home-brewed. Ladies did not expect to be addressed by strange men in the yard of a posting inn. Olivia gave him a freezing glance, just as she ought, but could not resist the temptation to speak her mind.

'I'm not in the habit of jumping out of carriages, sir. If you had been a little less impatient, I dare say you would not have called away the man who was on the point of helping me down.'

'Did I do that? I do beg your pardon, ma'am.'

He had taken off his hat and she got a better look at him. His chestnut-brown hair was well brushed and cut short in a Bedford crop, but still tended to curl round the edges.

This, and his very blue eyes, suggested a trace of light-hearted boyish impudence though he was probably over thirty, and powerfully built. He was eyeing Olivia with amused admiration. She was nettled by the amusement. The admiration she took for granted. She was not vain, but at twenty-two she could hardly help knowing the effect she had on most of the men she met.

She was a tall girl with dark eyes and dark hair and her skin had a vivid warm colouring. Her very unusual black eyebrows looked as though they had been smoothed on with two rapid strokes of an artist's brush.

The travellers studied each other for a brief moment before they were interrupted by the innkeeper, full of apologies. He knew Mr Tom Brooke had been driving four-in-hand and expected to end his journey to Parmouth in the same manner, but it wasn't possible. He would have to make do with a pair. There wasn't another sound horse in the place.

'Then it can't be helped,' said Mr Brooke philosophically.

'And as for the young lady, it's sorry I am to say so, miss, but you'll have to wait till my jobbing chaise gets back from taking old Mrs Preece to pay a morning call. The horses will be fresh enough, they weren't going far. I dare say you'd care to step into the parlour, miss, and take some refreshment.'

There was often a shortage of post-horses in small, isolated towns, and Olivia was prepared to put up with the inconvenience until a thought struck her.

'I arrived here before this gentleman. If you have only one pair, I think I am entitled to hire them.'

The landlord was plainly scandalised.

'But they are already harnessed and ready to start!'

As though this was any excuse. It was true that the curricle had been turned and two strong beasts had been strapped up with the pole between them. Olivia thought the inn servants had been far too hasty.

'I am anxious to reach Parmouth,' she said firmly, 'and I don't want to kick my heels here. . .'

'May I ask if you are travelling alone?' asked Mr Brooke.

'What is that to you, sir?'

It had just dawned on her that her cautious advisers might have been right. The innkeeper probably thought that a young woman travelling by herself to a fashionable watering place could hardly be a person of consequence, and that her needs could easily be passed over.

'I was merely thinking that if you are also bound for Parmouth,' suggested Mr Brooke, 'I should be glad to take you with me in the curricle. I know the road well and I will guarantee not to overturn you. Blackett here will give me a reference, won't you, Blackett? He knows that I am sound in wind and limb with no vices. He'll speak for my character as well as my driving.'

The innkeeper turned down his mouth and looked extremely sour that Olivia knew at once she must not accept a lift in Mr Brooke's curricle. Not that she would have done so in any case. It was enraging to think that Brooke as well as Blackett saw her as the kind of girl who might be persuaded to drive off with a complete stranger.

She said primly that she preferred to travel in a closed carriage, which was quite untrue.

'Then there's nothing for it,' said Brooke equably. 'You are entitled to the horses. First come, first served. They must be taken out of the curricle and harnessed to the post-chaise.'

Perhaps he hoped that this generosity would induce her to compromise, but he was wrong. She thanked him as a matter of course. He made her a somewhat ironical bow, and strolled away, the tankard still in his hand. Blackett was muttering to himself, clearly annoyed at having to get the horses changed from one carriage to another, but it was soon done, and Olivia was driven away on the last stage of her journey.

For about half a mile she could think only of her encounter with the man called Brooke, of the challenging note in his voice and the way he had looked her over. She could not help wondering with undue curiosity what would have happened if she had gone with him in his curricle. He would have flirted with her, that was a foregone conclusion, but would he have tried to do anything worse? And if so, how would he have managed it? His groom would have been with them in the curricle, but the servant of such a man would know better than to interfere with his master's pleasure. Had it happened, how would she have felt?

It was ridiculous and rather shocking to waste time on such imaginings. Olivia looked out of the window and studied the soft outline of rounded hills and rounded trees which were all beginning to slope downhill towards a still invisible coastline. She had never visited the West Country before.

Her father had been a soldier who had married the daughter of a wealthy East India merchant. He was stationed in Ireland when she died, leaving him with one daughter, the nine-year-old Olivia. In these circumstances Colonel Fenimore had done the most sensible thing by marrying again the following year. His second wife had been a handsome, good-natured Irish girl in her early twenties, the perfect stepmother for a lively, fearless child. As time went on Geraldine and Olivia had grown to feel more like sisters than mother and daughter. When Colonel Fenimore had himself died seven years later, they had both mourned him sincerely, and then gone on living together very happily in Ireland. Everyone had expected that Olivia would marry in her first or second Season, for she had inherited substantial fortune from her mother and she certainly had plenty of offers. Too many perhaps. She had found it more entertaining to stay single and enjoy herself.

In the end it was the widowed Geraldine who had married again. Her second husband, also a soldier, had carried her off to India six weeks ago. There was no question of their taking Olivia along with them. Two families of English relations were ready to befriend her. She had just spent a month in London with her married cousin Lizzie Wakelin and was now on her way to join the household of her uncle James Fenimore who lived with his wife and two daughters in the seaside resort of Parmouth. Here she had been offered a permanent home.

I wonder what the girls are like now? she thought. It was seven years since she had seen any of the James Fenimores, though they had always kept up a correspondence then, although she did not expect that her uncle and aunt would have altered much. Hetty and Flora must have changed out of all knowledge. Once dumpy and silent under the eye of their governess, they had now grown into young ladies of nineteen and seventeen. Hetty, she knew, was engaged to be married.

At this moment she caught her first glimpse of the sea, a glittering line like the blade of a knife across the horizon. Then a smooth blue pavement beyond the furze bushes on the hillside. Finally, as the road veered round the bulk of a small headland, she saw the whole of Parmouth spread out below her. There was a long, low sandy stretch of coastline, with a cluster of ancient stone buildings at the eastern end where the river Parr ran out into the sea. The enlarged village—now a small town—was situated on the open, gently rising ground behind the beach. Seen from above there was a neat display of small streets and all around, in leafy gardens, were groups of airy modern *cottages ornés* and summer lodges, facing south across the English Channel.

The postboy, being local, had no difficulty in finding the right house. There was a wide stretch of turf, smooth as a lawn, at the centre of the grand design overlooking the sea, and behind this a very pretty row of villas, one of which was Marine Cottage.

An iron gate stood open, there was a tiny carriage sweep, and Olivia had just time to take in an elegant, foreign-looking façade of white stucco with a miniature tower at one end and a peaked roof at the other, when the front door opened and her uncle and aunt came out on to the step to greet her.

'We have been listening for the horses!' exclaimed Mrs Fenimore, a large, smiling, talkative lady. 'My dearest Olivia, how glad we all are to see you. Such a long journey for you to make all by yourself; I hope you are not quite done up. Come in, come in, and let us have a proper look at you.'

If Mr Fenimore had anything to say, his words were drowned by his wife's, but he kissed his niece affectionately and seemed pleased. Behind were the two daughters of the house. Flora, the younger, all bouncing innocence, gazed at Olivia and exclaimed, 'Why, you've hardly changed at all!' and Olivia knew immediately that, in meeting a half-forgotten cousin still unmarried at twenty-two, she had been expecting a withered old maid.

The elder girl, Hetty, was much more reserved. She was fair and decidedly pretty, but her face was too thin. As they went into the drawing-room, Olivia wished her joy and asked when the wedding was going to be.

'In less than a month,' said Mrs Fenimore, answering for her daughter. 'You are just in time to join in the preparations.'

'I shall be delighted to help as much as I can. And does Mr——?' She had forgotten the bridegroom's name. What on earth was it? Something rather silly. Paperweight? No, that couldn't be right. Makepeace, that was it. 'Does Mr Makepeace live in Parmouth?'

'Oh, no,' said Hetty. 'He has a house in Cheshire. He will not be down again until just before the wedding.'

Mr Fenimore now got a word in edgeways and asked about Olivia's journey from London.

'I should have thought Lizzie and her husband might have spared a servant to accompany you,' he commented.

Lizzie Wakelin was his own first cousin and had married a rich man.

'It was quite unnecessary, sir. And they themselves were just off to Scotland.'

Olivia did not see any point in describing her little adventure at Brantisford. Mrs Fenimore said she must be wanting to go up and see her room.

'We dine at six, my love.' She hesitated. 'There is a ball at the Assembly Rooms tonight, they are held twice a week during the season, and we generally put in an appearance, but I dare say you will not care to go out this evening. You must be tired after your journey.'

'Not in the least,' said Olivia, who was hardly ever

tired. 'I should like to come with you to the ball if I may.'

So three hours later, having unpacked, changed and dined, she entered the Parmouth Assembly Rooms with her uncle and aunt, Hetty and Flora.

This agreeable pavilion had been completed only a few years before to cater for the very large number of people who now came down to Parmouth to enjoy a summer month or two by the sea. The ballroom was crowded and the company select. A good many of the men were in uniform. Some of the women were dressed in the height of fashion, and if others were dowdy hardly anyone was at all vulgar. Apart from the summer migrants who actually owned houses in Parmouth, many other visitors rented lodgings or stayed at the two good inns.

Some families lived here all the year round. The James Fenimores had no London house or country estate. In a sense they were not so grand as the summer inhabitants and certainly not as rich, but their permanent residence gave them a kind of importance and there were many friendly greetings as they sailed up to the top of the room, where Olivia's aunt presented her to Mrs Osgood and Mrs Channing, two ladies who like herself lived in Parmouth and presided as benevolent matriarchs at the assembly balls. Mrs Channing's son was standing beside her and asked Olivia for the first dance.

He was a pleasant, stocky young man, a little younger than she was and slightly in awe of her. At first their conversation was rather stilted. They commented on the length of the set, and the band, and he was just telling her how many glass pieces there were in each of the chandeliers when they were mercifully swept into action and had to go right down the country dance performing all the figures, with no time for banal conversation.

When they came to rest once more and had time to look around, Olivia caught sight of a man who had just come into the ballroom. It was the driver of the curricle. . .

She felt her heartbeats quicken—from surprise, of course, though why she should be surprised she could not imagine. Since she'd known he was on his way to Parmouth, she might have guessed he would be taking part in all the regular entertainments of the place. The sober black and white of evening dress acted as a foil to his burnished outdoor brightness and his air of keen interest as he gazed across the room. He had not seen her yet so she was able to watch him undetected.

Young Mr Channing had started a new topic—the scenery of the Parr valley—but broke off to say, 'Why, there's Tom! I wonder when he arrived?'

'Tom?'

'Mr Brooke. Over there by the door. I wonder when he got here? It's odd I shouldn't know, considering I live in his house. But I didn't dine at home this evening. I've been out fishing all day, and we had a lobster cooked fresh for us at the Admiral Nelson before I went home to change.'

He had overcome his shyness and become far more natural. Olivia sifted out the remark which interested her most.

'Is that gentleman related to you? I suppose he must be if you live in his house.'

'No, not related. He's a very old family friend and a most generous one. My father is in very poor health, he is supposed to benefit from sea air, and Mr Brooke has a house here which he has lent us to live in as long as we choose. He is only here occasionally himself. Of course he has houses all over the place.'

They now had to start dancing again. During their return progress up the set she realised that Mr Brooke had seen and recognised her. She felt rather than saw him staring at her, for she was determined not to catch his eye, but, when it was time for Bernard Channing to take her back to her aunt, Mr Brooke placed himself firmly in their way.

Bernard hailed him with enthusiasm.

'I say, this is capital, sir! I didn't know you were coming down so soon. No one told me.'

'How very remiss of them.' Brooke was smiling at Olivia while he spoke to the boy. Then he said, 'Don't you think you should present me to your partner?'

Bernard flushed. 'Oh, I beg your pardon. Miss Fenimore, this is Mr Brooke that I was telling you about. Miss Fenimore is Flora's cousin, sir. I mean she is Mr Fenimore's niece. . .'

'Which also makes her Mrs Fenimore's niece and Hetty's cousin too,' murmured Brooke. 'I think that is reasonably clear. May I ask you for the next dance, Miss Fenimore?'

Olivia hestiated, but only for a moment. It was clear that Mr Brooke was acquainted with her uncle's family, and, however doubtful his attentions might be to a solitary young woman outside a posting inn, she was sure he knew how to behave himself in a ballroom.

Sets were just forming for a quadrille, and as he led her to a corner of the room he smiled down at her and said, 'You might just as well have come in my curricle, might you not?'

Olivia had her own ideas about this. She said calmly,

'It was kind of you to offer but I was very comfortable in my chaise.'

'I dare say. However, I was not particularly comfortable being kept waiting nearly two hours at the Golden Fleece. Kicking my heels—I think that was your elegant expression.'

'Oh, dear. Was it so long?'

'Old Mrs Preece, having got hold of a carriage, seems to have paid off all her debts of civility for the past year. Is your father older than your uncle?'

He asked this question without the slightest pause or change of manner.

'My Uncle James was the elder by three years,' she replied, rather astonished. 'Why do you want to know?'

'Well, it is a matter of etiquette, isn't it? Your cousin Hetty has always been known as Miss Fenimore in these parts, but, if you belonged to a senior branch of the family, that would now be your privilege. As it is, however, I shall have to know your Christian name in order to address you correctly.'

'My name is Olivia,' she said, diverted by these tactics.

'Oh, that is charming. And very suitable. So romantic.'

Looking at him very straight, she said, 'I am not at all romantic, Mr Brooke, and I think I should tell you that I grew up in Ireland so that by now I am immune to flattery.'

'I suppose I might have guessed at your Irish upbringing from the nimble way you jumped out of the post-chaise. I hope you don't take that for flattery, Miss Olivia.'

Really, this man is an abominable flirt, she thought, slightly relieved that the dance was now beginning.

Quadrilles had become the rage in the last few years. Circles of dancers had formed all over the ballroom, four couples in each, ready to perform a whole sequence of figures within their own sets. Tom Brooke knew the three other couples in their circle and made introductions in a natural, unaffected way. Everyone was extremely civil, though one young married woman exclaimed, 'Hetty's cousin—good heavens!' and flashed an enigmatic glance at Brooke. Olivia wondered what she meant.

The quadrille was pure pleasure. Tom Brooke was a good dancer, as she had somehow known he would be. He might look powerful and solid, but he had all the spring and vitality of a born athlete. She could not have found a better partner. She looked round once or twice for her cousins and saw Flora swinging on the arm of Bernard Channing, both grinning with delight. She could not see Hetty and thought she must be in one of the more distant sets.

When the dance was over, Olivia said she must rejoin her aunt. Brooke escorted her as a matter of course. As they approached the top of the room where the older ladies sat, Olivia was startled to see her aunt sitting forward in her chair and gazing towards them with a long accusing face, full of doom and foreboding. Hetty was sitting beside her, head drooping as she plucked at her fan.

'Good gracious, is anything the matter?' asked Olivia.

'Nothing, my dear,' said her aunt unconvincingly. 'That is to say, nothing of any consequence.'

'Good evening, ma'am,' said Brooke. He turned towards Hetty. 'May I hope for a dance with you later in the evening?'

Hetty raised her head and Olivia saw that her light grey eyes were swimming with tears.

'No, sir,' said Mrs Fenimore before Hetty could speak. 'My daughter will not dance again this evening. She has a severe headache. In fact we are going home immediately.'

This was overheard by Flora, who had just come up with Bernard, and she began to protest.

'The ball has only just started and I have promised half a dozen dances. I don't want to leave yet and I'm sure Olivia doesn't—do you, Olivia? Can't we stay with Mrs Channing?'

Olivia, feeling very much the new arrival, said she would do exactly what her aunt wished. She realised that Tom Brooke had vanished into the crowd.

Everything now became very uncomfortable. Mrs Fenimore stood up, informing various watchful ladies that Hetty suffered from the most shocking headaches; she hardly knew what she was doing, poor child. She often cried from the pain. Hetty, looking white and doleful, allowed herself to be shepherded out of the ballroom. Flora followed, looking mutinous, and Mr Fenimore had to be fetched from the card-room.

They had come to the assembly on foot. Marine Cottage was barely three minutes' walk and they could see their way through the dusk. No one spoke until they were inside the house, and then it was the silent Hetty who burst out in angry sobs.

'I don't see why I have to be treated like a prisoner. I don't care what anyone says or what *he* thinks of me either. He is cruel and wicked but I don't care. And if anyone tells Alfred, he can break our engagement and I don't care about that either. I wish I were dead.' As an afterthought she added, 'I haven't got a headache.'

'You soon will have if you go on like that,' remarked Flora.

Mr Fenimore told her sharply to hold her tongue.

Olivia knew when she was not wanted. She escaped to the privacy of her own bedroom and tried to work out on insufficient data exactly what was wrong. She had a feeling that it was partly her fault.

Presently there was a tap on her door and her aunt came in, looking exhausted and at the same time slightly raffish, because her evening turban of pink gauze had slid over one ear.

'My dear child,' she said. 'I am sorry we have neglected you so, and on your first evening. Such a horrid introduction to Parmouth. It is all most unfortunate and no concern of yours—though I cannot help wondering how you came to be dancing with *that man*. Surely Mrs Channing did not introduce him to you as a partner?'

'No, ma'am. It was her son who introduced us. I had already gathered that Mr Brooke was a particular friend of his parents, so I saw no harm in dancing with him. Should I not have done so?'

'Don't be alarmed, my love. It is not of the smallest consequence. He is accepted everywhere in Parmouth. Indeed it is natural that he should be, seeing that most of our houses were built on his land. It was just the shock of seeing you together when we did not even know he was expected. I must say I am astonished that he should arrive just now. I am sure the Channings must have told him the date of Hetty's wedding. But he is bad, thoroughly bad. His reputation with women is dreadful.'

Mrs Fenimore sank on to the bed. Olivia went to sit beside her.

'Was Hetty in love with him, Aunt?' she suggested gently.

'I am afraid she still is.' Mrs Fenimore sighed. 'It happened last summer. He made a dead set at her, singled her out at all the picnics and balls, and the poor child was completely taken in. She was only eighteen and he has a great deal of address. I warned her not to set too much store on a seaside flirtation. I implored her to be more guarded in her manner, but, short of actually locking her up, we could not prevent their meeting. In a small place like this they were in company together every day. There was an expedition to Fawley Woods. I did not go—a great deal of walking was involved and I am not very good on my feet—but I thought Hetty would be properly chaperoned. Unluckily that man got her away from the rest of the party on some excuse or other and when Mrs Preece brought her home she felt obliged to tell me Hetty had not behaved just as she ought. Hetty, mark you! Not Mr Brooke. It is always the girl who gets blamed on these occasions. But when we scolded her she was not at all ashamed of herself and said she had done nothing wrong because she said she and Tom Brooke were going to be married.'

Mrs Fenimore paused for a moment before continuing. 'We were very much surprised and not altogether easy in our minds, considering some stories we had heard. However, plenty of men have been wild in their bachelor days and reformed their way of life on marriage, and at least we thought Mr Brooke must be very much in love if he wanted to marry Hetty, a provincial girl with no fortune. We waited for him to call on your uncle but he did not come near us. After two days your uncle went to see him at the Vale. They had a dreadful

interview. Brooke denied that there was any engagement, he said he had never entertained such a possi-
bility and that the word marriage had never been
mentioned between them.'

'He called her a liar, in fact?'

'Yes, but the worst of it was that when your uncle
came home—he was in a terrible state of mortification—it turned out Brooke had been telling the truth.
He had not asked Hetty to marry him, not in so many
words, but he was so—so insinuating and talked to her
in such a way, and my poor little Hetty was so innocent,
that she took it for granted that was what he meant.
She believed that they were engaged.'

The question flashed through Olivia's mind—could
any girl be as innocent as that?

'What happened next?'

'Mr Brooke took himself off to his great house in
Northamptonshire, leaving Hetty to face the
consequences.'

What consequences? wondered Olivia. Hetty's mild
adventure at the picnic was the sort of thing that caused
gossip at the time and was soon forgotten. It was not
serious enough to ruin her reputation, unless it had led
to something much more disastrous.

'You don't mean to say that Brooke had—er—tried
to seduce her?'

'Good gracious, no!' exclaimed Mrs Fenimore,
shocked. 'And if he had, Hetty would never have
consented to anything so wicked. She was expecting to
be married. That is why she most unfortunately told
her friends they were engaged. The story was all over
Parmouth in no time at all, so of course when he went
away and nothing came of it people said many spiteful

things and those who did not consider her a shameless husband-hunter saw her as an object of ridicule.'

A girl who had tried to trap a man and failed, thought Olivia. And now Hetty had got engaged to someone else. She ventured a question about Alfred Makepeace.

'She met him last winter when I took her up to London for a little change of scene, and in the spring he came down here and stayed for a month with the sole purpose of paying his addresses. He proposed and she accepted him at once. We were delighted. Mind you, I would not claim that she is excessively in love with him, but I think he has enough love to spare, and there is nothing like an affectionate marriage to cure a broken heart. Alfred is an excellent young man with all the domestic virtues. I am sure she can learn to be happy with him—if only she can suppress her feelings for that wicked monster. The mere sight of him this evening and she forgot everything but her unlucky passion and the disappointment of last year.'

'It must have been a great shock,' said Olivia. 'Once she has had time to think, I expect she will see things in their right proportion.'

'Dear Olivia, what a sensible girl you are. I can see you are going to be a great comfort to me,' said her aunt.

Lying awake in a strange bed, Olivia did not think very highly of her own good sense. She had certainly avoided any risk of a solitary ramble with Mr Tom Brooke, but after all she was twenty-two, not eighteen, and, though she had summed him up as a dangerous philanderer, this had not prevented her liking him and enjoying his company when they met again at the ball. She had not been clever enough to perceive any sign of

the heartless cruelty with which he had treated Hetty.
At least, she thought, I was saved from making one
mistake. Thank God I did not arrive at Marine Cottage
in Tom Brooke's curricle.

CHAPTER TWO

NEXT morning everyone behaved as though nothing had happened. Mr Fenimore retired to his study after breakfast. It was raining a little, so Mrs Fenimore, Hetty and Olivia settled down with their needlework in the drawing-room while Flora practised loudly and inaccurately on the pianoforte.

Just as the weather was clearing, two callers were announced: Mrs Osgood and her daughter Madeleine, come to enquire after Hetty. They hoped she had recovered from her headache.

Spying for scandal, thought Olivia uncharitably. But perhaps she was wrong. Mrs Osgood seemed a charming woman whose good manners and good taste were reassuring—one could hardly imagine her spreading vulgar gossip. She was about forty years old and must once have been very pretty. Madeleine Osgood was a beauty, though in quite a different style. She looked rather fragile with a pale, creamy complexion and a far-away expression in her pansy-brown eyes that were as soft as velvet. Apparently she was Flora's particular friend, though they did not look to have much in common, unless it was the attraction of opposites. When the Osgoods left they took Flora with them.

'What a very pretty girl Miss Osgood is,' said Olivia after they had gone. 'There is something very unusual about her.'

'That's because she is French.'

'French? But her mother is English, surely?'

25

'Mr and Mrs Osgood are not Mado's real parents,' said Mrs Fenimore. 'They adopted her when she was eight years old. It is quite a romantic story. Her real name was Madeleine de Cressy. Her father was an *émigré* who came over here at the time of the Terror but later returned to France, when things became more settled over there, taking his English wife and baby with him. She died, poor creature, and Monsieur de Cressy was killed in one of those horrid battles—I forget which. Somehow the child was conveyed to her mother's family in England in spite of the war, but there was no one able or willing to take charge of her. So the Osgoods stepped in, though they were not related. They have no children of their own, Mr Osgood is a great deal older than his wife. They both dote on Madeleine. It is a touching story, is it not?'

'Yes, extremely.'

'Which reminds me, I must go and talk to your uncle about the carpet.'

She bustled out of the room, leaving Olivia and Hetty alone together. Olivia was still wondering what the carpet had to do with anything when Hetty spoke to her for almost the first time.

'I suppose Mama has told you how stupid I have been. She was in long enough last night.'

Olivia kept her eyes on her sewing.

'She only wanted to explain why the sudden appearance of Mr Brooke came as such a shock to you all. And to find out how we happened to be dancing together. It was an unlucky escape that the person who introduced us was Bernard Channing, who is too young and scatter-brained to foresee any possible awkwardness.'

'Yes, I see. Did he—Brooke—did he say anything about me?'

'No, nothing. He would not, you know.'

'But he knew who you were. That must be why he asked you to dance.'

Olivia was sure he had asked her for quite a different reason, but could hardly say so.

Hetty had laid down her sewing. She took off her thimble and began spinning it round on the polished lid of her work-table. Her expression had melted a little. She was a fine-looking girl in a fairly conventional English way, though Olivia could not help wondering why that wretched man had chosen to flirt with her when he might have thrown out a lure to Madeleine Osgood. But last year Madeleine was probably still in the schoolroom, and in any case Mrs Osgood looked as though she could guard her ewe lamb more efficiently than poor Aunt Hester.

Hetty said, 'Mama told me I was to take you for a walk if the weather cleared. I suppose we shall have to go.'

'Don't you want to?' Olivia was longing to get out into the fresh air and explore.

'Everyone will be staring at me,' muttered her cousin. 'Everyone who was at the ball, and they are the only people who count.'

Olivia felt sorry for the poor girl who had made herself so conspicuous in such a small, enclosed society.

'You will have to face them sooner or later. Don't you think this would be a good opportunity? For perhaps we can persuade them to stare at me instead. New arrivals are always interesting, and I have got a very dashing bonnet upstairs. Lizzie said I should never have bought it because it was vulgar.'

This actually made Hetty laugh.

'Cousin Lizzie Wakelin is dreadfully *comme il faut*, isn't she?'

She was full of admiration for the bonnet when she saw it, and for the tiny artificial bunches of oranges and lemons stitched under the brim, which only someone as dark and striking as Olivia could carry off success-fully. By now the sun was shining steadily and the broad road behind the beach made an excellent parade for the fashionable crowd. Certainly there were plenty of people who recognised Hetty, but any undue interest could easily be put down to curiosity about the newly arrived cousin. Whenever acquaintances stopped and spoke, Hetty was able to ignore references to last night by introducing Olivia, who played her part by talking and smiling a great deal.

'That old lady thinks me shockingly fast,' she remarked, after she and her bonnet had been scrutin-ised by one sharp-eyed dowager.

'Surely you don't want to be thought fast,' said Hetty.

Olivia had always considered there were many worse fates but she realised immediately that Hetty would never understand this. She simply wanted to be suc-cessful and admired in a perfectly conventional way.

At this moment they were both distracted by the sight of a gentleman who was strolling towards them, alone and clearly enjoying the scene around him as he lazily swung his silver-topped cane. Hetty gave a gasp. Olivia gripped her arm, otherwise she might very well have turned and fled.

'Come along,' she said in a low voice. 'We have got to meet and pass him. I should like to cut him dead, but I think, with so many onlookers, that would only cause more talk. Just watch me and do as I do.'

When they were only a few feet apart she saw Tom
Brooke raise his hand to take off his hat. He was
smiling. There was no doubt he was a charmer, even if
a mocking awareness of a piquant situation was the
real reason for the smile.

Perfectly grave and cool, she gazed directly at him
and bowed the very slightest acknowledgement. It was
the way she had seen her stepmother depress the
pretensions of her Dublin dentist who had tried to
become familiar one night at the theatre when he was
tipsy. She had no idea what Hetty did but it no longer
mattered. Brooke had replaced his hat and walked on
without attempting to speak to them.

The girls had reached the end of the promenade
where the small bay was enclosed on the west by a
rocky ridge that straggled far out to sea. There was a
flight of steps leading to the beach.

'Shall we go down?' suggested Hetty.

'Yes, very well.'

Olivia had caught the note of pleading. If they
returned by way of the beach they would not have to
meet Brooke again or face all those inquisitive glances.

They shuffled through the soft, dry sand above the
tidemark and started to walk along the hard, smooth
surface, clean and printless, from which the salt water
had drained away an hour ago. On their right the blue-
green sea came sparkling up towards the land. The
sound and movement were incessant yet the pattern
was ever variable. This, thought Olivia, is what makes
the sea so mesmeric—you can't predict exactly what
will happen next.

It was no use trying to share this gem of philosophy
with Hetty, who was saying, 'You must think me the
most abject fool.'

'Because you fell in love with a scoundrel? It is not at all unusual.'

'I don't blame myself for falling in love. He is—he can be—very charming. Only I was stupid enough to think he would marry me. How was I to tell he was just amusing himself? How do girls tell? Don't girls in Ireland get into scrapes?'

'Sometimes they do. But it is different over there. There are very few rich husbands going spare. Most of the gentry and even the nobility are impoverished, so the unattached young men you meet in society can seldom afford to marry, and as they tend to be extremely handsome, with silver tongues in their heads, they soon become experienced flirts. And, as everyone knows this, girls are taught to be on their guard as soon as they come out.'

'How sad for them,' said Hetty, subdued.

'Oh, most of them marry in the end. There are plenty of long engagements.'

Olivia thought it pointless to explain that her own case was exceptional. Just because there was so little money in Ireland her mother's moderate fortune had caused far more of a stir over there than it ever would in England, where there were many far greater heiresses who could put her in the shade, besides all the men of independent means who need not be on the lookout for rich wives. She had been courted by far too many hopeful admirers and she had not felt inclined to trust her future to any of them, least of all an Irish earl whose ancient title made most English dukes look like parvenus, and whose beautiful house was rapidly sinking into a bog. Of course there would be fortune-hunters in England, but most of the male population would remain indifferent. That's one thing in Brooke's favour, she thought. His proposals might be dishonour-able but at least they would not be mercenary. He seemed to have plenty of money of his own. She must stop thinking about Brooke.

She managed this fairly easily, for after that first evening they were never in his company. Mrs Fenimore and her allies had a good intelligence service and it was easy to avoid any house where he was expected. The family did not attend the next two public balls. Prep-arations still went on for the wedding, in spite of Hetty's brave speech about not caring whether Alfred broke the engagement. She had no intention of being jilted if she could help it. She was determined to go through with the marriage.

'And of course we hope it will be the answer to all her troubles, but I cannot help wondering. . .' Aunt Hester confided to Olivia. 'Ought a girl to marry when she still finds the existence of another man so disturb-ing? I don't know how to advise her for the best—even if she were willing to take advice, which at the moment she is not.'

'Perhaps it is just as well. She ought to decide for herself.'

'If only she weren't so young! Your uncle has told her that we shan't be angry if she wants to call off the wedding, and that we shall always stand by her. Hetty simply said that she must marry Makepeace because she failed to marry Brooke, and no one here can forget it. I believe her main object is to get as far away from Parmouth as she can.'

Poor Mrs Fenimore began to cry and Olivia did her best to console her. She thought that if Hetty were her daughter she would stop the marriage at all costs. At the same time she dimly perceived what it was that

Hetty was running away from: the terrible humiliation of having to stay on here after yet another fiasco. Olivia thought that she herself would prefer this to a loveless marriage, but she realised that Hetty, though romantic, was not very brave, and that she desperately needed to stand well in the eyes of her world.

By now Olivia was curious to meet Alfred Makepeace. When he arrived a few days later, she was disappointed. She had been half hoping for a young Lochinvar who would sweep Hetty out of Brooke's orbit and Brooke out of Hetty's memory. Mr Makepeace was a pleasant young man of about twenty-six, well-looking in a quiet way but without Brooke's poise and dash, being younger than that man was, less experienced, less polished. He was besottedly in love with Hetty, and this, though admirable, put him at a disadvantage, for she was able to lead him by the nose and thought poorly of him as a consequence.

Aunt Hester was on tenterhooks. Now that Alfred was here it was impossible to avoid public functions or private parties. He knew how sociable the Fenimores were and would have found any change in their habits very surprising.

Luckily Hetty had got over the first shock of Brooke's reappearance. She had just enough pride and self-preservation combined to stop her making an exhibition of herself yet again.

They attended a party given by the Osgoods at the Villa Romana, which had a favoured site on the edge of a promontory overlooking the sea. Mr Osgood was a wealthy banker, a large, solemn man very well pleased with himself and his possessions. Everything in the house bore witness to his money and to the elegance of his wife's taste, though the most prized object in it was their daughter Madeleine.

Their drawing-room was crowded, though it seemed inevitable that when Olivia and Hetty entered side by side the first person they saw was Tom Brooke. He came at once to greet them.

'Miss Fenimore—Miss Olivia——' He glanced from one to the other with his delightful deceiver's smile, and then his glance rested on Alfred Makepeace, standing just behind them. 'You must be the fortunate fellow I have to congratulate.'

Olivia was prepared, if necessary, to make the introduction, but Hetty managed this, if a little awkwardly. Alfred seemed rather flattered by Brooke's friendly interest. Apparently no one was able or willing to move.

Olivia took the initiative.

'What a ravishing view there is from this window,' she heard herself gushing. 'Mr Brooke, do come and tell me what I am looking at.'

He followed her obediently and said, 'At the moment, Miss Olivia, you are looking at a rose-bush. Don't you have them in Ireland?'

'I didn't mean that,' she said crossly, 'I was speaking of the coastline.'

He named the nearest headland and went on, without a change in his voice, 'I wondered when we should meet again. Our paths never seem to cross, do they?'

'There is such a lot going on. It is not so very strange.'

'Of course it is not strange,' he said impatiently. 'You have been warned against me.'

He gave her a challenging look which annoyed her

all the more because she did find him dangerously attractive.

'No,' she said, staring him straight in the eye, 'I was not warned against you, Mr Brooke. I was simply told about you. That was quite enough.'

She was not able to see how he took this, because they were interrupted by Mr Osgood, wanting Brooke to talk to some local grandee.

The next time she caught sight of Brooke he was again talking to Hetty and Alfred Makepeace. Alfred was listening respectfully, Hetty was watching her faithless love with an agonising expression, like a deaf person lip-reading. Olivia moved across the room to join them but was again intercepted by Mr Osgood, who did not like to see a female unattended for a single moment.

'Is there anyone you would like to meet, my dear young lady? I dare say you find the room rather warm,' he fussed. 'The servants are bringing round refreshments. May I furnish you with an ice?'

Tom Brooke caught her eye as they were both struck by the absurdity of the last phrase.

'I'll look after Miss Olivia Fenimore, my dear sir. You have so many other guests to take care of.' And then, as the banker lumbered away, 'I wonder if I can guess what you are laughing at?'

'I expect you can. I was trying to decide what sort of a room one would wish to furnish with an ice.'

'Very few in this country, I imagine. Most of them are deliciously iced already for ten months of the year. On the other hand, there might be some rooms that could be cosily furnished with a Bath bun.'

She had found someone who enjoyed talking nonsense as much as she did, a great point in his favour whatever his faults might be. They went on happily like this until he changed the subject in the disconcerting way he had, with a pause or an alteration of tone.

'You are a sensible girl. Surely you do not think that two people who spend an afternoon together at a picnic should be condemned to a lifelong union which can bring happiness to neither?'

This caught her unprepared and she could only answer lamely, 'Perhaps they should have thought of that before they went to the picnic.'

'Perhaps they did,' he said darkly, 'and came to different conclusions. I do sincerely hope your cousin will be happy. She seems to have made a most sensible choice. Dull as ditch-water, I fear, but so devoted. And so suitable.'

And this time, of course, he had not been changing the subject.

'I think those opinions are uncalled-for, sir,' she said primly. 'He is an excellent young man and very—er—very kind.'

'That's just what I meant,' said Brooke, unabashed.

She felt herself flushing with anger. What right had this arrogant Don Juan to make Hetty fall in love with him and then pretend she had been running after him for his money?

Of course it might strike cynical people as a curious coincidence that Hetty's second and more serious admirer was also possessed of a large income. But then she was a very pretty girl.

It was increasingly hot in the Osgoods' bright pale glittering drawing-room. All the windows were open and a large moth flew in and fluttered round a branch of candle-light. One of the men tried to knock it away. Madeleine Osgood cried out in protest.

'Don't kill the poor creature. It is so pretty and so frightened.'

She looked as fragile as a moth herself in her diaphanous gauze. Walter Cottle, the Rector's son, fetched a wine glass, borrowed Madeleine's fan and was able, with a good deal of patience and dexterity, to capture the moth and set it free in the garden. He was a thin, eager young man, suspected of writing poetry. Madeleine thanked him with a pretty glow of admiration.

Olivia thought this was the pleasantest episode of the evening, most of which, it seemed to her, she spent in trying to detach Tom Brooke from the engaged couple. Whenever she was occupied with anyone else she found he had drawn close to them again—in a spirit of wicked mischief; he could have no other motive. She was so concerned for her cousin, it never struck her that she herself might be the quarry he was stalking in this round-about way, having realised that every time he spoke to Hetty, Olivia would come and interfere.

Hetty noticed and as soon as they got home she said so.

'You were having a great success with Tom Brooke,' she remarked crossly.

'She was trying to draw him off,' said Flora, before Olivia had time to answer. 'It was very thoughtful of her, with you turning white and shaking like a blanc-mange every time he came near you. Even Alfred must have noticed something sooner or later, though he is such a nincompoop.'

Hetty burst into tears.

By the time Mrs Fenimore had calmed one daughter, scolded the other, and sent them both to bed, she found that her niece had disappeared. Only her husband was left in the hall, tapping the barometer and saying with satisfaction that it was set fair.

'I wish it would snow,' said his wife unreasonably, 'if it would keep the girl indoors.'

'Do you mean to tell me Hetty is still hankering after Brooke? If so, she should break her engagement at once. She is treating young Makepeace abominably.'

'It's not Hetty I'm worried about. Well, at least, I am, knowing how unhappy she has been, but I believe that the worst is over now. She assures me she wishes to marry Alfred and that meeting Mr Brooke simply makes her feel uncomfortable. And that is chiefly because she knows everyone is watching them.'

'In which case,' said Mr Fenimore, 'what have you found to worry about now, my love?'

'Olivia. I could not help wondering all the evening whether *she* is falling under the spell of that horrid rake.'

'Olivia!' he repeated. 'I should say she has far too much sense. And too much knowledge of the world. She is not to be taken in like our poor silly little Het.'

'I hope not. I know she and her stepmother moved in the Dublin Castle set and that she had a great many admirers. All the same I should feel safer if that man were not staying with the Channings. I don't know why he had to come down here and disturb us all.'

'My dear Hester, he is not staying with the Channings, as you put it. He is in his own house; it is only natural that he should spend part of the summer here.'

'I suppose so.' Mrs Fenimore sighed. Then she had a good idea. 'How would it be if we sent Olivia with Hetty and Alfred on their wedding tour, instead of

Flora? I have been a little concerned about sending Flora—she is inclined to be too critical and outspoken. I really do think Olivia would be a far more tactful companion for Hetty.'

Olivia was at that moment blowing out her bedside candle with no idea of the plans that were being made for her. She had always laughed at the idea of a newly married couple wanting a third person to share their honeymoon. But then she had always intended to marry for love or not at all. In marriages of suitability and mild affection, both bride and bridegroom might find the presence of a third party removed a certain sense of strangeness and strain.

In the meantime Alfred seemed incapable of doing anything that would bring him and Hetty closer to each other. It was somehow typical that he got a bee sting on the instep that swelled up to the size of a football, so that he had to remain in his room at the Admiral Nelson, where he was staying until the wedding, swaddled in cold compresses and running a high fever.

'It is always worse feeling ill in hot weather,' said Olivia, who was sorry for Alfred.

'I call it poor-spirited to be laid low by a bee sting,' said Hetty, who was not as sorry as she ought to have been. 'At least we shall have the afternoon to ourselves. What shall we do?'

It was Sunday and they were walking home from church. Olivia looked at the sea, which shone like polished metal.

'I wish we could bathe. I used to in Ireland when I was a child. Isn't it absurd that we can never do it again until we become invalids and have to be taken out in those dreadful bathing machines and ducked by fat women with brawny arms?'

'Thank you very much, my dear cousin, I can do without that. Besides, sea-water is so sticky and the beach will be like a furnace. We should do better to go inland. Somewhere shady and cool.'

Hetty paused on the parade, twirling her parasol and gazing around her for inspiration.

'I know—we'll go to Rosamond's Bower.'

'Where is that?'

'The house up there, to the left of the chestnut trees, a little higher than the rest.'

The land behind the bay rose very gently and a great many of the charming new lodges and villas were visible in their green gardens and groves. Rosamond's Bower looked larger than most and was one Olivia had not yet visited.

'Who lives there?'

'No one at the moment. It belongs to Lord and Lady Canfield but they are not down here this year and they don't choose to let. There is a very picturesque garden with a fountain and a pavilion and a splendid view. We have permission to go there whenever we choose. And it will be deserted on a Sunday, no gardeners working.'

Olivia was attracted by the sound of this peaceful retreat, and they were on the point of setting out, after a light luncheon, when Alfred Makepeace arrived at Marine Cottage, hobbling bravely and saying that he felt much better and that he had come to spend the afternoon with his intended. Hetty was not very pleased to see him.

'We were just going out.'

'Don't let me prevent you,' said Alfred with a hangdog look. 'I would come with you, only I had better not walk very far on this foot. I can just sit in the garden until you return.'

'Nonsense!' said Mrs Fenimore firmly. 'Of course Hetty is not going anywhere now you are here.'

And even Hetty, self-centred as she was, knew that she could not abandon Alfred to sit in solitude five days before their wedding.

CHAPTER THREE

THERE was no reason why Olivia should give up her walk. Hetty had already explained exactly how to get to Rosamond's Bower, so she set off alone. Flora was spending the afternoon at the Osgoods'. It was a burning-hot day without a breach of air and the walk uphill seemed steeper than she expected. She hoped the delicious garden at the end of it would be a reward. She had her back to the sea. On her left, a little ahead of her, stood a miniature Gothic castle with pointed windows and a crenellated skyline, though as it was all sparkling white it was delightfully frivolous and not at all gloomy. This was the Vale, so called because it had views in two directions: out to sea, like all the houses in Parmouth, but also inland to the valley of the Parr. Olivia had never been inside the gate, for, although the Channings lived here and were particular friends of her family, the real owner was Tom Brooke, and while he was in Parmouth the Fenimores were keeping away.

She would have been interested to know that Mrs Channing was lamenting the fact at this very moment as she sat in the library at the Vale, gently scolding Brooke who was gazing out of the window.

'It is all very well for everyone to say that poor Hetty Fenimore brought all her troubles on herself, but if you had not encouraged her to flirt with you——'

'That is unjust. I never encouraged her. Quite contrary.'

'Well, you did not actively discourage her,' Mrs

41

Channing pointed out. 'And before you say that she should not have behaved so imprudently, please remember that she is very young and I think she hardly understood the situation in which she had placed herself.'

'Oh? And I suppose she didn't understand what she was doing when she got me to herself at that confounded picnic by pretending to have a stone in her shoe——?' Tom Brooke broke off abruptly. 'Damn it, I shouldn't have said that! It's the kind of story one should never pass on. At least I had the grace to keep it from her father when he came to ask me my intentions. Driven to it by his wife and daughter, poor devil, and horribly embarrassed. So please forget what I said just now about the picnic, Martha.'

'Of course. . .'

Martha Channing was not altogether surprised by Hetty's pathetic little ruse, but said in extenuation that a young girl in love for the first time was often very foolish.

'And now she has fallen in love for the second time, rather more successfully, having got her hand in,' said Brooke cynically. 'I gather the young man is very well off.'

'Yes, and it is inevitable that he should be. Hetty was bound to marry a man with money or not at all, for she has nothing of her own. I believe she will get a thousand pounds when her father dies, and that is all. I hope you don't despise her on that account also.'

'No, of course not,' he said quickly. 'What an arrogant brute you must take me for. I wonder you can put up with me.'

This threw her into a state of confusion. She could not approve of his attitude towards women. He had got the reputation of a rake in his early twenties, though she believed he had never broken the unwritten law which said that a gentleman must not seduce an unmarried girl. Yet he had no scruples about flirting with any of these girls who would give him the chance and showed no sign of forming a serious attachment and settling down. Yet she was hardly in a position to criticise any defects in his character, for as a friend he was amazingly generous. The Channing family owed him everything. Captain Channing was a victim of the war at sea. His health ruined, his career ended, he and his wife had very little money and five children. Tom had installed them at the Vale, kept the house running almost entirely for their benefit, besides helping with the boys' education. How could she criticise him?

While she was floundering through expressions of gratitude, Tom was still looking out of the window. He caught sight of a solitary figure on the road some way off, and picked up the telescope which was always kept there for anyone who wanted to watch out for ships at sea. He turned the glass on a much closer object and a tiny circular picture came swimming up to his eye like a painted miniature endowed with movement. He recognised the slim dark girl in the white dress and the straw hat tied on with a scarf, milkmaid fashion. She walked with a jaunty freedom, smiling and thinking herself alone.

Tom Brooke put down the telescope.

'It's time I took some exercise,' he said, interrupting Martha Channing's monologue.

She thought she understood—he could never bear to be thanked.

Olivia went on up the hill, happily oblivious. She reached the gate of Rosamond's Bower and wondered

whether she really had any right to go in without her
cousins. She supposed there could be no objection
since the family was away, but decided not to approach
the house, and instead followed a winding path that
climbed and twisted through a densely planted shrubbery. Some of the bushes were in flower, a few
aromatically scented, all at this season were thick and
green. That was how she came unexpectedly on the
fountain.

There was a white marble basin, and rising out of it
an arresting group of mermaids, dolphins, sea-horses
and other fishy symbols which had nothing much to do
with the medieval world of Henry II and fair
Rosamond, but was very pleasing all the same. The
fountain itself was not playing, but the shallow pool
was full of water and looked refreshingly cool on its
carpet of green lawn which was bounded on three sides
by shady bushes and trees. The fourth side had a small
marble pavilion set on a rising slope.

Olivia was charmed with her discovery. She made a
complete circuit of the basin, admiring the carved
figures and thinking it was a pity she could not enjoy
them in their full glory with the sunlight shining
through the misty spire of water which would lift above
them and slide back into the pool, gleaming on the
shapes of polished stone. Of course the fountain would
not be turned on when the owners were away.

As she was regretting this, she noticed a small metal
spigot, hidden under the lip of the pool. Suppose she
turned the water on, just for one moment. . .? Her
fingers explored the knob of metal as she yielded to
temptation. Then there was a rush and a roar and a
shaft of water descended on her with the speed and
violence of a summer storm. She was almost knocked

off her feet, and stood gasping for two or three seconds longer, too stupid to understand what had happened or to move away from the direct play of the jet. By the time she stepped back on to dry grass, she was drenched to the skin.

The fountain, instead of leaping up into the air, was shooting sideways through the shell-shaped trumpet of one of the mermaids on to the exact spot where she had been standing.

I suppose it serves me right, she thought, taking off her straw hat and shaking about a pint of water out of the brim. I had no business meddling with that wretched waterwork. But what am I to do now? She gazed down at her soaking white dress. How was she to walk back through Parmouth in such a state? She remembered stories about shameless beauties who dampened their muslins to make them cling close to the body underneath, seductive and revealing. Well, that was one myth disproved. Wet muslin did not cling seductively, enhancing the outline of the human figure. It stuck to the skin in wrinkled bunches and flapped round the ankles, draggled and dripping like an old dishcloth. Perhaps if she took off her dress and wrung out the excessive water, the thin material would dry fairly quickly. It was a hot day and luckily she knew she had the garden to herself. She peeled off the sopping garment, squeezed out every drop she could manage, and hung it on a lilac bush while she went through the same performance with her petticoat. She then noticed that the grass under her feet was getting damp. If she left, the fountain on the lawn would soon be flooded. She must turn the water off at once, before dressing again in the clothes that were drying in the sun.

She approached the marble basin warily, avoiding the cold spear of water as best she could, though it ripped across her arms and splashed her shoulders while she was wrestling with the tap, only to find she could not make it budge. She went on struggling for some time and had just turned away, thoroughly put out and not knowing what to do next, when a voice somewhere behind her exclaimed, 'Venus rising from the waves! What an edifying vision.'

Olivia stopped dead. She realised three things simultaneously. That the voice belonged to Tom Brooke. That, being on the far side of the fountain, he could see no more than the upper part of her back through a shimmer of spray. That his footsteps were coming towards her and he would soon see a great deal more. She took a flying leap into the shrubbery and remained there behind a curtain of leaves.

Brooke advanced on the fountain, though not to the place where she had turned the water on. He walked round the other side, where there must be some mechanism he knew about already, for a moment later the gush of water ceased and there was a blessed silence.

'That is one of George Canfield's more exuberant jokes,' he remarked. 'Not everyone appreciates his kind of humour. Do come and talk to me, Miss Olivia. I am going to sit in the pavilion and we will turn on the fountain to play properly as it ought. I am sure you will like to see it.'

'Not today, thank you, Mr Brooke. I shall be leaving very soon. I—I had no idea I should meet anyone else in the garden.'

'What a pity. I don't often find such charming

company on my visits to Rosamond's Bower. And I certainly don't wish to drive you away. Surely there is no need for you to lurk in the bushes. I can't believe you are afraid of me. Or is it your rigid sense of propriety that makes it impossible for us to hold a rational conversation because we are here alone?'

Olivia bit her lip. When he had startled her with his first remark about Venus, she had fled in dismay because she was undressed to her shift. She thought he must be aware of this. But suppose he had seen so little of her through the stream of water that he had failed to grasp the situation? In which case her retreat into the shrubbery must seem excessively missish and coy. She wished she could see him. She felt his expression would give away more than his voice, but she dared not leave the protection of the heavy green branches that hid her from view. It was natural that he should have come to her rescue in turning off the fountain, and equally natural, being Tom Brooke, that he was hoping for some lively conversation. In the ordinary way she would have joined him; she was not in the least afraid of him. It was so awkward—she would have to tell him something, make some excuse.

'Could I join you a little later, Mr Brooke?' she began. 'In some other part of the garden. Perhaps you would show me round?'

'It's such a very hot day,' he objected. 'I think I should rather stay here and admire the prospect before me. You must do as you choose.'

That's just what I can't do, she thought. Bother the man, why can't he go away and leave me in peace? How am I to get dressed if he insists on staying here and staring at the fountain, which he must have seen often enough before? And it isn't even playing. Then another thought struck her like a jet of cold water. She could not see Brooke and she was sure he could not see her, but included in the propect before him were her dress and petticoat hanging out to dry.

Of course he knew what she was wearing—or not wearing—and that she could not retrieve her outer garments without coming into the open and letting him see her in her shift. What a monster the man was. Any gentleman would have gone away immediately, but Tom Brooke was incapable of behaving like a gentleman. She heard movements and cautiously parted two of the branches in front of her. He was walking towards the small pavilion. He went inside and she heard the creak of a basket chair. ·

She could no longer see him now that he was out of the sun, but she heard him say in a most soulful manner, 'What a delightful spot this is. One is reminded of the Garden of Eden.'

I could kill him, thought Olivia. Garden of Eden indeed. She shifted uncomfortably in her hiding-place, brushing against a cluster of berries and spines that pricked her bare skin. How long would she have to remain a prisoner in this place of deep shadows where the sun did not penetrate? She was beginning to shiver after her unexpected cold bath, though she knew this was partly due to apprehension. In Ireland she had sometimes been in situations that high-minded females would consider shocking, but never in a fix like this. She supposed she was lucky that the lecherous brute was not chasing her through the undergrowth, though in a curious way what he was doing seemed almost worse: proposing to wait there until she was forced to come out and fetch her clothes, so that he could humiliate her by observing her unprotected body like a sultan inspecting a concubine.

Well, I won't do it, she thought, furious and disgusted. Though she had known Brooke was a rake, she had been secretly entertained by his impudence and his charm. She had not imagined him a degenerate who spied on naked women. Or perhaps he simply wanted to humiliate her in another way. He might be prepared to leave if she pleaded and begged him to do so. I won't give him that satisfaction either, she decided. I'll stay where I am and we'll see who tires of waiting first. A brave resolution, though Brooke had the advantage of sitting comfortably in the pavilion. It was not at all comfortable in the shrubbery and there was nowhere she could sit, for the ground was rough and gritty and covered with dry twigs. She had never realised how many things in nature were apt to scratch and prickle.

All this time she had been looking through her tiny gap between the branches, and although she could not see into the darkness of the pavilion she would certainly have been able to see her persecutor come out on to the grass beyond the fountain. He had not come, though he had given up taunting her. They seemed to have reached an impasse.

The next seven or eight minutes passed like a hundred years, and Olivia was feeling more and more dejected, when she heard a voice quite close to her, not a masculine voice but one belonging to an elderly, breathless countrywoman.

'Miss! Where are you, miss? There's no need to be afeared, for I've come to take you up to the house. Mr Brooke said you'd got yourself soaking wet with that dratted water-pipe of his lordship's. And here's your pretty dress all mussed up on a bush—well, I never did!'

The speaker now came into view—a small plump woman in a large apron carrying a bundle of white garments.

'Thank goodness you've come,' said Olivia. 'Let me have my clothes. Bring them to me here, if you please. I can't come into the open.'

'Here you are, miss,' said the obliging person in the apron. 'It's natural you should want to stay hid till you put them on. Not that there's anyone here to see.'

Scrambling into her petticoat, Olivia muttered, 'Mr Brooke is in the pavilion.'

'In the pavilion, miss? Not he!' said the woman in astonishment. 'Why, how could he be? Seeing he came up to my kitchen just now to ask me to come down here and find you. "For the young lady has turned the water-pipe on herself by mistake," says he. "Do you go and see to her, Mrs Bird." That's my name, miss. My good man and I are the caretakers.'

'But Mr Brooke went into the pavilion and never came out. I should have seen him.'

'He'll have gone through the door at the back,' said Mrs Bird placidly.

The door at the back! She had never thought there could be such a door. Garden buildings seldom had more than one entrance. This pavilion was probably larger than it looked. The point was that Brooke had behaved exactly as a gentleman ought. Having turned off the fountain, he had gone away at once, leaving Olivia in privacy and sending the only woman on the premises to her aid.

Yes, but while doing so he had made her think that he was going to stay in the pavilion with his eyes fixed on the shrubbery. He had done this deliberately to make her uncomfortable and if possible frighten her. He might not be quite the decadent libertine she had conjured up for herself, but her usually strong sense of humour had failed and she found she disliked him even more.

The caretaker was burbling on.

'If you come up to the house, miss, I'll make you a cup of tea, and you can wrap yourself in a shawl and sit by my fire while I go over the dress with a hot iron. It's not fit you should wear it as it is.'

Olivia declined the tea, the shawl and the hot iron. Her one idea was to escape from Rosamond's Bower as quickly as possible. It was true that her clothes were still damp and the dress extremely creased, but she hoped she could hurry back to Marine Cottage through the somnolent Sunday heat without meeting anyone she knew.

She thanked Mrs Bird gratefully for coming to her rescue and set off down the hill carrying her limp straw hat, which was quite unwearable.

She took it for granted that the unspeakable Brooke was somewhere in the house or garden behind her, so she felt a surge of relief when she came in sight of the gate. She was just about to pass through when a shadow moved among the trees, and he stood in front of her, barring her way. Olivia came to a standstill.

'Well met!' he said, smiling broadly. 'Shall we take that stroll you suggested? I dare say you don't feel as shy as you did up there by the fountain.'

'Will you please get out of my way?' she said coldly.

'Come, my dear, you know you don't mean that. Are you annoyed because I teased you a little just now? You did ask for it, you know.'

'Mr Brooke, I may have put myself in the wrong by trying to turn on the fountain, which I know I had no right to meddle with. It was an impertinence on my part, but I see no reason why you should take advantage of my embarrassment to treat me with familiarity and contempt. I don't think I deserved that.'

'Oh, I'm not talking about your mishap with the fountain. Anyone might have had the same impulse to turn it on. But what were you doing in the grounds of Rosamond's Bower? You are not acquainted with Lord and Lady Canfield, I think? Just so. And you are not the kind of young woman who trespasses in the grounds of perfect strangers. You came because you know that your uncle's family are welcome to come here whenever they choose, and if they told you as much I am sure they also told you that I keep an eye on the place when the Canfields are away, and that I come here frequently, especially on Sundays when the garden is deserted.'

Olivia was about to protest indignantly that she had known nothing about his visits to Rosamond's Bower. Then she had to bite back her explanation when she saw what it must mean. It was Hetty who had suggested their coming here together, though without saying that they might very likely meet Tom Brooke. It was not a lover's assignation or she would not have asked Olivia to come with her. The poor silly girl, five days before her wedding, was simply craving for a sight of Brooke and a few words with him in the presence of a third person because she had nothing more to hope for. No girl ought to be so abject, so lacking in pride. For that very reason Olivia could not bring herself to give her away.

Misunderstanding her silent discomfort, Brooke gave her a long cool stare, his blue eyes scornful.

'I am getting heartily sick of young ladies who enjoy contriving little adventures for themselves and then get into scrapes with their families for which I am held responsible. Girls who behave as you do deserve whatever fate befalls them.'

And, before she guessed what he meant to do, he reached out and caught her by the shoulders, pulling her into his arms and kissing her hard on the mouth with the ruthless skill of an expert. She tried to struggle but he was much too strong for her. When he lifted his head he was laughing again.

'There!' he said in triumph. 'That's what you wanted, isn't it, my dear? And much more of the same. Be honest and say so.'

'No, it is not!' she flashed at him furiously.

Confused and dizzy from her sense of outrage, she raised her hand and struck him across the cheek.

He let go of her with a speed that was almost comic and stepped back. They stared at each other. He had gone suddenly white, so that the mark of her hand showed up in a red streak. She was wearing a ring that had belonged to her mother, and because it was loose the diamond had slipped round to the inside of her finger and broken the skin over his cheekbone. A drop of blood had risen to the surface. She saw it with a horrified incredulity at what she had done.

'You harpy,' said Brooke in a low, menacing voice. 'I'll make you sorry you did that.'

This melodramatic threat immediately crushed her first impulse of regret.

'No, you won't,' she retorted, 'for I shall never willingly see or speak to you again.'

CHAPTER FOUR

THE wedding passed off without a hitch, much to Aunt Hester's relief, and afterwards the bride and bride-groom, accompanied by Olivia, set off for a house some miles inland which had been lent by some old family friends for the first few days of the honeymoon.

Olivia had originally agreed to go along as Hetty's confidential companion only because she thought this might reassure Aunt Hester. But virtue was being rewarded, for now she was thankful to escape from Parmouth. They were to be away a month, and when she returned she hoped Tom Brooke might have left the Vale.

They were all rather silent and nervous the first evening; there was certainly no sign of jubilation. Olivia was almost as nervous as the bridal couple, for she had not the slightest idea what she would do if Hetty went into a fit of strong hysterics or announced that she had made a terrible mistake. However there were no signs and no confidences.

Hetty and Alfred retired for the night and when they appeared next morning it was impossible to tell from their muted expressions how they had got on. It was, of course, even more impossible to ask.

Two days passed. A mood of boredom and apathy filled the large cold house and the only sound, Olivia thought, was her own voice uttering interminable plat-itudes as though she were talking to herself.

It was a great relief on Monday to set out on the tour

that was to take them up as far as Bristol and then northwards through all the counties on the Welsh border until they reached Alfred's home in Cheshire. They would be shut up in a carriage for hours on end, but at least there would be changes of scenery and places to visit and talk about.

Certainly everyone seemed more cheerful at breakfast and Hetty even went so far as to say that there was a village quite close called Maygrove which she would very much like to visit.

'I don't think it's on our direct route,' said Alfred, consulting his map and his traveller's guide, 'but I'm sure we can find it. What is it you hope to see there?'

'I believe it is very picturesque. The name is pretty, don't you think? And there is a beautiful old Church which Olivia particularly wants to look round. Don't you, Olivia?'

'Yes, indeed,' said Olivia with enthusiasm. She had never heard of the place but was keen to encourage any signs of interest from Hetty.

They set out in the handsome new barouche and behind them came a second chaise in which Alfred's servant and Hetty's maid were following with the baggage.

They took longer than they expected finding Maygrove, which was very much tucked away on a side-road, but it was a fine morning and they were all on their best behaviour, determined to be pleased with everything. At last they reached the sunny, silent village and drew up outside a modest inn which had an air of decent prosperity and a tidy garden, so Alfred went to order a light luncheon and then they set out on foot to explore.

'Did you notice the fine old house on our left?' said Hetty. 'I should like to have a closer look at that.'

They walked back about a hundred yards along the way they had come, and stopped to gaze between a pair of wrought-iron gates at a grey stone house, not very large but richly decorated, with mullion windows set in carved oriels. A high wall enclosed the house and a small piece of land which apparently contained nothing but grass and trees. The grass had been cut, but the trees straggled and needed thinning and there were little tufts of green on the short drive, suggesting that it was not much used. There was not a soul in sight.

'Elizabethan, I should think,' said Alfred. 'Or possibly Jacobean, and I dare say there are some fine rooms, though I should not care to be so shut in myself.'

'It's very quiet, isn't it?' remarked Hetty. 'Perhaps the house is empty.'

'There are curtains in the windows,' Olivia pointed out.

It was so quiet that they were actually talking in whispers, affected by the old house and its curious atmosphere—not of desolation but of privacy.

Then Alfred said, 'Shall we go and inspect this famous Church?'

They had passed it already in the village street, but when they went in it was a disappointment: a gaunt shell with whitewashed walls and nothing very notable about the contents. After their glimpse of the Elizabethan house Olivia had hoped for some fine tombs, but there was nothing of that kind, just a few slabs let into the floor, and the one impressive memorial dated only from the last century. It was a high-flown piece of classical extravagance with winged cherubs hovering over a weeping lady and a broken column, and a long eulogy carved on a stone scroll and setting out the virtues of John and Margaret Row who had lived at Maygrove Manor and died there in the 1760s.

Olivia dutifully read this epitaph with lukewarm attention until she came to the last few lines.

> . . .This tribute to the memory of her excellent parents was erected by their sorrowing daughter and only surviving child Margaret wife of THOMAS BROOKE ESQ OF CASSONDON HOUSE in the County of Northampton. . .

'Good heavens!' she muttered.

'What is it?' asked Alfred.

'Oh—nothing.'

She cast around for some distraction and drew his attention to an indifferent stained-glass window, the only one in the Church. But she had an idea that he too found time to read the epitaph. Hetty was sitting in one of the pews with a dreamy expression on her face.

Silly little fool, thought her cousin wrathfully. What did she mean by dragging us here? What was the point? Not an assignation, that was too fantastic to credit. Yet the connection with Tom Brooke could not be a coincidence. Olivia knew that Cassondon was the name of his family seat, a fine place somewhere in the Midlands. That Margaret was presumably his grand-mother. The beautiful Elizabethan house was undoubt-edly Maygrove Manor, and, since Margaret was her parents' only surviving child, it would have come into the Brooke family and eventually to Tom.

All this flashed through her mind while she was

apologising to Alfred for bringing him on a wild-goose chase. She must have been thinking about another Church somewhere else.

Alfred said in a toneless voice that it was of no consequence, and they all went back to the inn.

The innkeeper suggested they might care to be served out of doors. They agreed to this and Alfred went off to speak to his groom while the table was being laid.

Olivia took the opportunity of saying to Hetty, 'What induced you to bring us here? You must be mad.'

'Oh, he won't make anything of it,' said Hetty carelessly. 'Why should he? Brooke told me about the house. I always longed to see it.' And when a young maidservant came out with a dish of ham, she asked, 'Who does that big house at the end of the village belong to?'

'Why, to Mr Brooke, ma'am,' said the girl, looking nervous and surprised.

'And does he come here often?' persisted Hetty.

The maid had finished arranging the dishes on the table. She ran back into the inn without answering. There was no time to say anything more, for Alfred had reappeared, and they sat down under the shade of an old apple tree to a repast of ham and brawn, a salad of lettuce and green herbs, freshly baked bread and a bowl of plums.

One item had been forgotten and the innkeeper's wife herself brought it out to them, a porringer filled to the rim with thick creamy butter. She was an angular, fierce-looking woman, and as she put the porringer down she said to Hetty, 'I hear you was asking about Mr Brooke, ma'am. If you be friends of his, you can tell him we don't like the use he makes of his house, bringing those Jezebels here to give the village a bad name. It mazes me why Parson allows it.'

An urgent cry from the house summoned her back to her kitchen and she whisked herself off, muttering something about whores of Babylon.

'She seems very well versed in the Old Testament,' said Olivia, trying to speak lightly.

The woman reminded her of Jael, one of the most blood-thirsty characters in the Bible, who also brought butter in a lordly dish. But what she had said about Tom Brooke's use of his house had fairly put the cat among the pigeons as far as Alfred and Hetty were concerned. He began to speak and stopped. She looked as though she was going to cry.

The rest of the day's journey was very disagreeable. Once they had left the turnpike road, it seemed impossible for them to get back again, and they bumped around the country lanes, meeting wagons between the narrow banks or coming to a dead end in reeking farmyards. In the right company it would have been a mild annoyance, or even rather funny. With Alfred and Hetty sitting in a stricken silence, it was almost unbearable.

Olivia gave up trying to talk to either of them and spent the time wondering whether Brooke really kept a mistress, or, to be more exact, a succession of mistresses, in his grandmother's ancestral home. That must be what the woman at the inn had meant; she could hardly mean anything else. And, though Maygrove seemed an unlikely setting for a house of illicit pleasure, there might be points in its favour. It was not much more than fifteen miles from Parmouth, where Brooke spent a couple of months every summer. He could hardly install his current mistress at the Vale where, to do him justice, he had generously made a home for the Channings. In any case Parmouth was not like London where men could lead double lives in different parts of the city. Parmouth was small and intimate, full of well-bred, respectable people who met on an equal footing in public places and private houses. They would put up with a man's shameless flirtations, provided he did not run away with any of the married women or actually seduce the unmarried ones, but they would not expect him to introduce into their midst an actress or a notorious woman of pleasure. So if he could not exist without these luxuries, Maygrove would be conveniently situated for him while he was down here in the summer. Olivia thought such an arrangement was an insult to the beautiful old house.

They did at last regain the post road. So much of the day had now been wasted that they were glad to put up at the first small town where there was a comfortable inn. Hetty immediately went upstairs, saying she had a racking headache and was going to lie down. Olivia and Alfred were left together in the private parlour he had hired.

He demanded in a hollow voice, 'What am I going to do?'

'Give her a good shaking,' said Olivia, who was beginning to have a headache herself and felt thoroughly exasperated.

'How can I? She doesn't care for me, and if I treat her harshly she never will.'

'She'll never respect you if you don't.'

'I shouldn't have married her,' he said. 'I thought if I took her away from Parmouth she would forget that villain, recover her spirits. But I was a fool. How could I hope to replace him in her affections?'

He looked and sounded utterly dejected. Olivia studied him with a mixture of pity and irritation in which there was a strong strand of curiosity.

'How long have you been aware,' she asked cautiously, 'of the reason for—for Hetty's being in low spirits?'

'If you mean, how long have I known about Brooke, I was told of his existence almost as soon as I arrived in Parmouth in April. I first met her in Town last winter, and came to Devonshire with the sole purpose of getting to know her better. You would be surprised to learn how many there were in the place—agreeable people, self-styled friends of your family—anxious to tell me of the scrape that poor innocent girl had got into. In fact, to warn me against making her an offer. They only increased my desire to rescue her from her horrible situation and to try and make up to her for all she had suffered. She seemed quite easy in her mind when she accepted me. I felt certain I could make her happy, but I counted without Brooke's returning to spoil everything. When I came down for the wedding I saw at once how things were, but what could I do? I was prepared for her to break our engagement, but she didn't, and it wasn't for me to do so. She'd been jilted once. How could I subject her to a second humiliation? Now I begin to think I've ruined her life.'

'Nonsense! You've been treated abominably and it's time you stopped being sorry for her and told her so,' insisted Olivia.

He was startled. 'Do you think that would be wise?'

'Yes, I do.'

Up to now everyone at Marine Cottage, including Olivia herself and certainly including Hetty, had felt a faint contempt for this rather diffident young man, and it struck her that this was because he had seemed so totally unaware that his intended bride was going through a fever of unrequited love for someone else. They had thought him silly and obtuse and all the time he had been behaving like a hero of chivalry. Misguided, perhaps, but all the same heroic.

'You ought to have it out with her,' said Olivia. 'Make her see she has taken on responsibilities she can't wriggle out of. She cannot be a married woman and a spoilt baby at the same time. It's no good making allowances because she has been shabbily treated or even because you love her. You need to be firm and resolute, which, as far as I can see, no one ever has been with Hetty—that's her trouble. The one person who has refused to play her game is that selfish monster Tom Brooke, and I dare say that's why she became so besotted with him.'

Alfred gazed at her in silence, his pleasant features hardening into lines that were unexpectedly decisive. Then he got up and left the room. Olivia sat on by herself, hoping she had given him good advice. It would be dreadful if she had only made matters worse. She was afraid she had spoken her mind rather too freely because she was so cross with Hetty. She almost felt a twinge of sympathy with Brooke, who had flatly refused to be entangled into marrying such a stupid girl. And by the same token she felt angrier than ever with Hetty and others like her, who encouraged men of his kind to despise the young women who became their willing victims. And that is why he treated me so disgracefully at Rosamond's Bower, she thought. He took it for granted I was just another of the same sort. Fair game, in fact. Well, he was wrong. And she felt a small glow of satisfaction when she remembered the scratch of her diamond ring on his cheek.

After a while she wondered how Alfred was dealing with Hetty. She went upstairs and stood on the landing outside their door. She could hear Alfred's voice going on and on. When he paused, she caught the sound of Hetty weeping. He spoke again and then Hetty answered faintly. She sounded timid and conciliating, perhaps pleading for mercy. Olivia went into her own bedroom opposite, leaving the door slightly ajar and sitting down on the bed.

She now felt guilty. Aunt Hester had sent her to comfort and support Hetty during the first weeks of her marriage. What she had actually done was comfort and support Alfred, encouraging him to adopt a stern line with his errant bride. Had he perhaps taken her advice too seriously?

Presently she heard him come out of the room and walk away along the passage. She saw the back of his head and shoulders as he started down the stairs. She crossed the passage and went in to Hetty, not knowing what to expect. Her cousin was at the dressing-table, staring at herself in the glass with a kind of dumb dismay. She was white and dishevelled, her eyelids swollen from crying.

'I'm afraid you have had a difficult half-hour,' said Olivia. 'You must try to understand that Alfred has been at the end of his tether.'

'Oh, yes, I know.' Hetty was husky but she did not sound particularly cowed. 'Poor Alfred, I am so very sorry. And he has been so kind.'

'Kind?' echoed Olivia, who thought Alfred might have been too severe.

'He has explained all his own feelings and sensations

and how they have helped him to understand mine. He says he knows just how it was for me to be disappointed and rejected, and he has been so patient. I was ready to sink. He has gone to fetch a glass of wine for me because he says I need a restorative; he will be back directly.'

Olivia's relief was so intense, she was hard put to it not to laugh. How ridiculous her fears had been. Alfred had not taken her advice, he had done the exact opposite, exposing his own misery to the risk of Hetty's contempt; yet this had apparently won the trick. Men and women were most extraordinary, especially in relation to each other.

From now on the whole atmosphere of the honeymoon changed. Olivia could not pretend to herself that Hetty had fallen in love with Alfred, but she undoubtedly liked him, was growing fond of him, and was capable of sharing his interests. This was probably how she had felt when she had accepted his proposal in April, eight months after Tom Brooke had broken her heart and gone away. Now once again she was really making an effort to extinguish his memory. As time went by she and Alfred would concoct a romantic view of their marriage and how he had captured her heart in open competition with a notorious rake.

Meanwhile they all enjoyed their sightseeing, moving slowly up the western border of England and coming at last to the large, comfortable house that Alfred's grandfather had built in a rural setting just far enough from the city where he had made his money so that his son and grandson could grow up as gentlemen. It was a fine modern house, grander than anything Hetty had been used to. Marine Cottage would have fitted easily into one wing, and she was ready to be pleased with everything Alfred had to offer in the way of fine rooms, elegant furniture, heartfelt devotion and a landscaped garden that made her the envy of the neighbourhood.

Olivia stayed long enough to help her settle in and was back in Parmouth by the middle of August.

CHAPTER FIVE

OLIVIA's first duty on her return was to answer a great many questions and reassure Hetty's parents that she was leading a very pleasant life and was cheerful and contented with her lot. Presently she was able to ask for Parmouth news. The place was full of visitors, she was told, every house let. There were accounts of balls and expeditions. Madeleine Osgood figured in most of them, so did Bernard Channing. One name was not mentioned.

All the way down from Cheshire Olivia had been hoping that Tom Brooke would have left Parmouth before she returned. She did not want to meet him again, now or ever. Their last meeting had been too painful, and, as if that was not bad enough, there was the memory of the Manor House at Maygrove and what the woman had said at the inn. She did not even want to ask if Mr Brooke was still at the Vale. It would have been a perfectly natural question, considering his importance in Parmouth society; even so, she was afraid something in her manner might strike a false note. As no one spoke of him, perhaps it was safe to assume he had gone. Flora was talking now of a cricket match arranged for next day. Everyone would be there; all they needed was fine weather.

The weather was obliging, not only fine but hot. The match, an annual event, was between a group of local gentlemen and a team raised by the visitors. It was played on the wide expanse of turf which lay between the beach and the row of houses that included Marine Cottage, so the Fenimores had merely to step across the road and join the throng of spectators sitting or strolling about, some intent on the cricket, others deep in conversation. Olivia began to enjoy herself, meeting old acquaintances and making new ones. She was wearing a simple white dress, a style so fashionable that it had almost become a uniform. It particularly suited her slender height and her dark good looks. A golden aureole surrounded her head and shoulders as the sunlight penetrated her pale yellow parasol.

Out of the surrounding chatter, an occasional remark caught her attention.

'What happened to that very silly girl?' a woman's voice was asking. 'The one who was trying so hard to marry Tom last year? I don't see her anywhere.'

Olivia glanced instinctively towards her aunt and uncle but they were a little way ahead and had not heard.

She stopped behind the speaker, who was sitting on a bench facing the cricket pitch with a man on each side of her.

'Which girl do you mean, Susan?' asked one of the men. 'You know they are all trying to marry Tom, silly or otherwise.'

Olivia decided to take a look at Susan, so she stepped round to the front of the bench and was quietly inspecting the smartly dressed woman who was seated there, when the second man got to his feet and spoke to her.

'Good morning, Miss Olivia. When did you return?'

She found herself gazing straight into the eyes of Tom Brooke. She felt all the embarrassment she had been dreading, so it was pleasant to realise that he was

even more put out than she was. It was obvious that
she must have heard what his friends had been saying.
Their frivolous and faintly malicious remarks made him
out to be exactly the sort of conceited amorist she had
always taken him for, and he did not like it.

He gave them a severe glance and said, 'You have
not met Miss Olivia *Fenimore*, I think,' emphasising
her surname by way of a warning. 'May I introduce
you to Colonel and Mrs Twisden?'

Mrs Twisden said something civil, going rather pink,
and her husband got up hurriedly and bowed. Brooke
offered Olivia his seat on the bench, which she politely
refused.

'I did not mean to disturb you, sir.' She glanced
about her rather wildly and saw someone she knew in
the middle of the field. 'Isn't that Walter Cottle
batting?'

'Yes, but not for long, I fear.'

Walter had just given the ball a mighty crack. It flew
up into the air and came down in a neat parabola,
straight into the hands of the wicket-keeper.

'My turn to make an exhibition of myself,' said
Brooke in a voice of resignation.

She noticed for the first time that he was rather
strangely dressed in light, loose-fitting nankeen, his
white shirt open at the neck. She had not realised that
he was one of the cricketers. He picked up his long
thin bat with its hooked end and sauntered across the
grass in a leisurely manner. Taking his stance in front
of the wicket, he received the bowler's first onslaught
and sent the ball spinning away in the direction of the
sea.

Olivia pulled herself together and joined Flora, who
was lamenting poor Walter's mishap. They made their

way towards the end of the field and found seats in the refreshing shade of some tall chestnut trees. Brooke was hitting the ball with great precision and running between the wickets, exchanging places with Bernard Channing, the other batsman. Flora gazed at her old friend Bernard; Olivia gazed at Tom. She thought she had never seen anyone whose looks and movements held such a magnetic attraction, though she could not have said why. He was not the most handsome or graceful person she had ever seen. He was too individual, too charged with vigorous masculine energy for such smooth epithets. She had simply to watch him, fascinated, and be thankful that no one would find it odd of her to stare at him while he was the centre of interest. Though it was very odd indeed.

What a fool you are, she told herself several hours later, alone in her bedroom and getting ready for the ball which the cricketers were giving at the Assembly Rooms. What a fool to let yourself run the risk of being charmed by that man. She disliked and distrusted Tom Brooke for reasons which had nothing to do with her cousin Hetty or the sinister reputation of the house at Maygrove.

She forced herself to re-live the Sunday afternoon at Rosamond's Bower. She had managed to bury her memories of their last encounter but now these came rushing back—four different kinds of humiliation. The necessity of skulking in the bushes in her shift because she had taken off her dress to dry and Brooke was perfectly well aware of it. The infuriating discovery that she'd been frightening herself for nothing, and her paralysing weakness when he had held and kissed her against her will. The last humiliation she had brought on herself—by slapping his face with a vulgarity and violence she now found quite shocking. He'd said he would make her sorry for that, and indeed she was sorry because she had fallen below a certain standard of behaviour. Brooke must have meant something more definite, only what could he do? What further way could he find to torment her? She would much rather not have to meet him this evening, but there was no escaping the ball.

To raise her spirits, she put on a very pretty dress of cherry-coloured gauze, an exciting change from the eternal ladylike white.

As soon as they entered the Assembly Rooms, which were bursting with noise and light, she was approached by a Mr Frederick Walsh whom she had met that morning, a pleasant, quiet man who was said to be recovering from the death of his wife a year ago. He was the opposite of everything she disliked so much in the detestable Brooke.

She had seen Brooke immediately, the centre of attention and the hero of the cricket match, for the residents had won and he had made the most runs. Female voices were raised in adulation.

'Oh, Mr Brooke, how hard you hit that cricket ball. You nearly knocked my hat off, did you know? And you looked so fierce and ran so fast, I was positively trembling!'

'You'll have to avoid cricket matches in future, Miss Angelica. You know what a ferocious fellow I am.'

'Oh, Mr Brooke! You are always funning.'

Oh, Mr Brooke, Olivia thought derisively, how you despise your female admirers. Angelica Preece was one of a bevy of sisters whose affectations encouraged men to think poorly of their whole sex. While Olivia was observing the group Brooke caught her eye, and, abandoning his satellites, came over to speak to her.

'Good evening, Miss Olivia. Would you care to open the ball with me?'

No, I would not, thought Olivia, after the first moment of stupefaction. Luckily she had the presence of mind not to say so. But what was she to say?

Her feelings about him were so confused, their strong mutual attraction had been so distorted by the encounter at Rosamond's Bower, that she felt threatened by his mere proximity and she was determined not to dance with him.

Clutching at the only available straw, she said, 'I am obliged to you, Mr Brooke, but I am already promised to Mr Walsh here for the first dance.'

This was not strictly true. Though Walsh had made it plain that he wanted to dance with her, he had not specified exactly when. However, being a perfect gentleman, he offered her his arm as though to lead her on to the floor, but before he did so there was just a momentary pause of surprise which a man as acute as Brooke could not fail to understand.

'Then I must not keep you talking,' he said coldly, and walked away.

'I take it you don't wish to dance with him?' asked Fred Walsh curiously.

'I don't like being condescended to. He is so insufferably conceited. But I shouldn't have used you as my excuse. I do apologise.'

'Nonsense. You must know I am delighted. Though I don't think,' Walsh added conscientiously, 'that he was deliberately condescending.'

Olivia knew this was true. She could not explain that he had been doing something even more disagreeable:

trying to establish a physical contact which would make her even more uncomfortable by reminding her of something she wanted to forget.

The band was tuning up. Couples were spreading out across the shining floor under the chandeliers. Tom Brooke was at the place of honour at the top of the room because he was captain of the Parmouth Cricket Club who were this evening's hosts. Olivia had an unworthy feeling that she would have liked to open the ball. She crushed it down resolutely and turned her attention to Mr Walsh.

She had plenty of partners for the succession of country dances and quadrilles and saw very little of Tom Brooke, who always seemed to be in a different set. Halfway through the evening she again stood up with Mr Walsh and they went in to supper together. Afterwards there was an interval before the dancing began again, and someone suggested that Mrs Trelawney should be asked to sing.

Mrs Trelawney and her husband were regular visitors to Parmouth. She was a large, commanding woman with a beautiful voice, good enough for an opera singer. Accepting graciously as a matter of course, she sang the Countess's aria 'Dove Sono' from *The Marriage of Figaro* and followed this with Dido's Lament. Her husband then insisted that she must not tax her voice any further. When the mingled applause and disappointment died down, there were demands for other singers, but no one wanted to follow Mrs Trelawney. Two young ladies simpered and said they had no music with them. One of the men suggested that Miss Osgood would not fail them. He knew she sang charmingly.

Madeleine looked anxious and glanced at her mother.

'No,' said Mrs Osgood. Turning to Olivia, she added confidentially, 'It is too bad of them to pester a child of her age. My dear Miss Olivia, would you be kind enough to step into the breach? You are too sensible to mind if people draw comparisons. My poor little Madeleine might be put off forever.'

Which was not the most flattering way of persuading a lady to sing in public, thought Olivia, though it was typical of Mrs Osgood, who only saw other people in relation to herself and her daughter. Still, she had some sympathy with Madeleine and none at all with the older girls who would not risk performing after the extremely gifted Mrs Trelawney.

She herself was too honest about her own claims to be easily mortified, so she went forward without more ado, saying frankly that she had no music with her either, and that if anyone wished to go away before she began she would not blame them. Nobody went away.

The faithful Mr Walsh placed her chair for her at the pianoforte and then stepped back. She had already decided to give them one of Tom Moore's 'Irish Melodies', so unpretentious and unlike what had gone before. She had a good clear voice and she was used to singing to a roomful of people. She launched into one of her favourites.

A few lines in, from somewhere close behind her, a man's strong baritone joined in unexpectedly and they harmonised together in a duet. If Fred Walsh can sing like this, she thought, there must be unsuspected qualities behind his quiet exterior.

After the song had ended and the chorus of appreciation had died away, the unseen singer made the conventional apology which was usual on such occasions.

'I do beg your pardon, Miss Fenimore. It was a great impertinence.'

Olivia felt needles of ice running up and down her spine. She had not recognised the splendid baritone but the speaking voice was unmistakable. It belonged not to Frederick Walsh, but to Tom Brooke.

She turned and saw him standing just behind her and looking down at her with a rather mocking smile.

'Do forgive me,' he said. 'I can never resist the sentiments of that particular song.'

'You expressed them with great feeling,' she replied, thinking of the hours he must have stolen from so many nights with so many different companions.

She stood up, thankful that she would not be required to sing any more. The band was coming back and everyone was anxious to be dancing again.

Standing beside Brooke, she felt she would be perfectly able to dance with him now. She did not trust him any more, in spite of the warm, deceptive sincerity in his voice. She simply recognised that her panic-stricken refusal had been missish and stupid—what harm could come to her in a ballroom? She cast him a sideways glance as the music started. The mockery had hardened into something like hostility.

'You need not be afraid,' he said. 'I'm not going to ask you to waltz with me.'

For the second time that evening he walked off and left her, and this time she was entirely alone. Olivia was furious. Not since she was an awkward sixteen had she found herself in a ballroom without a partner.

In fact she was not left alone long enough to become an object of pity. She was rescued by a naval officer who said naïvely that he was in great luck, he had been trying to get near her all the evening. The ball dragged on for another two hours. She was glad when it was over.

CHAPTER SIX

DURING the next few days Olivia saw Tom Brooke only in the distance. Oddly enough, she did see the inside of his house, for now that Hetty was safely married there was no reason why the Fenimores should keep away from the Vale that was also the home of their particular friends, the Channings. Olivia really enjoyed this domestic interior more than the endless social round, which, for some reason, had begun to pall.

No one came to the Vale except old friends, on account of Captain Channing's health. He was a brave and clever man whose future had been ruined by several days spent in an open boat which had brought about a disabling chest condition. Thin as a wraith, he was condemned to sit in a chair, reading, studying and watching life go by, with all the patience he could muster. He was devotedly cared for by his wife. Bernard was their elder son. Interested in old buildings and a good draughtsman, he was hoping to train as an architect. There was a midshipman away at sea, and then three daughters aged eleven, eight and six.

Olivia and Flora often went to call on the Channings, sometimes accompanied by Madeleine Osgood. When she was there Walter Cottle from the Parsonage generally came too. He and Bernard were friends, two young men at a loose end in Parmouth without much money. Walter had done well at Oxford and was hoping to be ordained but was still too young.

One morning plans were being made for a picnic on the moor to celebrate Polly Channing's birthday. She was the middle daughter.

'I wish you could come with us, Papa,' she said, leaning against her father's chair.

'So do I, my love,' said the Captain, stroking her head as though she were a puppy. 'You will have to tell me about it afterwards. You will be quite a large party.'

'Oh, yes. Me and Fanny and Cilla and Mama. And Bernard of course, and Flora and Mado and Walter. And Miss Olivia,' added the little girl doubtfully. 'You will come, won't you, Miss Olivia?'

'I should like it above all things,' said Olivia, flattered at being included, for she was still almost a stranger to the children.

'So long as you don't mind that our picnics are not always very comfortable,' said Mrs Channing. 'You will be made to run about a great deal in the heather.'

'I shall enjoy that. How do we get up on to the moor?'

They would go in two carriages, she was told. There was an old open landau which lived in the coach-house at the Vale and which Mr Brooke allowed them to borrow. Bernard would drive this and Walter would drive his father's gig. The landau would take four persons besides the driver, if two of them were children. The gig would take Walter, one of the young ladies, and the remaining little girl.

'Then someone is going to have to walk,' remarked the Captain. 'I see no help for it. You cannot squeeze nine people into eight places.'

There were cries of dismay; they would be crowded as it was, for the baskets of food had to be got in as

well. Everyone started to count again and Olivia saw
that she was the one who would have to drop out, for
the idea of anyone's walking was not meant seriously;
they would take far too long to cover the distance.
Then a new thought struck her.

'I'll come on horseback,' she said. 'That will solve all
our problems.'

Mrs Channing was a little put out.

'Ride all that way by yourself? My dear, we could
not think of it. One of the boys, perhaps. . .'

But both the boys were required to drive the carriages, and Olivia pointed out that she could keep close
beside them all the way, and that she would be well
able to manage any horse hired from the local livery
stable. She had ridden in Ireland all her life.

So it was that four days later she collected a docile
liver chestnut hack from the stables behind the Admiral
Nelson and rode up to the Vale with Flora and
Madeleine walking beside her. The two carriages were
already being loaded with food and people. Everyone
was busy and active, children jumping up and down
with excitement, servants bringing hampers, Mrs
Channing making sure that it was Flora, not
Madeleine, who travelled in the Parsonage gig. Mrs
Osgood's daughter could not drive unchaperoned with
a young man, even in an open carriage and with a
sharp-eared little girl beside her.

There was an unexpected presence. Admirably calm
in all the commotion, Tom Brooke was mounted on a
large grey horse.

'Mr Brooke's coming with us,' Polly called out to
Olivia. 'Isn't it splendid?'

'Yes, indeed,' said Olivia insincerely.

Brooke raised his hat to her and said, 'So they've

given you that old slug. I hope you'll be able to manage him.'

She was ready to flare up when she saw he was teasing her, and smiled reluctantly.

'Hirelings are generally pretty tame. I suppose they have to be.'

'Yes, or the countryside would be strewn with casualties. But it's hard on those who do know how to ride. I'm sorry I had nothing to lend you, but none of my horses carries a side-saddle.'

The cavalcade was now starting along the road which led along the edge of the valley. Riding beside Brooke, Olivia felt obliged to say, 'I hope you were not pressed into coming on this expedition because Mrs Channing thought it would be dangerous or unsuitable for me to ride alone?'

'Well, she did think that, though I told her it was ridiculous. But don't let that trouble you. I always intended to come on this picnic. I am very much attached to all the Channings. I think we had better pass the carriages and ride in front to avoid the dust.'

Olivia felt she had been snubbed and that perhaps she deserved it. Whatever his faults, Brooke's attitude to the Channing family was beyond criticism.

It was a dull grey day, far from ideal for picnicking, and as the ground rose the view, which should have been miraculous, was disappointingly short and limited. Heavy clouds closed in, they could not see the sea. However, they had reached the edge of the moor, which had an air of romantic wildness, and there was some colour in the landscape, for at this time of year the rough rolling ground was pink with flowering heather. Until now they had kept to the road close to the carriages.

Brooke said, 'We can take a short cut across country here. Would you like that?'

'Yes, very well.'

They set off at a steady canter, Olivia having some difficulty in keeping up, for the slug was not used to this sort of exercise and thought himself ill-used. Brooke reined in his grey and laughed sympathetically at her efforts. Presently they came to a place not far from a loop of the road, where he said the carriages would meet them. They dismounted and tethered their horses to a solitary post and then sat down to wait.

'You must have had many more exciting rides in Ireland,' he said. 'Did you hunt?'

'Yes.' She was rather surprised by the question. Most English people seemed to be scandalised by the idea of women riding to hounds. 'Do you find that shocking?'

'Not in the least. Was your mother Irish?'

'No. My father was stationed over there, and after she died he married an Irishwoman as his second wife.'

'The other night, when you sang that ballad of Moore's, you put on a very pretty brogue. I wondered if that was deliberate or if it came to you naturally.'

'Faith and begorrah!' she flashed at him. 'Would your honour not be knowing I was dragged up in a bog?'

'Well, I have sometimes wondered,' he remarked equably.

He went on steadily gazing at her, his very blue eyes amused and untroubled. Olivia bit her lip. She had meant to ridicule his patronising manner. Instead he had reminded her of that dreadful occasion when she had taken off her dress in the garden at Rosamond's Bower, a thing no lady ought to have done, however wet. And then she had gone on to slap his face. She felt she could not endure any more humiliation from this hateful man. She would have liked to get up and walk away, only there was nowhere she could walk to in the middle of the moor, no escape from that critical observer.

At this moment, luckily, they saw the carriages approaching along the road. The arrival of so many talkative people gave her time to recover and presently to enjoy the picnic. It was a splendid repast, ending with peaches from the walled garden at the Vale and grapes from the vine which lived inside an elegant glass temple with its own private stove. When everyone had eaten too much the children wanted to run about, but Mrs Channing said they must sit still for at least half an hour, so they played complicated word games, everyone joining in. Tom seemed to enjoy the word games. He was very good with the children, who clearly adored him.

Once their mother had decided that no one was in danger of indigestion, he went with Polly and Cilla to inspect a clump of boulders and agreed with them that these might be part of an ancient fortress belonging to King Arthur. Then Fanny suggested a game of grandmother's footsteps, and everyone took part except Mrs Channing, who was repacking the baskets, and Olivia who stayed to help her.

'He is so easily pleased and unaffected,' said Martha Channing, fondly observing her landlord, who had been caught creeping up on Flora and sent back to base. 'And he has done so much for us. I don't know where we should be without him. He is so very kind.'

'He can sometimes be unkind.'

'You are thinking of your cousin. I am sorry to have to say it, but she did run after him, and, although perhaps he should not have played up to her, I am afraid that is the way most gentlemen behave when a pretty girl comes asking for compliments and admiration. I am sure he meant her no harm, and he certainly did not understand that she was going round among her friends boasting of their engagement as a settled thing. That was what placed her in such an uncomfortable position, you know, after he went away.'

Olivia had long ago realised most of this, but when she spoke of Tom's occasional unkindness she had been thinking of herself.

A few minutes later Tom came over to them, saying, 'I am sorry to be a wet blanket, Martha, but I think we ought to start for home. We don't want to get caught up here.'

'Are you expecting a storm?' asked Olivia, rather surprised.

The day had continued dull and dismal but she did not think it was going to rain.

'Not a storm. We are in for one of our thick mists. They come down very suddenly.'

She looked around her. When they had arrived at this point, two hours before, they had been able to see a good expanse of the moor, though not as much as they could have hoped for on a clear day. Now the land seemed to have shrunk as the horizon drew in and vanished in a hazy blur. In one direction she could actually see a patch of mist, like the foam on a wave, drifting across the heather.

Everyone else, even little Cilla, apparently knew what these signs meant, for they climbed into the landau and gig without argument. They drove away as Brooke fetched the two riding horses. Now, of course, he would offer to help her mount.

This situation offered all too many opportunities for gallantry. She did not really see him as a monster of depravity who would use his greater strength in forcing her to submit to his wicked desires. The whole idea was too Gothic to credit. But she did think him quite capable of pretending an assault on her virtue out of sheer devilry, just to see what she would do, and to punish her for hitting him when he kissed her before.

She decided not to give him the chance. It was almost impossible for a woman in a long habit to get into a side-saddle from the ground. However, one of the boulders would serve as a mounting-block, so she scrambled on to it and said coolly, 'Would you bring my horse over here, if you please?'

Brooke eyed her with some astonishment but did as she asked.

'You seem to set a very high value on your own fascination,' he remarked distantly, 'if you think I am unable to dance with you or help you get on a horse without engulfing us both in a tide of unlawful passion.'

She realised too late what a fool she was making of herself from his point of view. Having just taken the reins from him, she jerked them unintentionally. This annoyed the slug, a disobliging horse at the best of times. He served violently away from her, pulling the reins out of her grasp and setting off across the moor faster than she would have believed possible.

'Hell and damnation!' exclaimed Tom. He vaulted on to his own horse and set off in pursuit before even feeling for his stirrups. As he vanished into the thickening mist he shouted back, 'Stay where you are—don't move a step.'

This was all very well but she was not going to stand like a statue on top of the boulder so she jumped down and began to pace to and fro, feeling exceedingly stupid and only too well aware that she was putting Brooke to a great deal of trouble through a distrust of his motives which now seemed far-fetched and old maidish, not to say insulting.

But why should I trust him? she fumed. He behaved abominably last time we were alone together.

Soon a new anxiety took over. The mist really was closing in alarmingly. Clouds of whitish-grey vapour were rolling silently across the moor, swallowing up the ground. In a very short time she was quite isolated. She could see the hand before her face but very little else. The outcrop of boulders—they were a landmark, but even they had disappeared. She walked back the way she thought she had come but they were no longer there. She must have missed them somehow, gone too far, or not far enough. Or had she made a mistake and turned in the wrong direction? The hoofbeats of the two horses had died away long ago. Now she understood why Brooke had told her not to move. She had moved, and even supposing he could find his way back to the boulders she could not. She was lost on the moor and she would probably have to spend the night here alone.

She fought down an unreasonable panic. Nothing very dreadful could happen to her provided she stayed still and resisted the temptation to wander about hopelessly and fall down a ravine. She had been stupid enough already, she mustn't make things worse. She sat down in the heather, hugging herself to keep warm and trying not to think what it would be like up here at three o'clock in the morning.

After a measureless interval—perhaps a quarter of an hour—her common sense was rewarded. She heard the sound of trotting horses and a man's voice shouting, 'Where are you? Can you hear me?'

'Over here!' she called back. 'Over here!'

She went on calling. Then three dark shapes swam out of the mist. Tom Brooke was riding one horse and leading the other. He was in a very bad temper.

'Why the devil didn't you stay where I told you to?'

'I'm sorry. I only meant to take a few steps. . .'

'You shouldn't have done. It's always fatal. Now let's get you mounted again and no nonsense about it this time.'

He got down himself and lifted her bodily into the saddle with a grip that was far from amorous. She was reminded of her father picking her up when she had fallen off her pony after jumping a bank which he had told her not to. He had given her a good smack. She would not have been altogether surprised if Tom Brooke had done the same; she was sure he wanted to.

'Now follow me,' he said. 'Once we are on the road we shall be able to stick to it all the way home.'

He found the road without apparent difficulty and swung decisively to the left.

'How do you know which way to go?' she asked, subdued but curious.

'By listening for the sound of the sea. Over there to the south-west.'

She listened too and caught a very faint incessant seething she had not noticed before.

'I should never have thought of that,' she said respectfully.

'I've known the moor in all its moods since I was a child. I used to come down here and stay with my grandmother.'

They rode for a while in silence. Olivia was gathering the determination to speak.

'Mr Brooke.'

'Well, Miss Fenimore?'

'I owe you an apology.'

'I believe I owe you several. Shall we call quits?'

'If you wish,' she said with relief. 'Only there is one thing I should like to explain. I am not so foolish that I go round suspecting every man of looking for an opportunity to make love to me. But with you—I just thought—you might choose to torment me for your own amusement. As you did once before.'

'We neither of us showed to advantage that day. Due to a misunderstanding on both sides.'

Even in her chastened mood, Olivia was not quite prepared to admit that.

'I didn't misunderstand anything. You thought I was running after you, like all the other husband-hunting girls. So you treated me with contempt.'

'Not at all. What you wanted was to flirt with me on your own terms. You know, you shouldn't have done,' he added seriously, turning to look at her, this time without mockery.

'Why ever not?' she demanded, a good deal astonished. 'You were always trying to flirt with me.'

'That's different.'

'I can't imagine why.'

He said nothing, and she thought he was annoyed because she had challenged this male prerogative. The mist was growing a little thinner, or perhaps this was simply the effect of their coming down off the high ground. Away from the moor it might never be so thick. Here they could see hedges and trees silhouetted quite plainly. Everything else was drowned in a lavender-grey monochrome.

'It's hard to explain the difference,' he said after a while, and she realised he had been genuinely thinking out an answer. 'Flirting is a game between a man and a woman, in which either can invade the other's territory, hoping to gain a small victory or at least come off unscathed. But the players are governed by separate rules, as they are in life. A man can go as far as the woman will allow, knowing that she is entitled to send him packing at the first approach—and a rebuff of that kind can be very painful, let me tell you. A woman, on the other hand, must be guided by prudence as well as inclination because if she is not careful the man will consider himself free to do just as he pleases. If she sets no value on her own virtue, why should he? And if she leads him on and then changes her mind at the last moment, he will set her down as a common jilt.'

'Is that how you thought of me?' asked Olivia, mortified.

'No, because I didn't think you understood the situation you had got yourself into. I thought you needed to be taught a lesson.'

This was no sort of consolation. After a moment she said, 'Whether you believe it or not, I had no idea I should meet you in the garden at Rosamond's Bower. It never entered my head. I simply knew that the place was very picturesque and that my uncle's family had leave to walk in the grounds while the owners were away.'

'Never mind Rosamond's Bower. I had received encouragement enough at the Osgoods' party. You were determined to fix my interest that evening. You hardly allowed me to speak to another woman.'

Horrified, she began to protest. 'But that was because——'

Then she stopped. She had been going to say, that was because the woman he kept speaking to was her cousin Hetty, pathetically in love with him and liable to break down in front of her intended husband and the whole of Parmouth society. It flashed across her mind for the first time that he really did not understand Hetty's feelings and thought her quite cured of her passion for himself now that she had acquired another eligible suitor.

Olivia had disliked him for being heartless and vain. Now she saw him in a different light—not so much deliberately callous as obsessed with the idea that he was being pursued for his money. She was not as critical of this failing as some people might have been because she too had been pursued by fortune-hunters.

'What was it you were going to say?' he prompted her. 'Something about the Osgoods' party. Because. . .?'

Olivia felt she could not betray poor Hetty. She racked her brain for an excuse.

'I'm afraid I did behave badly because it was such a very dull evening,' she improvised.

He burst out laughing. 'And you thought I might enliven it for you because I was a little less dull than anyone else in the room? Well I suppose that is a compliment—of a kind!'

She liked him for this remark, which seemed to her the very reverse of conceited. They were now riding down a deep lane where the banks of fern pressed in on them as closely as the banks of mist had done on the moor.

She was still thinking how strange it was that he had remained completely unaware of Hetty's anguish and the harm he had done.

'May I ask you a question, Mr Brooke?'

'Certainly.'

'I admit that young women who flirt are frivolous and sometimes very unkind, but how is a girl to behave if her feelings are seriously engaged? How is she to treat a man who wants to dance with her and walk with her and talk about poetry and go through all the usual stages that lead up to an engagement? Is she supposed to play an active part or must she sit with a stony face like patience on a monument, waiting for him to make a formal declaration? I don't think many of us would get married at all if we did that. The men would be frightened away.'

'Well, of course,' he said, a little impatiently, 'you have answered your own question. If there is a serious attachment on both sides, of course she will encourage him.'

'And how is she to know it is serious?'

'If she is not sure of her feelings, she will be wise to hesitate.'

'I'm not talking about her feelings. I'm talking about the man. This well-brought-up girl who has been warned never to do anything improper or imprudent, never to flirt—how is she to know whether his advances are honourable or dishonourable or simply careless and meaningless, a matter of idle amusement? We are agreed that he will not have made any definite proposal without encouragement, so how is she to judge?'

He gave her a searching glance and asked, 'Have you ever found yourself in that predicament?'

'No, I have not,' she informed him hastily. 'I have been lucky in many ways. I was brought up by a young stepmother who knew all the ins and outs of Irish society and now I hope I am too old to be taken in.'

Her real protection, of course, had been her fortune. Most of the men had wanted to marry her, generally, for the wrong reasons. It had dawned on her that Tom had no idea she was a rich woman. The family at Marine Cottage were not at all wealthy and he thought she was just an indigent niece who had come to join them. In these circumstances her manners had perhaps seemed over-confident and brazen. Put out by this idea, she went on quickly.

'I was thinking of girls younger than myself who have seen less of the world. Gentlemen like you are only too ready to charm such innocent victims. They are fair game, I suppose, so long as you don't actually seduce them. It hardly matters if you raise their hopes or break their hearts. But don't you think it rather shabby to treat them with such open indifference?'

After this there was a rather painful silence which lasted so long that she began to wish she had kept her mouth shut.

At last he said, 'What a villain you must think me. Or not even a villain, perhaps. Just a selfish, care-for-nothing trifler. But I had no idea I had hurt your cousin so badly, and if I did I am very sorry for it.'

She made some sort of lame protest, knowing he would not believe her. She had taken care not to mention Hetty but her tongue had run away with her, and naturally he had guessed whom she was thinking of when she attacked him. As Mrs Channing had said, a good deal of the blame was on her side.

'I beg your pardon,' she said. 'I should not have expressed myself so freely.'

'Why not? Plain speaking is good for all of us. Don't back out now.' After a slight pause, he added, 'I hope Hetty is happily married. You have seen her quite lately, have you not?'

'Yes, I helped her settle into her new home.'

Olivia heard herself gushing about the happiness of Hetty and Alfred, but felt glad that basically she was able to speak the truth. Hetty was happier with Alfred than she would ever have been with this far more complicated and rather intimidating man, even if he had been in love with her.

They were nearly at the end of their journey, which had been taken up by this extraordinary conversation. They had discussed matters which most people would have considered quite improper between a young unmarried woman and a man who was not related to her. Perhaps the strangeness and isolation of the mist had affected them both. They had felt closer together and more removed from the world than they could once they were riding into Parmouth, where every house and garden was visible prosaically on an ordinary sunless afternoon. He escorted her back to Marine Cottage but refused to come in, saying he would return her horse to the livery stables.

'And I'll have something to say to Sampson, fobbing you off with such a brute.'

The slug, after his brief bolt for freedom on the moor, had relapsed into his usual state of grudging apathy.

CHAPTER SEVEN

AUNT HESTER was distressed that Olivia had been obliged to ride all the way home alone with *that man*. No doubt she was remembering the other unfortunate picnic last summer when he had gone wandering in the woods with Hetty.

'I can't think what Martha Channing was about,' she complained. 'She should never have left you alone with him.'

'It was not Mrs Channing's fault. They thought we were immediately behind them, and so we should have been if I hadn't stupidly let go of my horse. Mr Brooke had to catch him, and it was all very difficult because of the fog.'

'Well, I hope he behaved himself on the way home. He did not do or say anything improper?'

'No, of course not,' said Olivia, conscious that the boot had been on the other foot.

Uncle James, hidden behind his newspaper, spoke out like an oracle.

'You may depend upon it, my dear, Brooke is not the man to make improper advances unless he thinks he has received some encouragement.'

Aunt Hester sniffed. She could never quite admit that her dear Hetty had been very silly and unguarded.

Next day there was a change of subject. When the post arrived there was a letter for Mrs Fenimore in a hand Olivia recognised. It was from their rich and fashionable cousin Lizzie Wakelin. Lizzie's father had been a clergyman and no better off than the other Fenimores, but she had made a very good marriage. Her husband Preston Wakelin had large estates in Norfolk as well as a London house and they lived very much in the great world.

'Are they enjoying Scotland?' enquired Olivia, sipping her tea. Her aunt was reading the letter at the breakfast table.

'Apparently they did not remain long in Scotland. Their plans fell through. She says—good heavens!— she says they want to come down here for a few weeks and will I rent a house for her.'

'Cousin Lizzie is coming to Parmouth!' commented Flora. 'Just fancy. It's almost as good as the Prince Regent. She'll bring us into fashion.'

'We are quite fashionable enough already,' said her father. 'The place is becoming a perfect bedlam. And you'll never find a place for her at this time of year, my dear Hester. You'd better write and tell her so.'

'I can't do that. She's one of the family. I could not be so disobliging. And besides. . .'

Olivia could read her mind exactly. Parmouth was fashionable. Not like Brighton—though people were beginning to say that the smaller, more distant resorts were far more exclusive. Many of the visitors were exactly the sort of people the Wakelins would know. But it was not smart or fashionable to live all the year round at a summer watering-place, and in Lizzie's eyes the James Fenimores' dull, provincial existence was only redeemed by their happening to occupy a pretty villa and a respected position as local residents at a place where people of consequence gathered during two or three months in the year. With this advantage Aunt Hester should have been able to find a superior house for Lizzie and Preston, and so she could have done, given rather more notice. It was about the only favour she could ever hope to confer on them and she did not want to admit defeat.

'I'm sure there must be something available,' Olivia told her. 'Didn't Mrs Marling say they might have to give up Belvue on account of her mother's illness? Shall we go house-hunting after breakfast? I'd enjoy that because I am so fearfully inquisitive.'

'Would you, my dear? I should be grateful for your advice.'

They set out with reasonable hopes which were soon dashed. Belvue, unexpectedly vacant, had been snapped up immediately, and another house, suggested by Mrs Osgood, was not to be let after all. They were forced to apply to an agent, just like anyone else. This insufferable person enjoyed wondering at their simplicity and depressing their ambitions before grudingly admitting he did have two houses on his books. Predictably they were at opposite ends of the town. Aunt Hester and Olivia went off to inspect them. Yesterday's overcast weather had cleared and it was once again intensely hot.

Both houses were quite unsuitable. The first was dark, poky and noisy, the second ill-furnished and damp. They could not picture Lizzie in either.

'I don't know what we are to do,' lamented Aunt Hester after the second disappointment. 'We haven't room for Lizzie and Preston at Marine Cottage, and anyway they would not be comfortable. They are not accustomed to our simple style of living, our one-course dinners and the early hours we keep. Lizzie is so patronising. I dare say she does not mean it, but we should none of us be comfortable. Oh, dear, I am so hot, I cannot think properly, and my shoes are pinching dreadfully.'

By the time they got home she was too tired even to walk upstairs. She sat down on the drawing-room sofa, took off her bonnet and was about to unlace her boots when they heard the knocker on the front door.

'I don't want to see any callers,' whispered Aunt Hester. 'Tell Skinner to head them off.'

But it was too late. Skinner, opening the door, announced, 'Mr Brooke, ma'am.'

'What's he want to come here for? Send him away— Oh, Good afternoon, Mr Brooke.'

'I hope I am not disturbing you, ma'am.'

He came in with his usual air of energy and high spirits which seemed to invigorate everything around him. 'I wanted to make sure that Miss Olivia was none the worse for her adventure yesterday.'

'Adventure?' repeated Aunt Hester suspiciously.

'Being fogbound on the moor is an adventure to those who are not used to our peculiar climate.'

'Oh, yes. I see. It was certainly an awkward business,' agreed his hostess accusingly, as though it had been all his fault.

Tom looked straight at Olivia and said, 'I'm sorry you found it so awkward.'

'The only awkwardness was mine in being so clumsy as to let go of my horse. I have been telling my uncle and aunt how clever you were to catch him. Do sit down, Mr Brooke.'

Aunt Hester had forgotten to ask him. She only wanted him to go away.

He took a chair and said, 'I had another reason for calling. I had a letter from Canfield this morning. He is lending Rosamond's Bower to your cousins the Wakelins.'

'Rosamond's Bower!' exclaimed Aunt Hester, sitting up straight. 'And here have we been tramping the town looking at the most frightful houses! It never crossed my mind—I understood that Lord Canfield will never let.'

'He won't. He is lending the house because he knew they would never be able to rent one at such short notice. The Wakelins are old friends of his. He and I and Preston were all up at Oxford together—with the result that George Canfield thinks I am his man of business. I am always running little errands for him when there is anything he wants doing in Parmouth.'

'Well, I am grateful to you for bringing us such good news. My niece and I were wondering what to do, for there was nothing suitable to be had anywhere.'

'I'm sorry I wasn't in time to save you a useless search. I went out fishing early and have only just read my letters.'

Brooke stayed just long enough to explain to a now mollified Aunt Hester that his housekeeper would see to the hiring of servants as this was what Lord Canfield had suggested. He did not exchange another word or glance with Olivia. Rosamond's Bower was still a subject of embarrassment.

All the same it was a place she would now have to get used to, like it or not. The Wakelins arrived a week later, and the following morning the Marine Cottage family paid a formal call on their relations.

Lizzie Wakelin was a little, dark, vivacious woman, very well pleased with herself and at the moment pleased with her surroundings, as well she might be.

'Nothing could be more delightful,' she said exultantly. 'I am told we have the best house in the place and I can well believe it.'

Her husband reminded her to thank Cousin Hester for the trouble she had taken on their behalf.

'Oh, yes, it was very kind of you, my dear Hester,' said Lizzie blithely. 'Though, as it turns out, quite unnecessary.'

Preston Wakelin raised his eyebrows and glanced at Olivia. He was fond of his wife but sometimes embarrassed by the way she took other people for granted.

Olivia was interested to see the inside of the house. It was designed rather like a Cathedral with arches and arcades and fan-vaulted ceilings, though since everything was painted in the palest colours the room looked refreshingly light and new. More worldly than otherworldly, as Preston pointed out.

When the James Fenimores rose to leave, Lizzie begged Olivia to stay a little longer, and as soon as they had gone she began to express exactly the views that Aunt Hester suspected her of holding.

'Poor Hester, she won't get that girl off her hands as quickly as the other one. She was a little minx when I last saw her, though pretty enough in a commonplace way. Flora is quite plain and dreadfully provincial. But what can you expect? It's so bad for a girl, growing up in the mixed society of a watering-place.'

Lizzie and her widowed mother had lived in lodgings in Clifton until she was lucky enough to captivate Preston Wakelin on a visit to the assembly rooms in Bath. She had risen so successfully to the position of a great lady that she sometimes forgot, when talking to a member of her own family, that her listener was not to be taken in.

Olivia merely laughed and said there was nothing

wrong with Flora that growing a little older would not
cure.

They were joined by Preston's sister, Louisa
Woodvile, who was living with them while her husband
was serving with the Army in Spain.

She greeted Olivia with pleasure, and said, 'Do let
us go into the garden. It looks so tempting, I cannot
bear to leave it unexplored a moment longer.'

They went out through a french window, down a
flight of steps and along a grass path towards a summer-
house which stood at a break between the trees. There
was nothing of great interest in this garden shelter
except a door in the back wall, and as Preston reached
out to open it Olivia suddenly knew what they were
going to see on the other side. They stepped through
into a deeper pavilion furnished with some wicker
chairs and tables and saw before them a white marble
fountain.

This was the building Tom Brooke had entered on
that famous Sunday afternoon when Olivia was hiding
in the bushes, and he had gone through the very same
door in the opposite direction, while she thought he
was sitting there, waiting for her to display herself like
a nymph surprised in what Herrick called a sweet
disorder of the dress.

'How charming,' said Mrs Woodvile. 'The whiteness
of the marble is so perfectly set off by the darkness of
the greenery beyond. I wonder if we can have the
fountain turned on?'

As she spoke, a spire of water shot gracefully into
the air, glittering as it emerged from the shadows below
and sinking softly back into the basin. They laughed at
the extraordinary aptness of this display—all except
Olivia, as she recognised the man who was standing

beside the marble basin, doing something to one of the hidden taps.

'Well done, Tom!' Preston called out to him. 'You couldn't have timed it better.'

As Tom came towards them, Lizzie asked Olivia, 'Have you been introduced to Mr Brooke?'

'Yes, we have met several times.'

Olivia was annoyed with herself for feeling every bit as gauche as Flora.

Tom greeted Lizzie and Louisa punctiliously and then said, 'Good morning, Miss Olivia. I'm glad you've come to see the fountain play.'

It sounded like a mere civility but his eyes were brimming with amusement.

'Isn't there a special device attached to this fountain?' asked Preston. 'Some trick of George Canfield's?'

'George has a lamentable sense of humour. He thinks it amusing to see his friends drenched to the skin. I suppose it is in some circumstances,' said Tom reflectively. 'I'll show you how it works some time. But not now, I think.'

Lizzie said she had no patience with people who played silly jokes. She and Preston and Louisa went on admiring the figures on the fountain, now shining like crystal as the water streamed over them.

Tom said in a low voice to Olivia, 'It wasn't my doing, after all. You turned the water on yourself. But I did behave badly. Will you forgive me?'

He threw her a glance of such mingled penitence and laughter that her heart turned over. It was no longer possible to go on pretending that she was immune to his charm.

After this they began to see a great deal of each other. She was constantly with the Wakelins and so

was he, and she was included in various select parties
that she might not have attended otherwise. She felt
this to be a little invidious, but her uncle and aunt had
no objection, nor had Flora. Hetty would have sulked
at being left out. Flora had no social ambitions. She
thought Cousin Lizzie Wakelin tiresome and affected
and did gleeful imitations of her to amuse her cronies
Madeleine and Bernard and Walter. They amused
Olivia too.

She laughed airily and went off to enjoy herself.
Lizzie wanted to make up exploring parties and took it
for granted that Tom would act as their guide and
escort. This was all she expected of him, for although
she was matchmaking for Olivia she had set her sights
on a different quarry: Frederick Walsh the agreeable
widower, who, she said, really needed consolation as
well as a rich wife.

'Such a pity Fred cannot be with us today,' she said,
one fine morning, standing on the gravel sweep outside
Rosamond's Bower while they waited for the horses
and carriages to assemble. 'I cannot think what he is
going to do that is more amusing than coming with us
to Tatton Cove.'

'He's engaged to spend the day with the Millingtons,'
said Olivia. 'Sophie Millington is the attraction.'

This was true though she said it to bait Lizzie. The
Millingtons were a family with several pretty daughters.
Sophie was the prettiest.

'He is wasting his time,' said Lizzie severely. 'He
can't afford to fall in love with Miss Millington—she
has no fortune. And her mother ought to foresee the
danger and take better care of her.'

Tom and Bernard had arrived on horseback from
the Vale. Olivia could see Tom out of the corner of her

eye, and though they had been talking in low voices she was sure he could hear what they were saying. He had a somewhat ironic expression.

'I don't know what girls are expected to do,' she said. 'If they are disinterested you call them imprudent, yet if they take care only to fall in love with rich men they are accused of being mercenary.'

'No such thing,' said Lizzie crossly. 'Girls are expected to marry well if they can. It is the ones who try too hard, the brazen husband-hunters lacking in delicacy or reserve—they are the one who get a bad reputation. Men don't care for that sort of thing.'

Olivia remembered too late that Lizzie had shown great prudence in falling in love with Preston. Tom was looking more ironic than ever.

Lizzie's carriage had now come round, and a horse for Olivia from the livery stables. Other friends were waiting in the lane. They set out in a large party riding westwards and more or less parallel to the coastline.

'That horse is an improvement on the slug,' said Tom, coming up beside Olivia and surveying the neat bay hack she had been given today.

'Yes, and I believe I owe the improvement to you. The man at the stables treats me with almost embarrassing respect since you spoke to him.'

'So he should. You are a beautiful horsewoman.'

She was not sure whether this was a piece of flattery or an honest opinion. She *was* a good horsewoman, but would he have troubled to say so unless he was trying to make up to her?

She smiled briefly and rode on a little ahead of him. She wanted to think. She did not as a rule pay much attention to the worldly wisdom of her cousin Lizzie, but Lizzie had said something this morning which started an uncomfortable train of thought. Men did not like girls who tried too hard. That was true enough—witness poor Hetty's troubles. The motive, whether it was guileless infatuation or cold-blooded ambition, did not make much difference. Men liked to be the hunters. Tom thought Olivia had been chasing him. He believed, or pretended to believe, that she was at least uninterested, only wanting a flirtation—but he had given her a lecture on the dangers of flirting. Did he really consider her quite brazen?

Perhaps she had been too forthcoming. Her manners had been perfectly acceptable in Ireland, but then Irish society was so much more free and easy and, besides, an heiress who was trying to preserve her independence had either to be a perfect iceberg, which would be very dull, or assert her own wishes and preferences in a way which would never be mistaken for husband-hunting because she was rich and would inevitably receive many offers. But in Parmouth no one knew about her fortune. She had been glad of that; it had not struck her until now that her natural self-confidence might seem pushing and even vulgar in the orphan daughter of an officer in a line regiment who had been given a home by her relations at Marine Cottage.

These ideas occupied her all the way to Tatton Cove, a small sandy bay scooped out of the façade of an immense cliff which receded just here into the shape of a terraced amphitheatre.

There was a stream running down through a terrace in the cliff and a narrow path beside it. Horses and carriages were left at a nearby farmstead and the party proceeded on foot, some members making rather heavy weather over the steep and stony ground.

Tom offered Olivia his arm, but she said, 'I can

manage very well, thank you, Mr Brooke. I think there are other ladies whose need is greater than mine.'

She had several more offers of assistance but refused them all.

The pale fawn-coloured beach was fringed with rocks and the incoming tide was crashing and splashing vigorously. The sea and sky were both so blue that it was hard to make out the horizon.

'Very pretty,' said Lizzie, after some moments of silent contemplation. 'What else is there to see?'

'Nothing, I'm afraid,' said Tom, smiling.

'Good gracious, what did we come all this way for?'

Preston said hastily, 'This is where you are going to build your new watering-place, isn't it, Tom?'

'If I can buy the land and provided Walker's inspiration doesn't desert him.'

Mr Walker was the architect who had designed most of the villas at Parmouth.

This announcement caused a lot of interest and some argument, one lady saying it would be a crying shame to spoil such a prospect by putting up a lot of houses, and someone else remarking that there was not much point in a charming prospect if there was no one to see it.

Presently Olivia left the others on the beach and walked a little way back up the path. She found a convenient grassy hump and sat down by herself, staring out to sea. She still felt uncomfortable when she remembered some of her encounters with Tom. Yet surely he had done everything to provoke her, taking it for granted that everyone fell in love with him and despising girls with no money because they hoped to find husbands among the only men who could afford to marry them. Of course she did not like the idea that she might have sounded ill-bred and gauche, but the odd thing was she minded more having to think badly of Tom. That certainly was very odd indeed.

She had just come to this conclusion when she saw him walking up the path towards her. He stopped and looked down.

'You seem very pensive today. May I?' He sat beside her on the grass without waiting for an answer. 'I hope I haven't done anything to offend you?'

'No, of course not.'

Good heavens, just because I have kept quiet for once, he thinks I am offended. What a chattering hoyden I must have been, she added silently.

'No "of course" about it,' he said with a grin. 'I have annoyed you enough in the past, but I hope we are friends now. Tell me, do you think it would be a desecration to build on this site?'

'No,' she said slowly, 'though perhaps one ought to think so. I should not care to see houses sprouting on a mountain crag, for instance, nor at the heart of the moor. One does not want to domesticate natural grandeur. But the grandeur of the coast is invisible from the land, and if you are at sea I should think the sight of human habitation must be rather pleasant. Do the local people object?'

'Far from it. The land around here is too steep and exposed, poor farming country. On the far side of that headland there is a fishing village where times are hard just now—too many of the young and able-bodied men have been pressed into the fleet. There is an absentee landlord who does nothing for anyone.'

'And you would like to bring work into the neigh-bourhood?' she suggested, interested and impressed.

'Well, that is not my only reason, but it is one of

them. Most people think I am a quixotic imbecile, so I don't talk about it.'

Olivia did not believe this last statement. She knew from Mrs Channing that he always tried to conceal his acts of generosity.

She said, 'I don't know much about rural poverty in England—everyone over here looks so prosperous to me, but there must be bad patches. In Ireland it is dreadful. The condition of the people has often made me feel ashamed, and the Irish gentry all seem to think it is perfectly natural.'

'I suppose it is perfectly natural to them. They are a feckless race. And you feel as you do because you are not Irish.'

'In spite of my eccentricity and my brogue?' she asked before she could stop herself.

And then blushed. Had it been arch and vulgar to remind him of their sparring match on the day of the moorland picnic?

Tom did not rise to the bait, but he did not snub her either. He asked quite seriously about her life in Ireland, and listened while she told him about the small country house where she and Geraldine had lived very happily a few miles outside Dublin.

She felt they could have gone on talking for hours but for the impatience of their companions, who had seen all they wanted to of Tatton Cove.

All the same she now felt a curious shyness in dealing with Tom, and an awkward split in her consciousness, as though there were two people inside her: one going through the actions of talking to him, smiling at him, agreeing or disagreeing with him, while the other person was sitting in judgement on every word or gesture of hers, wondering what effect it had on him

and minding too much if she felt she had given a wrong
impression. Nothing like this had ever happened to her
before; she had never paused to consider what sort of
an impression she was making on anyone.

It would have been stupid to pretend she did not
understand the change in herself. She knew very well
what had happened. She had fallen in love. Only it did
seem unfortunate that, instead of displaying the bold
opinions, the careless self-esteem that might have
disgusted him, she was now in danger of driving her
love away by becoming nervous, insipid, a dead bore.

CHAPTER EIGHT

LUCKILY Olivia's diffidence did not last long. A few days later she was going into the library at Rosamond's Bower to hunt for Lizzie's reticule, which had been left lying about somewhere, when she nearly interrupted an interesting conversation between Tom and Preston.

'Your wife seems very anxious,' Tom was saying, 'to make a match between her cousin and Fred Walsh.'

The library door was very well-fitting, like all the doors at Rosamond's Bower, and slid noiselessly across the carpet. Olivia stayed where she was on the other side and became a shameless eavesdropper.

'Well, you know what women are,' said Preston easily. 'They are always trying to sort their acquaintance into pairs—it's as good as a game of cards where they are concerned.'

'Yes, but why choose Walsh? He's a very pleasant fellow, I've nothing against him. It's a good old family and the place in Gloucestershire could be much improved with a little money spent on it. But she is worth something better. I'm not speaking of her fortune, which I gather is considerable. She herself is too handsome, too lively, altogether too original to be wasted on such a man.'

'I don't think you need worry.' Preston sounded amused. 'Lizzie has got this notion in her head but Olivia is not a girl to be easily persuaded. I believe she has refused offers from half the peerage of Ireland.'

'I'm glad she has so much sense.'

Her head spinning, Olivia pushed open the door and went in. Immediately they saw her, both men looked thoroughly shifty. She pretended to notice nothing, found Lizzie's reticule on one of the window-seats, and went away.

New ideas were chasing through her mind. So Tom did know about her fortune. Had he been told recently by the Wakelins? Uncle James and Aunt Hester were not the kind of people to go around Parmouth boasting of their niece's wealth. But now she came to think of it, Aunt Hester would surely have confided in her great friend Mrs Channing. And Tom was on intimate terms with the Channings, who lived in his house. So he had probably been told the truth soon after she arrived and had never suspected her of trying to catch a rich husband. In which case his treatment of her—on what she thought of as the Day of the Fountain, for instance—had none of the arrogant superiority she had imagined and resented. He had been playing a game in which he saw her as an opponent worth challenging. He had called her handsome, lively, original. The last word daunted her a little. Most men did not care for originality in women.

She was starting down the hill an hour later when she heard quick footsteps behind her and a voice calling.

'May I walk you home, Miss Olivia?'

'That would be delightful, Mr Brooke.'

And she immediately thought, Did that sound silly and gushing?

They walked a short way in silence, then he said abruptly, 'Were you listening outside the library door?'

'Listening outside the library? Whatever made you think so?'

'Because you came in with such an innocent air, like a kitten stealing cream. Don't laugh. It was altogether abominable and eavesdroppers never hear any good of themselves.'

'I didn't hear anything very bad.'

'Yes, you did. You stand convicted of having refused to marry all those impecunious Irishmen who are in such desperate need of your good English money.'

'Yes,' she said with sudden enlightenment. 'That is exactly how they make one feel—that it is so selfish and unreasonable, refusing to take a simple step like getting married, when something really important, the transfer of a large sum of money, would be so beneficial to a set of undeserving people one doesn't care about. I suppose men in your position are subject to the same pressures.'

'Among other things. By the way, I think Fred Walsh is a good deal more deserving than your Irish suitors. What do you make of him?'

It was none of his business but she did not mind.

'I like him extremely though I find him a little too quiet and retiring. Tastes and interests depend a good deal on circumstances, don't you think? If I were a sorrowing widow, Mr Walsh is just the sort of gentle, amiable protector I might turn to.'

This made him laugh. He had the most delightedly amused and infectious laugh, his eyes sparkling with appreciation.

'I don't know what you find so diverting,' she said, trying to look serious.

'The thought of you as a sorrowing widow, my dear. How would you dispose of your first husband? Drive him to distraction, I shouldn't wonder.'

They were flirting again and very much enjoying themselves.

After this she forgot to be self-conscious and stopped worrying about the faults in her own character and whether they would put off a man who might be on the verge of falling in love. This was a great relief to her, and to him too, apparently, for that evening at the Assembly Rooms he commented on the change.

'I am glad to see you restored to your natural self. You have been very *piano* for the last week.'

'Have I?'

'Yes, and I was beginning to think I knew why.'

'Oh?' Olivia held her breath.

They were sitting on a small pink sofa between two pillars in a broad corridor which led into the ballroom, and were plainly visible from the ballroom itself, and to various couples who kept strolling past them to get a breath of fresh air from the open portico, for it was a hot night. This visibility made their tête-à-tête perfectly proper while giving them a degree of seclusion, for no one could hear what they were saying. There was a sofa beyond one of the pillars but that was unoccupied.

Tom picked up Olivia's fan and began gently swaying it to and fro to give her the illusion of cool air.

'I thought you might be wondering whether you ought to accept the Sorrowing Widower.'

'Well, I wasn't!' she retorted. 'Mr Walsh hasn't mentioned the idea and I'm sure he does not intend to. And it is one thing to make silly jokes, but you must be perfectly aware that if I received a proposal of marriage I should not dream of discussing it with someone who—with anyone else.'

There was an uncomfortable pause. Then he said, 'I

beg your pardon. You are right, of course. I had no business to speak as I did.'

They sat in silence. She knew her annoyance was perfectly justified; she also knew that it was partly due to disappointment because she had been expecting him to embark on something rather different.

A couple had come to sit on the unoccupied sofa beyond the pillar: one of the Preece sisters who haunted every Parmouth festivity and a young man with ginger whiskers to whom she had just become engaged.

Ariadne Preece was discussing a novel she had been reading.

'. . .and when Matilda gets to the castle, the Count is there before her. I forgot to say he had heard about the shipwreck from Ernesto. Or from his brother—the Count's brother, I mean, not Ernesto's. I don't think Ernesto had a brother. It is a little confusing, you must read it for yourself. . .'

'I don't have much time for reading,' said the young man. 'I tell you what, though. We have a capital library. You will enjoy that.'

'A circulating library?'

'No, I mean the books we have in the house. My grandfather's collection. I don't think there are many novels,' he added doubtfully. 'I believe there is a copy of *Tristram Shandy*. There's the band striking up again. Shall we go and dance?'

The engaged couple went off into the ballroom. Olivia and Tom stayed where they were. She waited for him to say something scathing, but when he spoke he was merely thoughtful.

'I have been considering something you said to me on the day of Polly's picnic, when we rode home from the moor: that under the rules which govern our society it is often difficult for men and women to recognise each other's wishes or intentions. There is something further you might have added. Some men and women will not even make use of the opportunities they do have. That couple have been thrown together for the last month, and I suppose they have been allowed to carry on a dialogue, or listen to each other talking in company for a couple of hours every day, and they have got engaged without discovering that they haven't a taste in common. He cares for nothing but sport and farming, she depends on gossiping female society, fashionable dress and a supply of new romances. People should not marry—I won't say on such a short acquaintance, I don't think time has much to do with it—but on such a vapid, meaningless acquaintance.'

'I entirely agree. One can only hope they will grow to have more in common. It is not a very promising outlook.'

'It would not be enough for you, I imagine,' he said with his challenging look.

Nor for you either, she thought.

At the end of the evening Lizzie scolded her for spending so much time with Tom.

'You are getting yourself talked about, and that never does any good. It is not just a question of behaving properly and not being thought fast—I know you won't make a fool of yourself. But sensible men will not fix on a girl whose mind is always wandering elsewhere. You've already lost Fred Walsh. And don't flatter yourself that Brooke is going to marry you, because he won't, I can promise you that.'

'I don't want to marry anyone at present,' said Olivia automatically.

She had been saying this to interfering well-wishers ever since she was seventeen and for the first time she was consciously lying. By now she did very much want to marry Tom and, without being vain or over-confident, she could not escape the feeling that he too was in love and seriously drawn to the prospect of marrying her, but she knew he would not say so until he knew whether they shared enough interests and opinions to ensure their happiness together. He had made this pretty plain and she respected him for it.

As the days went by it did seem that they were ideally suited. Both preferred the country to the town, enjoyed country pursuits, solitude and privacy. At the same time they both flourished in a social setting, were irresistibly charmed by pleasure and variety, but only in short spells. They had a love of music in common and a love of history. He had read a good deal more than she had, but she was able to hold her own in a political discussion.

One day they were standing in the library window at the Vale, looking down over that sea which had been watched so anxiously only eight years before. The scene was very peaceful, hardly a crest of white on the surface of the water and the one ship in view was a tall merchantman. Tom handed Olivia the telescope so that she could study it closely while he told her the names of the different sails.

Olivia said, 'It's very calm today. She's hardly moving.'

'"As idle as a painted ship Upon a painted ocean."'

'Where does that come from?'

'Did you never hear it before? Then for the next hour your fate is sealed. We shall sit in the garden while I read you "The Rime of the Ancient Mariner".'

He had the infinite pleasure of introducing her to the work of Mr Coleridge and Mr Wordsworth. She was an instant convert. It was one more enjoyment they shared.

They also had it in common that they had both lost their parents when they were quite young. Tom had no very close relations, which perhaps explained why, in spite of loving his home at Cassondon so much, he did not seem to live there very often.

It would be different when he married and settled down. She already knew he loved children, having seen him with the young Channings.

They were drinking tea one evening at the Vale when Tom got out a collection of prints, apparently to please Lizzie and her sister-in-law Louisa, though as the prints were mostly of Cassondon, and the two married ladies had actually been there, Olivia could not help thinking that it was her curiosity he wanted to satisfy. He kept looking across at her and paying particular attention to her comments.

Not that she said a great deal. It was difficult not to be effusive, and she felt that admiration, coming from her, might seem to have an ulterior motive. Cassondon was a very large house designed by Robert Adam in the previous century and placed in a beautiful setting, with a deer park in the foreground and a crescent of dark woods behind.

Lizzie talked away as she went through the prints. Presently she came to one which did not belong to the main set.

'What a romantic old place. Tudor, is it not? Where is it and whom does it belong to?'

Tom went round to look over her shoulder.

'It belongs to me. That's Maygrove.'

Maygrove. The name gave Olivia an unexpected jolt. She had somehow managed to forget that remote, secretive old house which she had seen with Alfred and Hetty on their wedding tour—perhaps because she had wanted to expunge her memories of that unfortunate day, when Hetty had dragged them there to indulge her foolish passion for a man who had never cared about her. Hetty was now living contentedly with Alfred, and all seemed to be going well. The Maygrove episode ought to be forgotten. But one incident came back to Olivia only too clearly.

Lizzie was still asking questions, and when she heard that the house was only an hour's drive from Parmouth she wanted Tom to take them there.

He refused. 'I am afraid that is not possible.'

'Why not?'

'The house is occupied at present. It would not be convenient.'

'But surely your tenants would not object? Can you not ask them?'

'No,' he said with finality.

Lizzie looked sulky and both Preston and Louisa hurried to change the subject. Olivia was not required to say anything, which was just as well. She was recalling the spiteful accusations of the woman at the inn. Something about whores of Babylon and Rector ought not to allow it. Was there an expensive Cyprian installed in the house at present? Tom had said the house was occupied, not that it was let. But he hardly had time to be visiting such a person. It was true that he did not spend all his days with Olivia, but they generally told each other now where they had been and with whom.

Tom came to sit beside her and started putting the prints back in the folio.

'You look tired,' he said quietly. 'Are you feeling quite well?'

'You mean I am looking washed-out because I stayed too long in the sun.'

'Then don't do so again. I have to go to Brantisford tomorrow on business with Osgood, but I shall see you at the concert, shall I not?'

At least, she thought with a revival of humour, he would not be going to a house of ill fame in the company of Mr Osgood.

By the following evening common sense had taken over. Why start worrying about an imaginary Cyprian? She had never doubted there were indiscretions in Tom's past, and village people had such long memories.

She sat with her uncle and aunt, thinking happy thoughts and listening to a rather dull concert. The German music was solid but not inspiring, the wind-players huffed and puffed, the fiddlers sawed labori-ously and Aunt Hester drooped in her chair and had to be nudged awake by Uncle James. She gave a guilty jump and tried to pretend she had been sunk in meditation.

The interval came as a relief and the audience began to stroll about, greeting their friends.

'Heavy going, isn't it?' Tom said to Olivia.

'It's very warm in here.'

'That's what I meant,' he said cheerfully. 'Stuffy. Shall we go out and get a breath of air?'

They stepped through the classical portico and by an unspoken consent took a short cut along a path that bordered the cricket field, facing a great expanse of sea and sky, the blue of air and water turning almost to lilac in the evening light.

'Shall we go down on the beach?' he suggested.

Olivia glanced to right and left. There seemed to be no one about. They descended the steps on to the sand and stood watching the restless shimmer at the tide's edge where the tide wavered and turned over in lacy ruffles. The constant, unequal movement acted like a spell, holding them motionless.

'We ought to go back,' she said reluctantly.

'To those braying asses? Whatever for?'

'My aunt will wonder what has become of me.'

'She'll think you've gone to sit with Lizzie and Preston.'

That was quite plausible. Olivia did not want to leave this magical solitude which enclosed them both and shut out everyone else. She turned to look at him as he turned towards her, and after that it was perfectly natural to lift her face to be kissed just as his mouth came down on hers. She felt a pleasure so extreme that it was almost like pain. He was holding her so close that each could feel the other's heart beating as though they had been grafted into one.

He raised his head to study her with a smile of such sweetness and brilliance, she felt sure he was going to say something momentous.

What he did say was, 'Your eyebrows were painted on by Van Dyck.'

Of all the ridiculous remarks. She was drowning in love and laughter as they started kissing again.

She did not know how long she stood there, caught in a state of rapture that was quite new to her.

Then suddenly it was over. Some roisterers had invaded another part of the beach and the blessed

peace was desecrated by whoops of tipsy jollity and
excited shrieks of unconvincing feminine alarm. The
vulgar horseplay was a disagreeable parody of the game
Tom and Olivia had been playing with such tenderness
and fire.

He released her quickly and they retreated up the
steps on to the promenade. She did not think those
people on the beach had seen them; they were much
too engrossed in their own amusements. There was no
one on the promenade itself and only a single curricle
coming along the road. They were certainly visible to
the driver of this carriage, but out of earshot, and
Olivia, her hand on Tom's arm, waited for what he
would say next.

She was disconcerted when he looked past her to the
oncoming vehicle and said, 'Good God, it's Lion!'

'Lion?' she repeated, uncomprehending.

Tom raised his arm in a kind of salute, and the driver
pulled up his team to a walking pace and then stopped.
He was a very young man, slim and handsome, with
fair unruly curls worn in the careless, romantic style.
He looked as though he had come a long way. His
clothes and his carriage were white with dust, he had a
servant up behind him and a good deal of baggage.

'What the devil are you doing here?' demanded
Tom.

'Looking for you, sir,' said the boy with an impudent
grin. 'Though I didn't think I'd find you so easily.
Would it be presumptuous to enquire what *you* are
doing?'

'Not in the least,' said Tom easily. 'Miss Fenimore
and I have been reviving ourselves with a breath of sea
air after enduring the first half of a very dull concert.

Miss Fenimore, may I present my godson Lionel Forester?'

Young Mr Forester bowed gracefully and gave Olivia a speculating glance she did not quite like.

'Why didn't you tell me you were coming?' asked his godfather. 'Or was the matter too urgent? I suppose you are in some sort of a scrape.'

'Nothing of the sort. I've been at Cassondon for a week or two—I knew you would not mind—and I've come down here entirely on your behalf because there is a piece of news I think you will want to hear without delay. And in private,' added Lion Forester with another meaning glance towards Olivia.

'I see. In that case I'd better come up to the house with you—if Miss Fenimore will excuse me.' Tom spoke to Olivia in a confidential voice and with a secret smile which had the power to charm away any disappointed flatness she might be feeling. 'Would you mind very much if I escorted you back to the concert and left you with some of your friends? I foresee that I'm going to have to deal with some kind of domestic disaster.'

'I hope it won't turn out to be too serious, Mr Brooke,' she replied with a very good imitation of bright unconcern. 'Of course you want to talk to your godson. And there is no need to escort me. I don't think anything very dreadful can happen to me between here and the Assembly Rooms.'

She thought he would insist on coming with her all the same, and hoped they might have a few words alone, but at that moment some more truants emerged from under the chestnut trees: the Millington girls and their brothers. They too had escaped into the beautiful evening but felt sure their parents would expect them to be back for the second half of the concert. And if

Olivia went with them they could all sit at the back and count how many of the music-lovers had fallen asleep.

'So you see I shall be well amused for the rest of the evening,' Olivia said to Tom.

He left her with obvious reluctance. It did seem extremely hard that they should be separated at such a moment. Surely he could have sent this unknown boy up to the Vale and followed later? But she did not know the circumstances and she would see him again tomorrow. Tonight she would think only of that precious interlude on the beach, re-living every memory before it was swamped by the even greater happiness she felt certain lay ahead.

CHAPTER NINE

IT CAME as a shock next day to discover that Tom and his godson had left Parmouth very early in the morning on their way to Northamptonshire. Olivia heard the news when she called at Rosamond's Bower. A message had been sent up from the Vale but the Wakelins had not seen the departing travellers and did not know why Tom had gone off in such haste.

'I dare say he's lost his entire fortune,' said Lizzie callously.

'It would need a revolution to dissipate Tom's *entire* fortune,' remarked Preston, 'and the herald of that kind of disaster would not be Lion Forester.'

'Who exactly is Lion Forester?' enquired Olivia.

The news of Tom's departure had taken her so much by surprise that she found it hard to keep her countenance, but she felt she had to say something.

'He's the son of an old friend of Tom's who died a couple of years ago,' said Preston. 'Tom is his godfather and trustee, almost a self-appointed guardian, since the boy's real guardian, his uncle, is an idle fellow who does nothing. Lion is a good-looking young scapegrace, always in some kind of trouble. I imagine he needs Tom's help to get him out of yet another tight corner.'

Lion himself had denied this when they met him on the promenade, she remembered, but then he would hardly want to admit to some social lapse or financial

crisis when encountering his godfather in a public place
and with a girl on his arm.

Olivia went to call on the Channings but they had
nothing further to add which would help to solve the
mystery of Tom's sudden departure. She would have
to possess her soul in patience and wait for his return.
This was extremely tantalising at such a time, but she
was not self-centred. Her chief concern was a wish that
she could have shared Tom's anxieties, whatever they
were. She hoped she would soon have the right to do
so. She felt certain by now that he was in love with her,
and by dinnertime she had sensibly convinced herself
that this tiresome interlude was of no importance in
the general scheme of things.

No one who saw her in the next week could have
perceived any change in her normal good temper and
cheerful spirits.

Before he went away Tom had promised to take the
Wakelins and Louisa Woodvile to see a ruined castle
belonging to his family at a place called Dalney, a few
miles from Parmouth. Olivia had of course been
included in the invitation. Now Lizzie decided that they
would go without him. She had been reading about
Dalney in the local guide. It was not an ancient ruin
precisely, nothing to do with William the Conqueror or
Richard the Lionheart, but it was a ruin all the same,
having been built by one of Tom's ancestors to defend
the coastline about the time of the Spanish Armada
and then allowed to fall down. It all sounded sweetly
pretty and picturesque.

Olivia did not really want to go on this expedition
with Tom acting as Banquo's ghost, but she saw no
way of getting out of it.

They set off early in the Wakelins' carriage, Olivia

sitting upright in the middle of the seat, the inferior place accorded to a spinster between the two married ladies, Lizzie and her sister-in-law Louisa each occupying a corner. That was another annoyance; Preston was a little ahead of them on horseback and if she had known in time she could have ridden too, instead of having to sit bodkin, which was never very comfortable.

The post had arrived just before they set out, and Mrs Woodvile had in her hand a thickish letter which she opened as soon as the carriage began to move.

'You will not mind my finding out what Catherine Wingfield has to say?'

'She seems to have a great deal to say,' remarked Lizzie, eyeing the lines of tightly compressed writing which crossed each other on the paper.

Louisa looked up. 'Sir Martin Laybourne is dead.'

She spoke as though this piece of news was not only surprising but important, and Lizzie responded in much the same way.

'Good heavens! I had no idea he was so ill. Everyone said it was just his dog-in-the-manger way of punishing Anne. When did it happen? I dare say it was in the *Morning Post*, only we never have time to read the papers properly down here.'

Louisa went on reading. Olivia had no idea who Sir Martin Laybourne was, so she said nothing.

After a moment Lizzie gave a little jump of excitement.

'So *that* was the reason for all the careering about in curricles! Only I don't understand why he was in such a hurry. Surely he did not mean to go straight to Anne?'

Louisa had been racing through her letter.

'On the contrary,' she said doubtfully. 'Apparently Anne has gone to him.'

'To live with him openly? I don't believe it! Though I suppose Catherine must know, seeing she is so closely connected to the Gerards. Do read out what she says.'

Olivia had fastened on a hint from the phrase, careering about in curricles. She thought they must be talking about Tom, but the recital of unknown names was confusing and she did not at once understand what was meant.

Louisa hesitated. 'I think you had better read the letter yourself.'

'My dear, you know I cannot so much as glance at a sheet of paper in a moving carriage without bringing on one of my dizzy spells. Do let me hear what she says.'

Louisa was still unwilling. 'It is rather confidential.'

'Well, what of it? We are all friends here. And you need not be prudish about Olivia *pas devant la jeune fille* and all that nonsense. She isn't a silly schoolgirl, are you, my love?'

'I hope not,' said Olivia stoically.

By now she was sure she was going to hear something she would not like. At the same time it was something she needed to know. Not to hear it would be worse.

Rather uncomfortably Louisa read aloud.

'. . .I am sorry to have to tell you something most unfortunate as regards poor Anne. After so many years of patience and discretion, her new freedom must have gone to her head, for she has lost her sense, burnt her boats, and left Welworth to place herself under Brooke's protection. Or at any rate under his roof for I am not sure whether he was there at the time——'

'He wasn't,' interrupted Lizzie. 'He was at the Vale. No wonder he went off in such a hurry.'

Louisa read steadily on.

'All the Gerards are greatly distressed, as you may imagine. It seems such a rash act and so unnecessary, when they had only to wait until she was out of mourning to put everything right. Such an honourable and suitable second marriage would soon have effaced the memory of her past indiscretion. As it is, their living openly in sin for however short a time, and scrambling into Church so soon after her first husband's funeral, can only ensure that their guilty connection can never be quite forgotten.'

'I find Catherine's preaching a little tedious,' commented Lizzie. 'She writes like a Methodist. But of course she is quite right about the scandal, and I must say I am surprised at Anne. She must be absolutely sure of Tom.'

'And very much in love,' said Louisa.

'Oh, that certainly. And I tell you what I think. I expect Anne had been warned of Sir Martin's approaching death, without knowing the exact date, and that she and Tom had made their plans accordingly.'

Olivia heard them talking as though at a great distance. She was struggling with the stunning sensation of what she had just discovered: that Tom, all the time he had been charming her into love with him, had been committed to another woman, so committed that when her husband died everyone took it for granted that they would marry. They had been actually waiting for him to die. The shock, the total reversal of all her hopes and feelings, was almost paralysing. She had never fainted in her life; briefly she wished she could. Just to let go the consciousness of the hateful present would have been a relief.

Lizzie had leant forward in her eagerness to discuss the fascinating news with Louisa, so there was now enough room for Olivia to lean against the back of the carriage and receive a little support while she gained command of her emotions. Eventually they stopped and she saw with a dull surprise that they had driven into quite a different landscape—low green hills, a small hamlet clustered beside a stream and, before them, on a rising slope with a view of the coastline, the miniature tower and castellated walls of a roofless building that looked as though it had probably been destroyed by fire. There were broken arches and rocklike platforms of masonry. The only part of the castle still intact was a handsome gatehouse.

They all got out and stared about them, though Lizzie had no time just then for the picturesque—she was too busy telling Preston that the newly widowed Lady Laybourne had gone to live with Tom at Cassondon.

He was very much surprised, agreed that they must intend to marry as soon as possible, and found a reason for Anne Laybourne's rash flight.

'Since she and Martin had no children, the title and property pass to his brother, who is no friend to Anne—on account of her association with Tom.'

'I hadn't thought of that,' said Lizzie.

She began to take an interest in her surroundings,

and presently she and Preston moved off, arguing about barbicans and portcullises.

Olivia was left standing without the energy to do anything or go anywhere on her own iniative. She was aroused by the gentle voice of Louisa Woodvile.

'It's not a very distinguished castle, is it? Shall we stay here and contemplate it from a distance?'

'Very well.'

They found a grass bank and sat down in the sun, gazing at the crumbling chunks of stone.

'I suppose the Elizabethans built it as a sort of Martello tower.'

'I dare say. . . Mrs Woodvile, since I could not help hearing what was in your letter, may I ask you about this lady whose husband has died? I understand Mr Brooke is in love with her. Is it an attachment of long standing?'

'Nearly ten years. That is why he has never married.'

Olivia felt a weight of cold despair sink through her like a stone. Louisa was earnestly prodding the turf with the point of her parasol.

She said, 'I'm afraid that a man of his kind, apparently unattached, sometimes causes pain without meaning to. Women have been misled by his lively and unguarded manner.'

'I suppose I am lucky not to be one of them,' said Olivia, boldly denying the truth. 'We did have a little flirtation, which as it happens did no harm. Even so, I should never willingly have encouraged the most transient attentions from any man who was bound in honour to another woman. Or bound in dishonour, which I suppose was the case. Lizzie warned me against him without saying why; that is what enrages me. I am not so young that everyone has to pretend I don't know what goes on in the world. She admitted as much herself when she asked you to read aloud from your friend's letter. Why could she not tell me about Lady Laybourne?'

Louisa spent a little time apparently thinking over her answer. Then she said, 'I have always felt it dishonest and irrational to condone certain actions so long as they are not openly recognised. It seems to me that one should either condemn sin altogether or accept the failings of others without presuming to judge. But there it is—I can't change the customs of society. And Anne Laybourne's friends have always had a particular reason for trying to protect her reputation. Many of these illicit arrangements are entered into without bitterness by all parties. With the Laybournes it was different. Anne Gerard was married at seventeen to a man more than twice her age, who I believe cared for her sincerely but was never able to make her happy. Their characters did not suit and unluckily they had no children. Tom Brooke was their near neighbour—the Laybournes' home, Welworth Abbey, is only five miles from Cassondon.

'When the love-affair first began Sir Martin pretended to know nothing but he became increasingly unkind to his wife. I don't know the details, only that he kept a Sword of Damocles perpetually hanging over her: he threatened that if the scandal became public he would turn her out of doors, though without divorcing her, so that she would be unable to make a second marriage. And that, you know, would have left her utterly disgraced. You can see why everyone has been so anxious not to link her name with Tom Brooke's.'

'Yes, I do see,' said Olivia slowly. 'And I suppose

Mr Brooke himself has been the person most anxious
to protect her.'

'That is very true. In fact they were so discreet, and
their manner towards each other was seen to be so
guarded when they happened to meet in the ordinary
comings and goings of society, that I for one believed
the affair to be over—until about three years ago when
Sir Martin, claiming to be ill, incarcerated himself and
his wife at Welworth, and the story went round that he
had caught her with her lover and was keeping her
more or less a prisoner. People said his illness was
simply a face-saving pretence, though here I feel they
were mistaken. After all, the poor man is dead. But I
suppose Tom and Anne must have been in touch all
along, or she would never have gone to Cassondon so
soon or with so little ceremony. And now I come to
think of it, if Tom knew Sir Martin was dying, this
would explain his spending so little time in
Northamptonshire recently. He would not wish to
revive an old scandal or give additional pain.'

Olivia thought he did not care how much pain he
caused outside Northamptonshire. Carefully modulat-
ing her voice, she asked, 'What sort of a woman is
Lady Laybourne? Are you much acquainted with her,
ma'am?'

'I've known her all my life, and she is not at all what
you are probably imagining. A beauty, in a quiet style.
Affectionate with an excellent understanding. And, in
spite of everything, good. Very good people don't
always avoid doing wrong. They simply pay more
heavily.'

Olivia was hurt, angry, bewildered and too much
distressed to marshal her thoughts properly. She had
lost the only man she had ever loved or wanted to

marry. Sufficient reason to be unhappy. And then everything had happened so suddenly. She had just heard the name Laybourne for the first time when the dreadful truth came out. A moment earlier she had been living in a world of illusion: joyful, confident, looking towards a delightful future. How could she have been so complacent, such a fool?

It was a good thing she was able to be angry, for the anger acted as a stimulant and prevented her breaking down. Anger and pride got her through the rest of the visit to Dalney and back to Marine Cottage and the not very observant company of her relations there.

She went on raging inwardly against Tom for deceiving her and herself for having been deceived. Perhaps she was as much to blame as he was. What had he actually said about marriage? Very little, when you came to the point. All her hopes had been founded on intimate glances, hinted preferences and confidences exchanged in what had seemed like a climate of perfect sympathy, and that last evening, when he had held her in his arms and kissed her, she had taken it for granted that he was on the point of proposing, would have done so but for the interruptions. How rash and silly and trusting she had been.

Of course at the time she had known nothing of Anne Laybourne, and she now tried to cast this shadowy rival as the villain of the piece; an immoral, ageing harpy who had got hold of Tom and corrupted him when he was quite young. But it would not do. She knew this was a totally false picture of the woman described by Louisa Woodvile, who was not even very old—twenty-nine to Tom's thirty-two, so Louisa had told her. She was ashamed of her own agonising jealousy and knew that if she had been told of three

strangers in similar circumstances her sympathies
would have been with Anne. She would have wanted
the man to keep faith with his early love instead of
deserting her for someone new. She was more widely
informed and more tolerant than most unmarried girls
because she had been brought up by a stepmother only
ten years older than herself who had discussed with
her, in private, subjects not considered proper for
innocent young ladies. For this very reason she should
have known how to avoid the snares of a dangerous
philanderer. She, who had felt so superior to poor
Hetty. Instead she had made the same mistakes with
the very same man, which was so humiliating.

At least she could avoid the sequel. She would not
make a public exhibition of her own folly and
wretchedness.

So she kept her place among the pleasure-seekers—
dwindling now, the Parmouth season was nearly over—
and tried to find something to occupy every vacant
hour.

She bought a donkey for the Channing children and
took them for rides, leading Neddy round the orchard
at the Vale, with Fanny, Polly and Cilla taking turns to
sit astride, grasping handfuls of his dusty, woolly coat
and hallooing him to go on.

One day the rides were especially hilarious. Polly
slid off the donkey and landed in a soft heap on the
grass. While they were laughing and picking her up,
Neddy ate the cotton flowers off Cilla's sun-bonnet.

When they finally went indoors and Olivia sent the
children up to their midday dinner in the nursery, she
had earned a temporary release from pain and was
feeling almost her old self when she opened the library
door and found that Lizzie was calling on Mrs

Channing, which was not unusual, and that they were having a heated argument, which was.

Lizzie was in full spate. 'I think he is the greatest villain unhung. He has behaved with barbarous cruelty to the gentlest and sweetest of women, and I for one hope I shall never set eyes on him again. I'm only surprised to find you don't agree with me, considering what a high value you set on the domestic virtues. But perhaps you think that a woman who has made one unfortunate mistake deserves to be cast off, even by the man responsible. He is to go unpunished, I take it, while she is ruined.'

'I never said that.' Martha Channing was sitting up straight and was very red in the face. 'Only that no one in our family has the right to condemn him, whatever he may have done. When I think of his continual generosity, of what our situation would be if he hadn't taken us in——'

She stopped, her eyes full of tears.

'You are perfectly right, ma'am,' said Preston, who was leaning on the back of his wife's chair. 'And, Lizzie, you have no business to be abusing Tom in front of Mrs Channing, and in his own house. Of course she is not going to listen to you.'

'Perhaps you may have been misinformed,' suggested Mrs Channing with an air of pleading.

'Nothing of the kind,' snapped Lizzie, unrepentant. 'I myself have now received a letter from another member of Lady Laybourne's family. Mrs Gerard is a most reliable correspondent.'

At this moment she caught sight of Olivia, standing transfixed in the doorway, and dragged her into the controversy. 'I warned you against Mr Brooke, didn't I, my dear Olivia? I could see that you thought me

interfering, but I was right to put you on your guard.
What do you think he has done now? He has rejected
the woman who has loved him for years at the very
moment when he ought to have honoured his obliga-
tions and married her. Withdrawn his protection and
humiliated her so publicly that she has been forced to
enter a nunnery.'

Olivia was so horrified by all these accusations that
she could hardly grasp what Tom had done. Her mind
fixed on one detail so bizarre that it seemed as though
they had all been transplanted into the pages of a
Gothic novel.

'How could Lady Laybourne go into a nunnery? She
has not left the country?'

'No, of course not. The Laybournes have had a party
of French nuns living in one of their houses ever since
the Revolution. Anne has been very good to them, so
I hope they will be kind to her now, though it is not
very likely. I expect they will make her wear sackcloth
and do penances all day long.'

'But is she a Roman Catholic?'

'No, she isn't,' said Preston, 'and Lizzie is talking
nonsense. These nuns are French ladies of good family
who escaped to England at the height of the Terror.
They will know how to behave towards a Protestant
benefactress.'

'They will try to make a Papist of her,' said Lizzie
darkly. 'But never mind that. The worst thing is that
she should have to go to such people for succour. It
shows what a disgraceful situation Tom has placed her
in. There is no one else she dares turn to.'

She showed signs of making another attack on Tom's
character. Mrs Channing looked stubborn and defen-
sive. Olivia felt she could not listen any longer. She

made some disjointed remark about the children and
the donkey and cravenly slipped away.

She felt quite weak as she started down the hill, as
though she had been ill and her legs could hardly carry
her. It was strange that what she had just heard had
come as an even greater shock than the original news
of Tom's being in love with Lady Laybourne. She had
lost the lover she was confidently to marry, and at the
time that had seemed intolerable. Yet in a sense she
had not entirely lost Tom, because there in her mind's
eye he still was: the same delightful, fascinating person,
only in love with someone else. He was an incorrigible
flirt, she had known that all along, and he had never
tried to make himself out better than he was. Because
Olivia was naturally generous—and also because she
was infatuated—she had managed to convince herself
that she was principally responsible for her present
wretchedness and that hardly any blame rested on
Tom.

She could think so no longer. His treatment of Anne
Laybourne was so much worse than anything he had
done to her or Hetty. He had tempted her into years
of adultery and, according to Louisa Woodvile, pangs
of genuine guilt. She had suffered the unkindness of a
jealous husband and been more or less imprisoned in
his country estate. And then, when she was at last free
to become his wife, Tom had abandoned her.

Olivia did wonder for a moment whether Tom had
some excuse, whether Anne had tried to force his
hand. But that would not do. Both Lizzie and the far
more sensible Louisa were convinced that she would
never have gone to live with him openly unless they
had planned to marry after her husband's death.

By now Olivia was nearly back in the streets of

Parmouth and realised for the first time that tears were running down her cheeks. She stepped aside into a patch of woodland, pushed aside a tangle of leafy branches, and came to rest against the trunk of a thick tree, clinging to the rough surface while she sobbed her heart out.

Only for a few minutes. She hardly ever cried and knew it did her no good. She soon felt able to go on, her face decently hidden by the wide brim of her bonnet. It was midday and there were few people about.

She had one thing to be thankful for. Her uncle and aunt and Flora had driven up to Brantisford to see some old friends, so once she reached Marine Cottage she had the rare luxury of being alone.

A plate of chicken sandwiches and a jug of lemonade were placed for her in the morning-room. She was not hungry but she swallowed a little of the lemonade to cool her burning throat. She wished she could talk to the only person she had ever confided in: Geraldine. But Geraldine was half the world away, somewhere on the high seas or perhaps even in India by now.

A letter would have to do. It would be a release to unburden herself on paper. She fetched her small writing-box of polished wood and began, soon becoming so absorbed that she did not hear the voices in the hall, or turn her head even when the door behind her opened.

'I hardly dared to hope I'd find you alone,' said Tom. He was dressed for the road and his boots were powdered with dust. His hair was ruffled and his skin was brown. He brought with him the active male assurance that came from hours spent in the open air.

He was smiling and his eyes, as always, were intensely blue.

She felt her heart lurch.

'What are you doing here?' she heard herself ask in a strange, thin voice.

'Everyone seems very surprised to see me, I don't know why. I said I'd be back.' He went to lean against the mantelshelf, one foot on the fender. 'I had some unfinished business to see to. Can't you guess what it was?'

He was still smiling.

'No,' said Olivia flatly.

She had retained enough presence of mind to sprinkle some sand on her letter and close the writing-case.

'I've come to finish what I was just about to begin when that scamp Lion made his ill-timed appearance. To ask you to marry me.'

'To ask me what?' She could not believe she had heard him properly.

'My dearest love, surely you must have guessed. You who have received offers from half the aristocracy of Ireland, I understand. Perhaps I am acting like a coxcomb, trying my luck where so many have failed, but you did give me an idea that you liked me.'

This piece of false modesty cleared her brain wonderfully, with its unmistakable reference to the way she had encouraged his lovemaking. She felt herself growing cold with anger.

'Please don't address me in those terms, Mr Brooke. You have no right to do so and I wonder you dare speak to me of marriage.'

'What do you mean—no right?' He straightened up and the smile vanished.

'I believe there is another woman who has a prior claim to be called your dearest love.'

He flushed. 'I see people have been talking. What have they told you?'

'Enough to make me certain that I never want to see you again.'

'That's a trifle peremptory. What have they said, Olivia?'

'That your—your connection with Lady Laybourne was so serious and long-established that everyone took it for granted you would marry her when her husband died. She herself must have thought so, since she threw discretion to the winds and went to live openly in your house.'

She was watching him closely and she saw that he was disconcerted. He could not have expected the news to reach Parmouth so quickly and in such detail.

After a moment he said, 'If you imagine Anne Laybourne is living with me at Cassondon, I can understand your resentment. I assure you this is not so.'

'Thank you, I know that already. Everyone knows it. Her wretched situation seems to have become public property. I gather she has been forced to go and hide in a Convent.'

'Good God, how spiteful people can be!' he exclaimed. 'Determined to see everything in the worst possible light. And of course I am cast as the villain. But I did not think you would condemn me unheard. You at least are not a prude.'

Olivia bit her lip. The reminder that she was not a prude sounded more like an insult than a compliment, coming from him. She was dimly aware that he might not be responsible for everything that had gone wrong between himself and Anne Laybourne; there were probably faults on both sides. Only Tom was the kind of man who took advantage of a woman's folly and then put the blame on her for being a fool. She was thinking not of herself, but of someone who had been far more defenceless.

She said, 'I don't know why you should come here expecting me to give you the benefit of the doubt. I know very little of the character of Anne Laybourne but I haven't forgotten the way you treated my cousin.'

'Oh, I might have known you would drag up the pathetic example of Hetty—as though there was any comparison! That's the trouble with romantic young ladies—you never have any sense of proportion.'

The note of derision in his voice was the final straw. There was no longer the slightest chance that she would listen to any of his explanations, or feel kinder towards him because he said he wanted to marry her. This could be no more than a momentary whim. He was tired of Lady Laybourne and perhaps he thought he could get out of marrying her more easily by claiming that he was already engaged to the girl who happened to be his latest fancy. Olivia found him altogether detestable.

They were staring at each other in a state of freezing hostility. By now their dislike was mutual. At last he moved towards the door and turned slowly for a parting shot.

'I told you once that girls who led men on and then refused them were apt to be known as common jilts. But you are something different again—a most uncommon jilt. A girl who is able to refuse an honest offer of marriage as though it was an insult. I suppose I ought to congratulate you.'

CHAPTER TEN

THE grey rain came down on the grey sea, stabbing the grey surface of the water with steely pin-pricks. The change in the weather had coincided with the end of the Parmouth season and the disappearance of the visitors. The older inhabitants said this was unusual, but it helped to emphasise that other change in Olivia's life and hopes, and made her feel as though she had been literally living in a different world. The happy scenes of two or three weeks ago were now remote.

The Fenimores were making their way along the promenade to Sunday morning service under a fleet of flapping umbrellas. Olivia did not want to go to Church or to any other public place where she ran the risk of meeting the man who had now become a threat to the small amount of confidence she still possessed.

For Tom had not gone away with the other smart summer people as she had somehow expected, and sure enough when they entered the Church she immediately saw him, sitting in his reserved pew with Mrs Channing, Bernard and the little girls. As the Fenimores' pew was three rows behind his, she could not avoid seeing the back of his head all through the service, and this distracted her from the source of comfort and fortitude just when she needed them most.

As Mr Cottle ended his sermon, she calculated the chances of their getting away without having to speak to Tom. But it was hopeless. The rain was now coming down so hard that no one wanted to leave the Church

and they all clustered in the porch, waiting for a break
in the storm.

'Shocking weather,' Tom said to her uncle.

They were the first words Olivia had heard him
speak since he had called her an uncommon jilt, and
they were hardly inspired, but she could see that he
too was embarrassed, which gave her a kind of painful
pleasure.

'We don't often see you here after the summer is
over,' Mr Fenimore reminded him.

Tom said something about local business, a hold-up
in his plans for the new houses at Tatton Cove.

Olivia thought he had a much better reason for
remaining at Parmouth. He would not want to return
to his natural haunts while his treatment of Anne
Laybourne was causing so much disapproval and comment among his circle of friends.

She forced herself to look directly at him and found
that he was studying her. There was an instant of
confusion, almost of complicity, before they both
turned away. She busied herself in putting on her
pattens. The rain was easing off, soon they would be
able to escape.

As they splashed their way home she tried to analyse
what she had seen in Tom's expression. Resentment,
bitterness, what you might expect from a rejected
suitor whose pride had been hurt. But there was
something else as well, and she realised that if he was
indeed skulking at the Vale to avoid his friends in the
great world he must particularly dislike meeting anyone
still in Parmouth who also happened to know the truth.
He would keep out of her way, and now that the
Wakelins had left Rosamond's Bower their paths would
not cross nearly so often.

This did not prevent her feeling very low, and it was a struggle always trying to seem bright and contented at Marine Cottage. Her aunt had said several times that she hoped Olivia would not find life in Parmouth too humdrum now the summer was over. It would be dreadful to appear moody and listless, the typical heiress, when they had always been so kind to her. It would almost be better to admit the truth and become an object of pity.

Almost but not quite. She could not admit to anyone the misery of crushing down her unwilling love for Tom under the weight of disillusion and disenchantment.

She thought she might feel better if she had rather more to do, and then the opportunity came. Hetty had been writing happily from Cheshire about her recent pregnancy, but now a letter arrived from Alfred. He was anxious about her health. She never complained but it seemed to him that she was suffering a good deal more discomfort than most ladies did at such a time. His mother was dead and he had no sisters. Could Mrs Fenimore pay them a visit and give him her advice?

Of course Aunt Hester was all eager anxiety. She set off in a post-chaise, thankful that she could leave everything at Marine Cottage in Olivia's capable hands.

Olivia was quite satisfied with this arrangement. She liked responsibility and was well able to manage the house, the servants, her uncle and Flora. Apparently there was only one thing she could not do: chaperon Flora to evening parties. In fact she still needed a chaperon herself, which seemed ridiculous, considering how sedate and world-weary she had begun to feel. However, it was useless to complain, and Mrs Osgood had already promised to take them both under her wing at the first of the monthly subscription balls which took place in Parmouth through the autumn and winter.

The balls were held at the Assembly Rooms built for the entertainment of the summer visitors, and this was not altogether a happy arrangement. The rooms were far larger than most of those in country neighbour-hoods and as a result the company always looked a little thin on that great expanse of polished floor, which was like the rest of Parmouth out of season: far too expensive-looking and empty, and the ladies and gentlemen—though they undoubtedly were ladies and gentlemen—not quite fine enough for the gilding and the blaze of chandeliers.

One thing had been worrying Olivia all day. On the whole she thought not, but if he did attend, would he feel obliged to ask her to dance, and, if so, ought she to accept, simply to stop people gossiping? They had danced together so constantly in those rooms.

On arriving at the ball, however, one quick glance was enough to reassure her. There was no one here from the Vale. But this meant there were not quite enough men to go round, and after standing up for the first two dances she decided to make use of an ankle she had twisted, not at all seriously, on her morning walk. It hardly hurt at all, but if she exaggerated a little she could go and sit by Mrs Osgood, and the younger girls would get enough partners. She did not feel in the least noble; there was no one here she wanted to dance with in the place where she had once been so exquis-itely happy.

'You must find this a sad decline after your triumphs in the summer,' remarked Mrs Osgood. Here was someone else prepared to think her spoilt and discon-tented. It was too bad.

She smiled sweetly and said, 'I hope you don't think I went out and twisted my ankle on purpose, ma'am, in order to sit in a corner and give myself airs.'

Mrs Osgood had never quite succeeded in patronising Olivia. She gave up trying and began to treat her almost as a confidante.

'These monthly balls have certain dangers attaching to them. In such a limited society young people are sometimes drawn into unsuitable associations. I make it a rule that Madeleine must never dance more than twice with the same partner at any ball. I dare say I am over-particular,' said Mrs Osgood with the complacent smile of someone who was quite sure she was right, 'but one cannot be too careful.'

Olivia looked along the set and saw Madeleine dancing with an airy grace on the arm of Walter Cottle from the Parsonage—that intense young man without money or connections who would certainly be classed as unsuitable. He was gazing at her with hungry adoration. She seemed as happy and carefree as a child.

'I should think,' said Olivia frankly, 'that such a very pretty girl must always find more would-be partners than she has time to dance with.'

'How kind of you to say so. Yes, she has been very much admired. There have been a few little difficulties, but never of her making. She understands exactly what I will permit and what is forbidden and she is never disobedient. The fear of displeasing me is enough to deter her from even the slightest misconduct.'

That girl is almost too good to be true, thought Olivia, watching the immaculate beauty return smiling to her mother as the dance ended. She was accompanied by Flora, who was flushed and jolly, with a tear in her skirt. Each of these very young ladies was irritating in a different way to someone of twenty-two who was suffering from the pangs of an unsuccessful love-affair.

It was at this juncture that Olivia saw a newcomer appear in the doorway at the far end of the room. He was a tall young man, very fair, and she was sure she had seen him before. Then Bernard too emerged through the doorway, and this gave her a clue. The fair young man was Lionel Forester, Tom's godson, that bringer of bad tidings who had come posting down from Cassondon and ruined her happiness.

Behind his two young protégés came Tom himself. Olivia felt her heart pounding uncomfortably, which was ridiculous. Tom was nothing to her now. Only the whole situation was so awkward.

She gathered in the next few minutes that Lion had just arrived at the Vale. When he heard there was a ball that evening he was mad to go to it, only he had to wait for his clothes to be unpacked and that was why they were late.

Lion turned to Olivia, recalling that they had met before, and asked her for the next dance. Of course she had to refuse on account of her twisted ankle. There was nothing else she could do with Mrs Osgood listening beside her, but it was mortifying to catch Tom's smile of cynical incredulity. Did he really believe she had refused Lion in case he himself should ask her later? She remembered the clumsy way she had avoided dancing with him at the cricketers' ball and how he had paid her out, and her mortification grew.

Lion had by now been presented to Madeleine. He gazed at her as though he could hardly believe his luck, and was soon leading her on to the floor. Mrs Osgood watched them with pride. Flora was glad to be dancing with her great friend Bernard. Tom remained standing a few feet from Olivia, apparently lost in thought.

Presently he spoke to her directly.

'I am sorry you are unable to dance, Miss Fenimore. I know it is one of your great pleasures.'

She listened for a note of sarcastic disbelief, but could detect nothing but a chilly formality.

'One has to survive these hardships, Mr Brooke.'

'I am sure you will do that. You are a model of fortitude.'

'Will your godson be staying with you long, Mr Brooke?' asked Mrs Osgood cunningly.

'That depends. He wants to join the Army and I hope I can get him into a good regiment through the offices of my friend General Durnford.'

Tom stood watching the dancers for some time. He took no further notice of Olivia and presently walked off to the card-room.

In bed that night Olivia gave way to a flood of almost hysterical weeping, stuffing her head into the pillow so that Flora could not hear her in the next room. There was no use pretending; she was still in love with Tom. Achingly, shamingly in love. It was like an illness. Those precious minutes on the beach had given her an indication of what passion must be like at its full extent. She understood for the first time why girls ran off to Scotland with devil-may-care adventures, why women like the wretched Anne Laybourne betrayed their husbands at the risk of being punished for the rest of their lives.

If Tom had asked me to run away with him, she thought, I might not have been strong enough to refuse. But the heartbreaking truth was Tom had never faced her with such a temptation. He had not tried to seduce her, left her for another woman or simply made her the object of a heartless flirtation. What Tom had done was make her an offer of marriage, which she had refused because of the way he had treated the mistress who seemed to have a prior claim on him.

But why did I do that, she asked herself, for a woman I don't even know and should probably detest? What is Anne Laybourne to me? An adulteress who got what she deserved.

I said all those dreadful things to him because I had only just received the shock that very morning of hearing how that unfortunate creature had been rejected and humiliated by the one person who ought to have stood by her. If he had come twenty-four hours later, I should still have refused him, but more temperately, and he might have asked again. Now he never will.

Yet, in spite of all her regrets, a small voice at the back of her mind said, You could not swear to love, honour and obey a man who behaved as he has done without a sign of remorse.

The next time she saw Tom she was walking up the hill that led to Brantisford with Flora, Madeleine, Bernard and Lion Forester. He overtook them on horseback and stopped to pass the time of day.

Looking at her directly, he said, 'I am glad you have recovered from your sprained ankle,' and she could not for the life of her tell whether he was being serious or sarcastic. It was all part of the tragedy that they seemed to have lost their lightness of touch.

It was soon clear that Lion was greatly taken with Madeleine and she with him. He had been rusticated from Oxford but this did not seem to matter very much as he was not at all scholarly and genuinely wanted to join the Army. So he was to remain at the Vale while Tom negotiated to get him a commission. He was quite a wealthy young man though at present his property was being held in trust.

All these facts were soon known to the Osgoods, so that in spite of Mrs Osgood's strict rules it was apparently quite fitting for the carefully chaperoned Madeleine to meet Mr Forester every day, provided she never saw him alone. Bernard and Flora went with them everywhere and it was taken for granted that Flora's cousin would be there too and could be regarded as an unofficial duenna 'because she is so sensible'. And so old, thought Olivia derisively. But I must not let myself get soured, it is very wrong and stupid. Being crossed in love is such a dismal occupation.

Bernard had time on his hands because he was waiting to take up an appointment in the office of Mr Walker, the architect. He accepted the presence of Lion in a good-natured, uncritical way. His friend, Walter Cottle, felt very differently.

Walter, the Parson's son, intended to take Holy Orders, but he was not quite old enough, so he too was at a loose end and until lately he had filled his days with being happily if hopelessly in love with Madeleine. The sight of her falling under the spell of the smooth-tongued, handsome and altogether detestable Lion was more than he could stand. He now avoided his old friends, wanting to know what was going on but unwilling to join in.

'What are your plans for today?' he asked suspiciously, meeting Olivia one morning as she was coming out of the library.

'We thought we might take a long walk inland, up the valley as far as the mill. Why don't you come with us?'

'And play second fiddle to that Bond Street lounger? No, I thank you,' said Walter, deep in gloom.

'You can keep me company and bring our numbers up to six. There need be no question of second fiddles.'

The young man declined this offer rather ungraciously, but slouched along beside her for some way, the wind off the sea blowing keenly through his raven locks, in order to give his views on the vile character of Lion Forester and the dangerous effect he was likely to have on Madeleine's unsmirched purity. Olivia found him feeble and exasperating but had too much fellow-feeling to say so.

He left her before they reached Marine Cottage, where the quartet were assembled and waiting. They set out, walking in a loose group, sometimes all together, sometimes as a trio and a couple. The couple were invariably Lion and Madeleine.

They had turned away from the sea, glad to be out of the wind and in the shelter of a deep Devon lane. Above them on the hill were two fine white houses: the Vale, and, higher still but plainly visible among the trees, Rosamond's Bower. Olivia averted her gaze.

Presently she discovered that Madeleine was telling the others about her early memories of living in a Convent in France during the lifetime of her real parents. Olivia listened with some interest. She had almost forgotten that this beautiful, unusual-looking girl was actually the Osgoods' adopted daughter and that her father had been a Frenchman.

Lion remarked that there were a number of Convents in England now.

'The nuns are French *émigrées*. Though I do know an English lady who has been forced to take the veil.'

'Forced?' repeated Flora with a delicious shudder. 'Against her will?'

'More or less. She became the centre of a scandal and was disowned by those who might have protected her.'

'Do you mean her parents?' asked Madeleine.

'Her parents were dead. She wasn't a young girl, my dear. She was a widow, old enough to know better.' Lion caught Olivia's eye. 'I dare say you can guess who I am speaking of.'

She did not answer. How much did he know? Was it possible that Tom joked with his godson about his tangled love-affairs? Surely not. It must be all guess-work. But I believe Walter is right, she decided, there is something objectionable about this young man.

She spent the rest of the morning keeping as close as she could to Lion and Madeleine, close enough to hear what he was saying. It was tedious work. Lion looked annoyed and tried to shoulder his way ahead of her or edge her into the muddiest part of the lane, but he said nothing that anyone could take exception to. Madeleine did not appear to notice that she was being chaperoned. She was too busy gazing at Lion.

After this Olivia tried conscientiously to keep a particular eye on Madeleine when Lion was around, but nothing was ever said or done that she could find fault with, and she did not want to go as a tale-bearer to Mrs Osgood, whom she did not care for, and who undoubtedly hoped that throwing the young couple together in this innocently domesticated group would lead to their forming a serious attachment. Young Mr Forester's birth and expectations made him a good and equal match for the banker's adopted daughter, and it was on the cards that Tom would agree, though of course she could not ask him.

He seemed to be fixed in Parmouth, though taken up with his building plans at Tatton Cove. Acording to Bernard, there were doubts about the cliff site, fears of a possible subsidence.

At all events she had no intention of seeking Tom out, and when Flora and Madeleine said they meant to walk up to Rosamond's Bower she made an excuse for not going with them. She supposed they had an assignation with the two young men, but that couldn't be helped. There was safety in numbers, and one thing she was not prepared to do: she would not run the risk of meeting Tom in that horrible garden.

CHAPTER ELEVEN

SURE enough, as the girls climbed the hill, Bernard and Lion were waiting for them. The garden of Rosamond's Bower was quite unlike its summer self. Bare trees now swayed like tall ships drifting in a sea of autumn leaves, in every colour from lemon through russet and gold to deep copper.

'It is sad the house is empty again,' said Madeleine as they walked round the outside of the white villa and tried to peer through the shuttered windows.

'What a soft heart you have,' said Lion, smiling down at her. 'I never met anyone before who was sorry for an empty house. What would happen if we took you over to Dalney Castle? Would you burst into tears in the ruins?'

'No, I shouldn't,' she replied, blushing a little but ready to stand up for herself. 'I only think this house is sad because it is so beautifully furnished and hardly ever lived in. Ruins are different. They are romantic and all the sadness is a long time ago in history.'

'Did you go over to Dalney yesterday with Bernard?' Flora asked Lion.

'Yes, and I explored a great deal while he was sketching. We spent most of the day there.'

'Wasn't it very cold?'

'No,' said Bernard, who had been standing with a pencil in his outstretched hand and one eye closed, measuring the south façade of the house in what he hoped was a professional manner. He was making architectural studies in as many styles as possible while waiting to start work in Mr Walker's drawing-office.

'We asked the caretaker to light a fire in the gate-house,' he added, 'and the people from the inn sent us up a hot dinner. We were very snug.'

'I wish we could have been there,' said Flora rather wistfully.

'I tell you what,' said Lion. 'Why don't we go over there again, Bernard, and take the girls with us?'

'Oh, I wish you could,' said Madeleine eagerly. 'Only they would never let us join you on such an expedition. At least Mr Fenimore might let Flora go, but my mama would never agree.'

Her eyes filled with tears of vexation. There was a short silence, then the other three all spoke at once.

Flora said perhaps it would be all right if Olivia came with them. Bernard said they might be permitted to drive the girls to Dalney and back if they did not stop for a meal.

Lion ridiculed both these ideas.

'We don't need Miss Olivia, and just to drive there and back would be very tame. We should all be frozen stiff. A dinner *à quatre* in the gatehouse would be half the fun. Can't you girls contrive to get away for a few hours in the middle of the day without anyone noticing?'

'If only we could,' breathed Madeleine.

'I don't see how we can,' objected Flora. She was usually the more adventurous of the two, but today it was Madeleine who, after a little frowning concentration, came up with a plan.

'Suppose I told Mama that you had asked me to spend the day at Marine Cottage? She would be bound to say yes. And then on the same day you could tell your papa and Olivia that you are coming to us. We could all go to Dalney and no one would be any the wiser. We should have to be back before dark.'

'Bravo,' said Lion, 'I couldn't have thought of a better dodge myself.'

'Would it work?' asked Flora doubtfully.

'I dare say it might,' said Bernard. 'You girls often spend whole days in each other's houses, don't you? Only what would happen if Mrs Osgood and Olivia were to compare notes?'

'They wouldn't. They don't have long conversations, like two ladies of the same age.'

'There you are, then,' said Lion. He was satisfied, though Bernard was not.

'Suppose they were to meet in the town on the day itself? One of them might say something which would give the game away.'

'Well, it would be too late by then.'

Madeleine had a better solution. 'If we went on Monday there would be no risk of their meeting, for Mama is going to visit old Mrs Preece at Parr Cross and she won't take me with her because she doesn't want me to become too friendly with the Preece granddaughters—Angelica and her sisters. She thinks they are vulgar.'

Flora was faintly surprised. Not so much by Mado's ingenuity, or by her willingness to deceive her doting mama—she knew better than anyone what a trial Mrs Osgood could be with her eternal fussy precautions, but although Mado had often regretted her mother's strict rules she had never questioned the notions of good conduct and ladylike propriety that lay behind them. It was the safeguards she found unnecessary, not the opinions. But now, when she implied that her

mother looked down on the Miss Preeces, there had
been a note of derision in her voice which Flora had
never heard before.

They went on discussing their plans while they
sauntered through the gardens, and presently the two
couples became separated, taking different paths
through the shrubbery.

When they were alone Lion stopped, slipping an arm
round Madeleine's waist.

'Are you pleased with me for arranging such an
adventure for you? Will you reward me for being so
clever?'

'How am I to do that?'

'You know very well how. By letting me do as I
wanted yesterday, and the day before. And every other
day before.'

'No, I cannot, Lion. I must not. Kissing is wrong.
Everyone says so.'

'Everyone as interpreted by your mama. I can just
hear her admonishing you. "Now, my dear Madeleine,
it is very naughty to let a wicked, rough man pull your
hand out of your muff and kiss your fingers and your
wrist."' He suited the action to the words before going
on to kiss her cheek under the rim of her beaver
bonnet, remarking, 'This is even worse, isn't it? And
yet you don't run away from me in spite of your serious
moral scruples.'

'How silly you are,' protested Madeleine, half laughing and half angry. 'I know we are behaving improp-
erly, only it cannot do any harm. It is not like the other
sort of kissing.'

'So that is what your mother told you!' He pretended
to be suddenly enlightened. 'She said, "That handsome

young man can do anything he pleases so long as he does not kiss you on the mouth." Anything else!'

'Of course she didn't—she would not speak in such a way. She has too much delicacy of mind.'

'Far too much for my way of thinking. I have the greatest respect for your parents but they have brought you up to be a perfect little goose. You seem to have no idea what is going on outside your nursery. You know we are at war, you know I am going to join the Army. Does it not occur to you that in a month or two from now I may be dead?'

'Oh, no, Lion,' she whispered.

'Oh, yes, Madeleine. Think of me, bleeding to death on a battlefield and remembering the hard-hearted girl who denied me the one thing I desired.'

At this moment, when she might have flung herself into his arms, they both heard the crackle and creak of twigs made by someone approaching through the undergrowth. They jumped apart, expecting to see Bernard and Flora. The person who appeared round the side of a holly tree was Lion's godfather.

'What are you doing here, sir?' Lion asked, struggling to hide his annoyance.

'Just looking over Lord Canfield's property for him. I sometimes think I shall apply to him for the post of land agent. More to the point,' said Tom, smiling sweetly, 'what are you two doing?'

'We came up here with Flora and Bernard. They are about somewhere.'

Lion and Madeleine stared around as though they had accidentally mislaid their two friends.

'Then we may as well go and find them.'

Tom placed himself firmly between the boy and girl, offering his arm to Madeleine, who took it nervously.

They were soon joined by the other couple and left Rosamond's Bower together.

Later that day Olivia went by herself to keep an appointment with Mrs Chapman, the dressmaker. Mrs Chapman was a treasure, an unlikely find in a place as small as Parmouth. She had come down from London with her husband, a clockmaker, and their two small daughters, so that he could open a shop of his own selling timepieces to the neighbourhood and the summer visitors. He was a good craftsman but it would take him a year or so to establish a local reputation and a thriving business. Meanwhile his wife continued her own trade. She had made Hetty's trousseau and enjoyed working for Olivia, whom she admired for her striking good looks and her eye for the latest fashion. She was not one of your insipid young ladies who always managed to look prim and inoffensive.

To reach the private part of the house it was necessary to go through the shop. Olivia went in and greeted the clockmaker, who was attending to a customer.

'Mrs Chapman is expecting me,' she said. 'I can find my way.'

But apparently this would not do. Mr Chapman hurried forward, saying he would fetch his wife.

'If you will excuse me for a moment, sir.'

'Certainly,' said his customer, turning round, so that he was facing Olivia.

Mr Chapman disappeared into the back premises. For the first time since his ill-fated proposal Tom and Olivia were alone together with the bitter words of that encounter echoing in their memories.

'How do you do, Miss Olivia?' said Tom politely.

'I am well, thank you, sir.'

'Won't you take a chair?'

This struck her as slightly ridiculous. Was he trying to put her at her ease in a shop belonging to one of his tenants?

She said, 'I don't suppose Mrs Chapman will be long.'

There was a pause. Then they both started talking at once, apologised and fell silent. Tom had been examining a pretty little carriage clock which had its brass skeleton entirely visible through the glass that formed its body. He laid it down on the table.

'There is something I wanted to say to you.'

Olivia could not imagine what it would be. Nothing he could say was likely to gratify her, unless he declared that her just assessment of his character had touched his conscience and that he now intended to make an honest woman of Lady Laybourne, and of course she knew in her heart of hearts that this moral pronouncement would not satisfy her in the least and would merely add a disgraceful and unwarranted jealousy to all her other miseries. So it was a good thing he was not going to say anything of the sort.

What he did say was, 'I believe you are more or less in charge of the walking parties that Madeleine and Flora and the boys have become so addicted to. An honorary chaperon, in fact.'

'I don't know about being in charge,' she said defensively. 'I am certainly older than the others, if that is what you mean.'

'Yes, I expect it is what I mean,' he agreed. 'You've told me yourself how many difficulties there are facing very young girls before they have had time to gain much experience. Did you know that Madeleine was wandering about Rosamond's Bower, alone with my scapegrace godson? I interrupted what I took to be the start of a promising love-scene.'

Olivia felt a momentary shock. Then she rallied quickly.

'I think you must be exaggerating. They cannot have been alone for more than a few minutes—Flora and Bernard were there too. I know Madeleine has been rather dazzled by Lion, ready to fall seriously in love, which is, I am sure, what her mother is hoping for, and it is not for me to interfere. But, as to anything improper, she has been much too well brought-up. I don't know what you mean by a promising love-scene——'

She broke off, knowing only too well what he meant. He simply stood there and she was too sensitive not to imagine the irony that might or might not be present in his glance.

She was stung by an acute sense of grievance. She was not responsible for Madeleine, not related to her, not her governess. Why should she be expected to spy on a quiet, well-behaved girl who would never get into trouble of her own accord, because Tom's graceless, predatory godson, living in Tom's house, undoubtedly under Tom's influence, was given the run of that notorious garden where Tom himself had taken part in at least one disreputable incident? It was typical of the unfair treatment always meted out to women.

'If you think Lion is not to be trusted,' she said acidly, 'then I suggest he is the one who needs supervising, not poor little Madeleine. Though I don't suppose it would do any good. If every respectable girl in the place were locked up, he would find someone to corrupt, probably a married woman.'

Her gibe caught Tom unawares, he drew a sharp

breath, stopped looking at her and looked at the ground instead, biting his lip.

In a muted voice he said, 'I did not mean to offend or criticise you, Olivia. I seem to have been remarkably clumsy. That was a stupid thing to say and in very poor taste. Of course Lion knows how to behave himself with a young girl like Madeleine. I only meant to warn you that she may be in danger of taking him rather more seriously than he takes himself at present. Nothing more.'

He picked up the clock again and absently began to wind it. He had sounded so unlike himself, tentative and rather sad, and her anger immediately melted.

And then, most inconveniently and before she could answer, Mrs Chapman came in, apologising for the long delay. There had been some sort of domestic catastrophe, a lot of broken glass on the stairs, but now everything was shipshape; would Miss Fenimore be pleased to come for her fitting?

Reluctantly Olivia was obliged to go without a chance of speaking again to Tom, and when she returned through the shop he had left.

She walked slowly home, dissatisfied with her own performance. Tom's gentle manner had brought about a change of feeling, and she reminded herself that, however deeply she disapproved of his rake's progress, her right to comment had ceased when she refused his offer of marriage. He had been just as angry as he was at that stormy interview, and there was no doubt she had hurt his pride, but he had learnt to control his rancour and she now felt that his warning about Madeleine had been entirely disinterested, with no underlying intention to wound or jeer. She should have taken it in the right spirit. She would at least follow his advice and make a point of always going on the walks and rambles.

It wasn't a very amusing prospect, so she was glad to hear, a few days later, that Flora had been invited to spend Monday at the Villa Romana. In answer to a casual question, Flora added that Bernard was going over to do some sketching at Dalney Castle and Lion was to go with him.

So that was all right. The reluctant chaperon could take a holiday.

CHAPTER TWELVE

FLORA met Madeleine on Monday morning as arranged. It was a fine, dry day, rather cold, but they were well wrapped up and they walked briskly towards the edge of the town, where Bernard and Lion would be waiting for them.

'I got away quite easily,' said Flora. 'Did your mother suspect anything?'

'No, why should she?'

Why indeed? Their families did not expect them to be devious and deceitful.

'I feel rather mean,' said Flora. 'They are all so trusting.'

'That's just it,' said the new Madeleine. 'They are not quite trusting enough. They trust us to walk about Parmouth unaccompanied and to talk to the men we dance with at balls, because they know we can come to no harm. We are never trusted to do anything that might turn out to be dangerous or wrong. They are continually giving us good advice on how to behave and yet they can never trust us to take it.'

This was true at any rate as far as Mrs Osgood was concerned. She was over-protective. Flora knew that her own mother and Olivia both thought so. She did not think her father would have forbidden this expedition since Bernard was going to be there and she regarded him as a sort of honorary brother.

They had now reached the place just beyond the town where their companions were waiting for them:

Lion with his own curricle and pair, Bernard with the phaeton he had hired from the livery stables. There was also a third conveyance and three figures standing in the road.

'It's Walter!' exclaimed Flora. 'Who asked him to come?'

She was alarmed at seeing an outsider. Not that she disliked Walter, but the fewer people who knew about this escapade, the better.

Walter said to Madeleine, 'You don't mind my coming, do you?'

'Of course not.' She gave him her sweet smile.

'And may I drive you?'

'In that old tub?' said Lion with a jeering laugh. 'Don't be a fool, man. You'll never get there in one piece. And Mado has already accepted a seat in my curricle. Come along, girl. I'll lift you up.'

He held out strong hands to her and swung her on to the high perch above the two great wheels. Madeleine gave a little cry of delight. Walter Cottle watched them unhappily. He had a lean, hungry look and a chin that always looked dark, even when he had just shaved.

'If you overturn her, I'll kill you!' he muttered.

'You'll have to catch me first. You won't find it easy in that thing.'

In the meantime Bernard had handed Flora into the phaeton and got up beside her. Walter got into the Parsonage gig by himself and they set out. They were not taking grooms; it had been decided that they had better not risk servants' gossip about the presence of the girls.

'Who asked Walter to join us?' Flora enquired.

'I did,' said Bernard. 'He overheard me ordering the

phaeton and demanded to know what I wanted it for so I swore him to secrecy and told him of our plan.'

'You shouldn't have done that.'

'Nonsense. He's as safe as houses, old Walter. Only then he wanted to come too, and I could hardly refuse.'

'I don't think it's a very good idea. He and Lion will wrangle all day and it will be very tedious, besides being horrid for Mado.'

'Mado enjoys it, don't you think?'

Flora was startled by the strangeness of this idea and did not answer.

Dalney was less than an hour's drive. They expected to be there by half-past ten and to spend a long morning exploring the ruins. They were to dine in the gate-house—Bernard had made all the arrangements—and start back in time to reach Parmouth before dark.

They climbed the long, slow hill which led out of the combe in the direction of Brantisford, and for a time the three carriages were all bunched together, for no one could do more than walk. Presently they took an easterly fork off the Brantisford road, the ground levelled out and they went spinning through a fine sweep of open country, the sea just visible on their right. Lion whipped up his horses, was undoubtedly showing off to Madeleine. Bernard was not such a dashing driver but the phaeton and pair kept up pretty well. Walter was left far behind with his one horse pulling the heavy gig. Flora was sorry for him but this could not affect her own enjoyment.

The two couples reached Dalney more or less together and stabled their horses at the inn, which was the most important building in the small hamlet. The castle stood a little way off on its mound. The girls were not disappointed by its small size and lack of importance; they had been coming here for picnics since they were children, but this did not spoil the romantic excitement of exploring roofless turrets, running up and down flights of broken steps and peering into holes which might once have been dungeons.

At first they moved about as a quartet, but presently split into their inevitable pairs. Bernard tried to teach Flora all he knew about architecture, Lion told Madeleine that a girl who claimed to be in love must be willing to prove it.

They were quite hungry by the time Walter joined them, morose and complaining.

'You might have waited for me. You knew I couldn't keep up with your sporting turn-outs.'

'Then you shouldn't have come,' said Lion, adding with brutal frankness, 'I find you very much *de trop*.'

Walter turned to Madeleine with the eyes of a beaten dog. 'Is that your opinion also?'

'By no means,' she said, far too kind-hearted to let this pass. 'You know I am always glad to see you, Walter.'

'In that case,' said Lion, 'no doubt you will be happy to drive home in the Parson's gig.'

He sauntered off, leaving her torn with indecision between infatuation for her new love and loyalty to her old friend. Flora wanted to say something helpful but did not know what.

Bernard had missed this exchange, he had been talking to a servant from the inn.

'Everything has been brought up to the gatehouse,' he reported. 'Shall we go and dine?'

The small crisis was averted.

They trooped into the gatehouse, which contained a poky entrance and a spiral stair leading up to the two great rooms, one above the other, over the arched gateway. They climbed to the upper chamber so that they could admire the beautiful south aspect of a green valley sloping towards the coast. This room was hardly furnished, apart from some faded wall-hangings and a very old-fashioned daybed. The room below was much more impressive. Here they found the richly orna-mented plaster ceiling that Bernard had been trying to draw, two enormous leaded windows that might have belonged in a Church and a monumental stone fire-place. There was a log fire dancing in the grate and a modern table in the centre of the room on which their dinner had been arranged: lobsters, pheasants, braised ham, oyster patties and a quince tart with clotted cream.

'How did all this get here?' wondered Flora as they drew up chairs to the table. 'So many good things to eat, and the pretty painted plates—they did not come from the inn.'

'We bought most of the food over yesterday,' said Lion, 'and the innkeeper had it cooked for us. The dinner service belongs in the gatehouse.'

'I shouldn't have thought it necessary,' remarked Walter, 'for a man to keep all this valuable china in an empty house to eat off perhaps once a year.'

'Then you had better state your objections to Mr Brooke,' said Lion. 'I dare say he will tell you to mind your own damned business, but you won't care for that. High-minded moralists never do.'

'Do stop sparring, you two,' said Bernard amiably.

Flora rather agreed with Walter about the china. All the same, it was looking a gift horse in the mouth, when circumstances were making their meal so agreeable.

Soon they were eating and talking merrily. Even Walter was enjoying his dinner though he did not say much. The inn servants had been sent away, they were waiting on themselves. Lion had put himself in charge of the wine also brought from Parmouth, having been smuggled out of the cellar at the Vale without the owner's knowledge. There were bottles of sherry, claret, champagne and brandy.

Flora was not accustomed to drinking wine. She asked rather nervously for a glass of water. Lion made rather a fuss about providing this. Bernard said stoutly that she should drink water if she wanted to.

'Though I think,' he added in a protective manner, 'you could take a little champagne if you do not dislike it.'

She saw that Madeleine was sipping the pale, bubbling liquid with an air of calm unconcern, and allowed her own glass to be filled. Soon she found that she liked it very much.

After that the meal was a great success. Everyone was very witty and amusing. It was extraordinary how the absence of any older person contributed to their sense of ease and well-being. Even Walter brightened a little, and Lion kept him generously supplied with claret. Madeleine, between them, was entrancingly vivacious, her clear skin flushed, her eyes glowing as she gazed up at Lion.

Presently the sun went in and the day began to darken.

'We shall soon have to start for home,' said Bernard, regretfully. 'I'd like one more stroll round the ruins before we go.'

'Can I come with you?' asked Flora.

'Yes, do. Is this your cloak? Put it on.'

The other three paid no attention to them. As she followed Bernard to the door, Flora had a sudden qualm. Ought she not to stay with Madeleine? They had daringly defied convention by coming here and there was a tacit understanding that they were chaperoning each other. She glanced back. The trio at the dinner table seemed to be safely anchored. Lion and Madeleine were talking quietly, Walter was leaning forward, his elbows on the table, apparently listening.

So long as they are both with her, she can't get into any difficulties, thought Flora. Safety in numbers—it was a favourite maxim of her mother's. She hurried to catch up with Bernard.

After the warmth of the gatehouse, the air outside was cold and raw. She caught her breath, almost ready to retreat, but Bernard took her hand and ran with her across the smooth turf. Now her blood was tingling and she was able to enjoy being out on this autumn afternoon. A little mist was coming in from the sea and the ruins had acquired a mysterious strangeness which was more romantic that the hard-edged architectural shapes of midday.

She was sorry when Bernard said they ought to be starting for home.

They went back into the gatehouse. The dining room was unexpectedly quiet. The fire had died down and there was only one person there: Walter, lolling across the table, his head on his arms.

'Good gracious!' exclaimed Flora. 'What's the matter with him? Has he gone to sleep?'

'He's drunk,' said Bernard. 'Silly cuckoo. It's my fault, though—I should have stopped him drinking all that claret. And where are the others?' Bernard shook Walter's shoulder and, getting no immediate response, picked up the water jug and gave his friend a liberal splashing. 'Where are Lion and Mado?'

'Wah!' gulped Walter, bobbing up like a puppet and gazing stupidly around him.

'I think they must be in the room above,' said Flora.

She had heard voices and a sudden sharp sound, then silence. She went out on to the spiral stair and called, 'Mado! Lion! Are you there? It's time to go home.'

There was another longish silence before they appeared round the stone twist of the spiral. Lion came first, looking rather sulky and not troubling to give his arm to Madeleine, though in fact it was difficult for one person to assist another in such a confined space. When she was able to see Madeleine clearly, Flora had a shock. She was chalk-white and she moved awkwardly, with an expression of bewilderment and strain, clutching the stone handrail yet hardly noticing where she put her feet.

'Madeleine—what's the matter? Are you not well?'

'She was overcome by the heat,' said Lion.

'Yes,' said Madeleine in a toneless voice. 'That's why we went upstairs.'

Lion did now put out a hand to support her but she turned her face away and made no response.

Leaving the gatehouse, they were obliged to go down to the inn on foot.

Flora, walking beside Madeleine, said, 'Can I help you? Please tell me what is wrong?'

'Oh, do stop asking questions.'

This ill-tempered reply was most unlike Madeleine but she sounded at the end of her tether. Flora did not know what to do. Bernard was attending to Walter, wondering whether he was fit to drive himself home in the gig. Walter now seemed wide awake and quite sensible, but they were a sorry little party. The good spirits of an hour ago had been dissipated.

Flora wondered whether Madeleine ought to travel on the high seat of the curricle. Should she offer to change places? She tried to pluck up courage to suggest this, humbly aware that Lion would not care for the exchange, and in the end she left it too late. One of the inn servants had helped Madeleine up to her seat beside Lion and they were ready to drive away. Walter had now taken possession of the gig, so Flora got into the phaeton with Bernard.

As soon as they were under way, she asked him what he thought could be the matter with Madeleine. He had been too taken up with Walter to notice either of the others.

'What should be wrong?' replied Bernard.

'I wondered if she could have drunk too much champagne.'

'Madeleine? I should think it most unlikely. I don't suppose she had more than one glass. It doesn't seem to have done you any harm.'

Flora subsided, always ready to believe that Bernard knew better than she did. She still thought that Madeleine had been affected by something more than a touch of faintness caused by the heat of the log fire. Probably there had been a lovers' tiff. Or a tragic love-scene between those two who were so soon to be separated. Or the tragic scene leading to a lovers' tiff because their future was so uncertain. She hoped they would make it up on the way home.

Lion was driving fast and furiously. Flora and Bernard watched the curricle bouncing and swinging ahead of them. Walter and the gig had been left far behind.

Just before they reached the turning on to the Brantisford road the curricle stopped so suddenly that the phaeton nearly ran into them.

'What the devil do you think you're doing?' shouted Bernard, extricating his horses and drawing level with the curricle.

'Go on ahead of us,' Lion shouted back. 'I shall stop here if I want to.'

Bernard swore under his breath but drove on all the same. As they passed Flora noted that Lion and Madeleine seemed to be arguing.

They left the byway and joined the road that ran from Brantisford down into Parmouth. Presently they heard the clip-clop of Lion's horses approaching from behind. Flora was vaguely aware of the dark figure of a man standing on the grass verge. They passed quite close to him, but she was thinking of something else.

'Bernard, do you like Lion?'

Bernard grunted. 'I used to but I'm beginning to change my mind. He wants everything his own way, thinks of no one but himself.'

'I hope he thinks of Mado. Isn't he in love with her?'

Before Bernard could answer, they heard a scream, followed by a clatter and commotion which made Flora spin round in alarm. Lion's horses had swerved violently and for a moment she thought the curricle was going to overturn. Bernard, keeping his eye on the road, asked her what was happening.

'I think something must have startled the horses. They're all right now.'

At least they had recovered their equilibrium, with both wheels touching the ground and both horses moving in the right direction, but Madeleine was still screaming and clutching Lion's arm and he was telling her to let go.

'Stop, Lion! You must stop.' She sounded quite hysterical. 'You hit someone, you know you did.'

Lion did stop, but only because they had now reached the phaeton.

'For God's sake, hold your tongue,' he told her. 'No wonder the horses took fright with you screeching like a parrot. We never hit anyone. You imagined the whole thing.'

'There was a man,' persisted Madeleine. 'I saw him.'

'I saw him too,' volunteered Flora. 'There was a man.'

'Well, he's not there now,' said Lion, as they all craned to look back along the pale road.

'Then where did he go?' asked Bernard.

'Jumped over the hedge and made off.'

'Why should he do that?'

'Because he was a poacher and didn't want to be seen. Who else would be slinking along here at this hour? Get down and look for him if you don't believe me. I'm going home.'

There were no further protests. They had all begun to realise that they were later than they intended and that if the girls did not get home soon there would be trouble.

They drove on by common consent. It was several minutes before Flora realised that she would not have another chance of speaking to Madeleine that day. It had been decided that each girl should be driven as close as possible to her own home and left to walk the last few yards alone.

When they returned from each other's houses the visitor was always escorted by a servant from that

house. One of Mr Osgood's tall footmen would follow
Flora back to Marine Cottage, or the Fenimores'
homely Joan would plod along behind Madeleine on
her way to the Villa Romana. The accompanying
servants would wait just long enough to see the young
ladies admitted at their own front doors, so today they
could arrive home with an air of perfect innocence—
unless any unforeseen delay led to awkward enquiries.

By now Flora only wanted to get home. She had
enjoyed almost everything about the expedition to
Dalney, but the latter part of the adventure had
unsettled her and she was beginning to feel guilty.

CHAPTER THIRTEEN

OLIVIA had spent a quiet day at Marine Cottage, where nothing interesting had happened. She had occupied herself in planning a dinner party they were giving later in the week. The Fenimores did not entertain much, but it seemed they always gave a dinner at the beginning of November, and this year Olivia was to deputise for her aunt. The Osgoods and the Walkers had accepted invitations. Captain and Mrs Channing had refused on account of his health, but Bernard was coming with Tom and Lion.

This had driven Olivia into a sort of panic, for which she thoroughly despised herself. It was ridiculous, at her age, to be frightened of having a man to dinner because she had refused to marry him, and as the evening darkened she began to be impatient for Flora to come home and give her something else to think about.

'I was beginning to wonder what had happened to you,' she said as her cousin came into the drawing-room. 'My dear, you look frozen to death. Is it very cold outside?'

'I suppose it must be,' said Flora vaguely, drawing nearer to the fire. 'I'm not late, am I?'

'Only a few minutes. And we are dining early because Mr Cottle is coming to play chess with your papa. So how did your day go? How was Madeleine?'

Flora did not have much to say on the subject of Madeleine or much to talk about at dinner. She ate very little and said she was not hungry. Her father, noticing this, chose to be jocular and suggested that she must be in love.

'Good gracious, Papa—whoever is there for me to fall in love with?'

He threw her an anxious glance and said no more, perhaps feeling he had been tactless.

They had barely finished dinner when Mr Cottle arrived for the promised game of chess. He was very like his son, though older, fairer and more contented. Perhaps it would be more correct to say that Walter would be very like his father when he had lived some years longer and forgotten the pangs of unrequited first love.

'Here I am, sir,' he said gleefully, 'come to avenge my last defeat! You won't get the better of me this time!'

Mr Fenimore nearly always did get the better of him, but he never minded.

As soon as the men had gone into the study, Flora announced that she was tired and thought she would go to bed.

'Are you feeling ill?' asked Olivia, surprised.

Flora said there was nothing the matter with her. Olivia did not entirely believe this, but there was no sense in fussing. Let her have an early night and the morning would show whether she was developing any uncomfortable symptoms.

Left alone, Olivia returned to the drawing-room fire. She would have been glad of someone to talk to, someone to distract her from the subject that filled her mind, but it was no use repining, she had better go on with her library book. Having already finished the first volume, she would have to go upstairs and fetch the second.

She was crossing the hall when she heard the sharp rap of the knocker on the front door. She paused at the foot of the stairs. Although it was a gentleman's house and several servants were kept, etiquette and formality did not loom very large at Marine Cottage. Since she was nearer the front door than anyone else, she went to open it. Standing outside was Tom Brooke.

'Oh,' she said, falling back a pace.

He showed no particular emotion and merely asked, 'Is Cottle here?'

'Yes. He's playing chess with my uncle.'

'May I come in?'

'Of course. I beg your pardon.'

She stood aside, confused. He passed her and went into the drawing-room, casting his long driving coat over a chair. Olivia followed him, thinking this was off behaviour, even for Tom, but since he was there she asked him to sit down, which he did, saying abruptly, 'Do you know where Walter Cottle was going today? You don't happen to have seen him?'

'No, I'm afraid not. Why do you ask?'

'It is the most damnable thing, and I have got to break the news to his father.'

'Good God!' she said. 'What has happened? Has there been an accident?'

'There has been an accident but Walter was not the victim. I was driving home from Brantisford just before dark—I was about a mile short of Parmouth—when I heard the groans of someone in pain coming from the roadside or the ditch just beyond. My groom heard them too. I pulled up and he got down to investigate. There was a man lying in the shadow of the hedge, bleeding from a scalp wound and half stunned. I think he had only just recovered his senses and was barely able to say he had been hit by a cart or carriage, before again losing consciousness.'

'Poor man, what a terrible thing to happen. But how fortunate for him that you came by. Did you recognise him?'

'Yes, I did. It was my tenant, Peter Chapman.'

There was a brief pause while they both recalled their meeting in the clockmaker's shop.

'I do hope he is not too badly hurt,' she said. 'What did you do then?'

'Bell and I got him into the curricle, and Bell led the horses while I walked beside, holding Chapman as he lay on the seat to prevent his falling. About fifty yards further on we were held up by a gig drawn right across the road with its one old horse cropping the verge. In the driver's seat, believe it or not, was Walter Cottle, apparently fast asleep.'

She stared at him. 'How very extraordinary!'

'You may well say so. It was not much past five o'clock. However, the matter became a little less extraordinary when I went to rouse him. He was reeking of brandy.'

'Oh, I see. At least I don't entirely. It doesn't sound like Walter.'

'I agree. But there's no doubt he had been, and still was, extremely drunk, and it's usually these abstemious fellows who do the most damage when they go astray. I asked him where the devil he'd been to get in such a state, and whether he knew he'd knocked down poor Chapman. He gaped at me and swore he remembered nothing—how he came to be there in his father's gig or anything else. I could tell from his manner that he was

lying. I put him in Bell's charge and commandeered the
Parson's gig—it was the safer conveyance for getting
Chapman home. He was still unconscious and very cold.
I got him indoors and we sent for the apothecary, who
shook his head and said it was too early to tell what his
injuries were. Mrs Chapman was very good in spite of
her distress. I imagine she is a capable nurse. Their little
girls were frightened and crying.'

He paused a moment, gazing into the fire, and Olivia
watched him with an approving sympathy for all he had
done and felt. Everything else that had happened
between the two of them was forgotten for the time
being.

'After that,' said Tom, 'I felt obliged to go round to
the Parsonage. Bell had delivered Master Walter there,
as instructed, but his father was out and he was sitting
in the hall, unable to go upstairs and tell his mother
what he had done. There were no further protestations
of innocence, though when he ran into Chapman he
may very well have been too fuddled to notice. I don't
believe he would have driven on and left him
deliberately.'

'No, I am sure he would not.'

'One of the servants was able to tell me that Parson
was visiting Mr Fenimore, so I decided I had better
come round here and fetch him—and break the news
as gently as possible, for I don't think Walter is in a fit
state to do so. Which will explain,' said Tom, looking
at Olivia with his very clear blue eyes and a sudden,
deprecating smile, 'why I have been pouring out the
whole story to you, because I dread telling it to Cottle.
I am afraid he will take it so much to heart. His son
involved in such an accident with one of his own
parishioners.'

'And he has always been so proud of Walter. No one wants to be the bearer of such news. It is a wretched business.'

But it had to be gone through all the same. Olivia escorted Tom to the door of her uncle's study, showed him in and came away. She thought she had never seen him to better advantage. All his good qualities had come to the fore without a trace of the arrogance, frivolity and cynicism which ruined his relations with women. If only I could have him simply as a friend, she thought. But Tom Brooke did not seem to want the friendship of the girls who fell in love with him. And when it came to frivolity, what was she about, mooning over her broken heart, when two families near by, the Cottles and the Chapmans, were in such deep trouble? Presently she heard her uncle showing his visitors out. He retired once more to the study and she decided to go upstairs.

On the landing she heard Flora call out through her open door.

'Olivia—come and talk to me.'

Olivia went in. Flora was wide awake, lying in the dark.

'What is Mr Brooke doing here? Why did he come?' she demanded.

'Were you hanging over the banisters? I thought you were too sleepy to keep your eyes open.'

'I heard his voice in the hall. Do tell me, did he come to see Papa?'

'No, he was looking for Mr Cottle.' Olivia thought quickly. 'Have you any idea where Walter was going today?'

'Why should I? He hasn't been near the Villa Romana, if that's what you mean.'

Flora sounded a little shrill, as though she thought she was being accused of something.

'Has he quarrelled with Madeleine, perhaps?' Olivia suggested.

'Not quarrelled precisely. Mado doesn't quarrel. Only he is jealous of Lion Forester.'

That would acount for the drinking bout, so out of character.

Flora was now sitting up in bed. Olivia could see her outline, dimly shadowed on the wall by the light of her own candle.

'You must tell me,' she was saying urgently. 'Why are you asking all these questions about Walter?'

Having aroused her curiosity, Olivia felt it would be unreasonable to refuse, so she began by saying, 'You must not repeat this to anyone, unless we find that it is generally known. . .'

When she heard Tom's account Flora was very much upset, begging to be told that Mr Chapman was not badly hurt and even suggesting that Walter might not be responsible for the accident—after all, Mr Brooke had not seen it happen. Olivia did not pay much attention to this piece of partisan loyalty.

Next morning news of the accident was all over the town. The Fenimores' cook had it by breakfast time from the baker's boy whose father heard it at the Mariner's Rest from a man whose brother worked for the apothecary. Peter Chapman was lying on his death-bed and Parson's son, young Mr Walter, was to blame.

'On his deathbed?' repeated Flora, horrified, when this piece of information reached the breakfast-room.

'I don't think that is at all likely, my dear,' said her father. 'The good burghers of Parmouth take great delight in believing the worst.'

Flora still looked unhappy. After breakfast she announced, 'I must go and talk to Madeleine.'

'I'll come with you,' said Olivia.

'There's no need for that,' said Flora ungraciously and apparently not wanting her cousin. This did not induce Olivia to change her mind. She had an idea something odd was going on.

However, neither of them saw Madeleine that day, for on their way to the Villa Romana they met Mrs Osgood by herself.

'I have kept Madeleine in bed,' she explained. 'Poor child, she is not at all the thing. She was awake half the night and is still very poorly. She is lying down with a hot brick at her feet and can take nothing but a little arrowroot.'

The girls both said they were very sorry and sent messages to the invalid.

'I think she must have eaten something that disagreed with her,' said her mother. 'You seem to have suffered no ill effects, Flora.'

This was said with a touch of resentment, which Olivia thought pretty cool, considering that any meals shared by Madeleine and Flora yesterday must have been prepared by Mrs Osgood's cook.

Flora asked, 'Have you heard about Peter Chapman's accident, ma'am? Does Madeleine know?'

'We make it a rule never to listen to gossip,' said Mrs Osgood grandly. 'And if you think that Madeleine would make herself ill over young Cottle's troubles, then you are a very foolish girl.'

Olivia thought with a touch of malicious amusement that Mrs Osgood might not repeat gossip but she certainly did listen to it, for the mention of Chapman had promptly suggested Walter Cottle.

They parted from the high-minded lady and turned towards the shops.

'I cannot decide,' Olivia said, 'whether to call on Mrs Chapman or not. My dress is supposed to be ready today and I meant to collect it, but I don't want to seem vulgarly curious, and the poor woman will have more important things to think about.'

'You will occupy very little of her time.'

'More to the point, I shall be able to pay her what I owe, and I dare say she will be glad of the money. I had better go.'

They crossed the Parade, skirted the open sweep of grass and entered Trafalgar Street, a sequence of small shops behind the Admiral Nelson Hotel. The shutters were firmly closed across the windows of Peter Chapman Clockmaker, and Olivia would have turned away, but at that moment the door was opened by Mrs Chapman, showing out the apothecary. She looked weary and dejected. Olivia paused on the pavement.

Flora was evidently unable to bear too close a contact with tragedy. Muttering to her cousin, 'I'll meet you at the library,' she fled.

Mrs Chapman saw Olivia and managed a painful smile.

'Miss Fenimore, I have your dress waiting for you. Do be pleased to come in.'

Olivia made a little speech of commiseration, adding, 'I don't wish to disturb you if it is not convenient.'

But Mrs Chapman insisted on taking her into a room at the back where Olivia's new lilac silk was neatly folded in a linen wrapper.

'I must not allow myself to get behindhand,' said the dressmaker, 'especially now.'

She glanced at the various garments with tacked

seams and ragged edges, lying ready to be fitted and
finished. She would have to earn for them all while the
shop was closed. Her husband made, or at least assembled, the clocks he sold, putting together the various
pieces of the mechanism from a Birmingham foundry,
installing them in a case made by a local craftsman,
and painting the faces himself. Each one bore the
words 'P. Chapman, Parmouth'. He also did repairs
for anyone with a clock or watch that had gone wrong.
These were skills which a sick man could not delegate.
Olivia made sympathetic enquiries.

'You are right,' said Mrs Chapman. 'No one can take
on Peter's work while he is ill. Mr Hudson thinks he
has suffered nothing worse than a concussion—provided his lungs have not been affected by the cold. We
don't even know how long he was lying there. He had
walked up to Ridge Farm to look at old Mr Smith's
long case clock which wasn't chiming properly. I had
been wondering for an hour or more what was keeping
him when Mr Brooke came in to tell me what had
happened. He was kindness itself, and so gentle and
sensible when he and his groom carried Peter indoors.
Peter might have died, you know, if they had not
rescued him. Mr Brooke took charge of everything;
sent for the apothecary, went himself to fetch my
neighbour, even managed to distract the children. And
do you know, Miss Fenimore, when he was on the
point of leaving, actually on the doorstep, he suddenly
turned back, saying there was something he had just
thought of? I must not trouble my head over the rent
because we need not think of paying until Peter is
recovered. How many landlords would be so generous?
But then he is so truly a gentleman.'

'Yes, indeed,' said Olivia, who felt a curious surge

of pride when she heard this panegyric applied to the man she had rejected and whose conduct in other ways she found so despicable.

She left Mrs Chapman with expressions of hope and goodwill and went on her way to the library, which she could reach most conveniently by going to the top of Trafalgar Street and turning right at the Assembly Rooms. There was an apron of charming rural greenery in front of the white portico, but Olivia was so busy thinking about the Chapmans' misfortunes and Tom's generosity that she did not notice the figure of a man standing quite still in the shadow of an evergreen.

A voice said urgently, 'Miss Olivia—can I speak to you?'

She stopped and found herself gazing with very mixed feelings at Walter Cottle. He had placed himself like a sentry at a good observation point for watching the Chapmans' door. He had a hangdog expression and looked dreadfully ill.

'Can you tell me how Chapman goes on?' he asked in a low voice. 'I saw you come out of the shop. I ought to enquire myself but I haven't the courage. I must be an object of such detestation to his wife.'

Oddly enough as it now seemed, Mrs Chapman had not mentioned Walter. Was that Christian forbearance or common sense? The accident was past and irreversible, she was concerned only with her present anxieties and future problems, with Tom's generosity over the rent rather than Walter's wickedness in driving on a public road while he was drunk.

Olivia said, 'I don't think Mrs Chapman is given to hating. Her husband has suffered a concussion, they hope there is nothing worse, and I am sure he is being carefully nursed.'

'Thank God!' said Walter. 'I have been feeling like a murderer, and even if he has suffered no permanent injury I can't escape from the knowledge that I might have killed him. I shall never forgive myself.'

He sounded suspiciously husky; she thought he was going to burst into tears. She would have liked to say something comforting but it was hardly possible; of course he knew he was to blame.

Instead she said, 'I don't think you ought to be standing around on such a cold day. You don't look at all well.'

'That's the brandy,' he said with a slightly theatrical groan. 'I've never been so drunk before. In fact I don't think I've ever been really drunk. I thought I'd slept it off. I shouldn't have tried to drive home, only I thought they'd start worrying. I'd borrowed the gig from my father, said I wanted to go to Brantisford.'

She would have liked to ask exactly where he had gone but thought this would be intrusive, coming from her. Why he had got drunk was not at all hard to guess. He was hopelessly in love with Madeleine and miserably jealous of Lion. He was also inexperienced, the good son of the Parsonage. It was understandable that he should take himself off for an orgy of solitary self-pity somewhere outside Parmouth and where there was no friend to stop him making a fool of himself.

'The dreadful thing is,' he was saying, 'I don't even remember running into Chapman. I must have gone to sleep again. I was in a kind of stupor when Mr Brooke found me. What a disgusting way to behave! You can imagine how it has shocked my parents.'

'Is your father very angry?'

'No, but he is disappointed in me. And mother cries all the time.'

Olivia was by now feeling genuinely sorry for Walter and said as many cheering things as she could manage without feeling too much of a hypocrite.

As they were on the point of parting, he asked diffidently, 'Has Flora heard the whole story? And Madeleine?'

'Flora was very sorry to hear it. I have not seen Madeleine.'

She did not add that Madeleine had taken to her bed, in case he built this up into a display of sensibility on his behalf. From what Mrs Osgood had said, Madeleine was suffering from a stomach upset which had come on last night before anyone at the Villa Romana had heard of the accident. Advising the unhappy Walter to go home and keep warm, Olivia hurried on to the library, where Flora was waiting for her.

She was talking to Bernard and they were both looking so grave that she assumed they were discussing the accident. Or perhaps not, for as she approached them she heard Bernard say, 'Lion insists it is all nonsense and that I should be a fool to stir up trouble.'

'What is it that Lion insists is nonsense?' asked Olivia, coming up behind them.

They swung round on her, looking startled and almost guilty.

After a moment's hesitation Bernard said, 'Oh, nothing to signify. I made a stupid bet, that is all.'

A vague suspicion made her ask, 'Had your bet anything to do with Walter?'

'With Walter? Of course not. Why should it?'

'I met him just now, and I wondered where he had been to be driving down the Brantisford Road yesterday afternoon apparently quite drunk. He didn't tell me. I suppose he was mooning about by himself, lamenting his lost love. I am sorry to speak ill of a friend of yours, Bernard, but I shall be thankful to see the back of Lion Forester.'

'So shall I,' said Bernard, which surprised her.

Flora asked anxiously about Peter Chapman, and Olivia repeated everything she had been told. They listened with serious, worried faces. They both seemed much affected by the accident, which had cast a shadow over the whole of Parmouth. The Cottles were held in high esteem and so in their different way were the Chapmans.

It was in this depressing atmosphere that Olivia had to get ready for the dinner party at Marine Cottage.

CHAPTER FOURTEEN

THERE was a modern dining table at Marine Cottage which would seat twelve when all the leaves were in. There would be eleven at the dinner party—the Fenimores themselves, the Osgoods with Madeleine, the Walkers and the three men from the Vale: Tom, Bernard and Lion.

Olivia thought privately that there would hardly be room for the servants to get round the table, but she did not argue. She had a great deal to do. Her aunt's jolly, red-faced cook was a champion roaster of beef and boiler of puddings, and perfectly capable of following a recipe, but the idea of French sauces frightened her and she had to be sustained with constant encouragement. Olivia helped out by concocting creams and desserts, made sure that the best dinner service had been properly washed, the linen napkins properly starched, the silver cleaned and the glass polished. She had ordered pot-plants from the nurseryman—Flora could help her put them in bowls and jardinières and arrange them in the drawing-room.

Flora had been remarkably useless so far that day and when Olivia went upstairs to look for her she was not at all pleased to find her cousin putting on her bonnet and pelisse in order to go and call on Madeleine.

'You can't call on her now,' she said crossly. 'Don't be ridiculous. Madeleine will be arriving here with her

187

parents in a few hours' time and you will have the
whole evening to talk in.'

'You don't understand. I must see her alone.'

'Why?'

Flora remained obstinately silent.

'Has this something to do with Walter?' hazarded
Olivia. 'Are you afraid she may be blaming herself for
his silly behaviour? Why should she be so over-scrupu-
lous? You've told me yourself that she has never given
him any encouragement to be in love with her, and if
she has found someone she prefers it is not for Walter
to complain. I don't happen to care for Lion Forester
and I dare say he has simply been amusing himself,
but, as to Walter's getting so abominably drunk and
nearly killing poor Chapman, that is a different matter
and no one can say it was Madeleine's fault.'

'Of course it was her fault!' Flora almost shouted.
'And mine too. Walter is being blamed for something
he didn't do and Mr Chapman would never have been
knocked down if it weren't for us.'

And she burst into tears.

'My dear Flora, what can you mean? What has it to
do with you?'

'It was all because of our going to Dalney,' sobbed
Flora. 'It was very wrong to deceive you, and you will
be so angry and so will Papa.'

'To Dalney! But when did you——? Oh!'

Olivia stopped. Light was beginning to dawn.
'Bernard and Lion were going over there together,
weren't they? I suppose you and Madeleine went with
them, while you were meant to be spending the day at
the Osgoods'. And Mado told her mother she was
coming here—was that it?'

Flora nodded and gave a doleful sniff.

'Well, that is very dreadful but it not the end of the world,' said Olivia. She put an arm round Flora and persuaded her to sit down on the bed. 'Do take my handkerchief and try to stop crying. . . There, that's better. Will you tell me a little more? I still don't understand how this concerns Walter.'

Flora gave a confusing account of the expedition. Olivia gained an impression of the drive to Dalney with Walter trailing far behind, of a harmless morning spent among the ruins and a convivial meal in the romantic gatehouse where the young men drank a good deal and it was altogether too much for the inexperienced Walter.

'It's plain he wasn't fit to drive,' she said, frowning. 'And neither Bernard nor Lion had the sense to stop him. I don't think either you or Madeleine could be expected to recognise the danger. It really was most unlucky that he ran into Mr Chapman on the way home.'

'That's the worst part of it,' said Flora miserably. 'You still don't understand. I'm practically sure it wasn't Walter who knocked him down. It was Lion.'

And she went on with the story of Lion's bad temper and bad driving, of her conviction that she had seen a man close to the hedge, and how Lion had denied hitting anyone and sworn it was Madeleine's fault that the horses had swerved. And what pricked her conscience now—how they had driven on without investigating, because they were afraid of awkward repercussions if they were late.

'So you think,' said Olivia slowly, 'that Chapman was already lying by the roadside when Walter drove past some time later, too fuddled to notice him.'

'Yes, and when Mr Brooke came on them both, one

after the other, he naturally took it that Walter had caused the accident. And everyone believes him, including Walter himself. So what do you think we ought to do?' asked Flora. 'Bernard and I both feel that it is quite wrong to let him take the blame. Lion says it is all fudge and that he never knocked anyone down, but I'm sure he is lying. Bernard would have spoken out before now if it weren't for getting me and Madeleine into trouble. I don't care for myself, because Papa is not so very strict, and anyway I don't believe he or Mama would have minded my going to Dalney with Bernard to look after me. Only Mado's parents are different. That is why I must talk to her before we decide what to do. I went to the Villa Romana yesterday, only she and her mother were out in the carriage.'

'And you think she would be too frightened to admit the truth?'

'I don't know. She is so besotted over Lion—though I think they may have had a quarrel on the way back from Dalney, and that was why he was driving so badly. It is going to be so awkward when we all meet this evening. Oh, dear, I wish we were not having this dinner party!'

'So do I,' said Olivia, who had been wishing it all along. 'But, you know, I think it's quite possible Madeleine won't come—if she doesn't wish to meet any of you, especially Lion. She was not feeling at all well on Monday night and Tuesday, as a result of your trip to Dalney, of course, but her mother doesn't know that, and if Madeleine wants to keep away she has only to invent a sore throat or a headache.'

Flora brightened considerably, and, although Olivia knew Madeleine's absence would not solve anything in the long run, there was nothing to be gained by further discussions and regrets. One of the maids was at the door with a question about candles, the pot-plants still had to be dealt with, and then it was time to change.

Olivia put on the new lilac dress. It was very becoming, thanks to the skill of Mrs Chapman—but this thought brought back the whole wretched business of the accident and the events leading up to it. She felt irrationally guilty, as though she should have prevented those silly girls jaunting off to Dalney with the young men. Tom had warned her, everyone believed that she was keeping an eye on both Flora and Madeleine, and, however unreasonable this might be, it was perfectly true that she would have gone about with them more, and paid a closer attention to what was going on, if she had not been in such low spirits, wanting to avoid Tom himself, disliking the company of Lion Forester with his impudent references to Lady Laybourne, backing away from any suggestion of a visit to Rosamond's Bower. She wouldn't have wanted to go to Dalney either, come to that, for it was there she had first heard the story of Tom's duplicity. She might have been able to scotch the whole plan if she had known of it, or, if she had felt obliged to go along with them, she would at least have made certain that no one took the road while unfit to drive.

She went downstairs to play the part of hostess with none of her usual confidence.

The Walkers arrived first, and in bringing them close to the fire, exchanging remarks about the weather, she slipped into the easy social manner she had been accustomed to since she was younger than Flora. She, poor girl, was more than usually nervous. Uncle James was genial. He quite enjoyed entertaining once he faced up to it.

When the trio from the Vale came in Olivia's self-possession was put to the test, for she had to go forward and welcome Tom.

'Good evening, Miss Olivia,' he said in his pleasant voice, looking her over with the swift appreciation and the quicksilver smile she had not seen since the summer.

'Good evening, Mr Brooke,' she responded in what she hoped was an example of exquisite calm.

He seemed in better spirits than the two young men who followed him. Lion looked sulky and Bernard worried.

When Skinner announced, 'Mr and Mrs Osgood and Miss Osgood,' Olivia felt a slight sinking of the heart, for she had really hoped that Madeleine would stay away. Catching sight of the girl beyond her parents, she could not think why her mother had let her come. Beautiful Madeleine had somehow shrunk into herself, her head drooped, she had lost all her usual grace and her voice was almost inaudible.

Mrs Osgood, graciously arrayed in Brussels lace, explained that Madeleine had not been feeling quite the thing.

'But such a gathering as this will do her all the good in the world. Will it not, my love?'

'Yes, Mama,' muttered Madeleine obediently.

Out of the corner of her eye Olivia had seen Lion give Madeleine a resentful stare and turn away. She had not looked in his direction. Uncle James offered Mrs Osgood his arm and led the way into the dining-room, the others falling in behind them while Olivia speedily rearranged the dinner table in her head.

She had assumed that Lion and Madeleine would want to sit together, but this was clearly a mistake.

Flora was right, there had been a quarrel. She saw
Madeleine safely established between Bernard and Mr
Walker before turning herself to Mr Osgood, a not
very amusing dinner companion. She ought to have
had Tom beside her. Strictly speaking, Mr Brooke of
Cassondon should have taken precedence over the
banker and the architect, but they were much older
men and he was not one to stand on his dignity. So she
had put him as far as possible from herself, next to Mrs
Osgood, and because the numbers were uneven he had
ended up with Bernard on his other side. So there was
no one for him to flirt with. He was looking rather
amused. Did he think she had done this deliberately?

It was a stiff, unmanageable party from the start.
There was nothing wrong with the food, the wine or
the pleasing arrangement of the table, only the guests
refused to rise to the occasion. Four of them had been
apparently struck dumb. They shared a most
uncomfortable secret, and since Olivia now shared it
with them she could guess how they felt. She gazed
down the length of white linen and sparkling silver to
her uncle's end of the table where there was a normal
amount of animation. Tom was conversing agreeably
with Mrs Osgood and Uncle James was listening to Mrs
Walker, who never stopped talking anyway. But there
were two silent couples in the middle—Lion and Flora
on the right, Bernard and Madeleine on the left. Mr
Walker, on Olivia's left, was patiently trying to get a
word out of Madeleine, and this left Mr Osgood free
to pontificate, addressing Olivia loudly enough to dom-
inate the whole table. He liked the sound of his own
voice. He soon got on to the accident.

'A most unfortunate occurrence. Chapman is a
person of exemplary character, I believe, and most

industrious. I do not know what will become of his
family if he does not recover—I understand there are
several young children, and clockmaking is not a
business that could be carried on by his wife. Or his
widow.'

Olivia felt rather than saw the tension in the faces of
Madeleine and Flora. She tried in vain to change the
subject by saying something totally irrelevant about the
news of the war. Mr Osgood prosed on, unheeding.

'One cannot offer charity to a respectable tradesman.
The lowest sort of people will always ask for anything
they can get, but a man in Chapman's situation should
not be robbed of his modest place in society by financial
assistance which he has not earned.'

Olivia looked to see whether Tom had heard this,
and gathered from his scornful expression that he had.
Naturally he would not say that the Chapmans were at
present living rent free at his expense.

She sipped her wine and in a moment of inspiration
began talking about the number of excellent shops that
had been attracted to Parmouth. This diverted Mr
Osgood, who took a personal pride in the watering-
place where he was such a prominent citizen, and he
continued with this subject while the first course was
removed and replaced by dishes of hot and cold game,
salads and savouries. She noticed Madeleine refusing
everything she was offered. Then, unfortunately, Mr
Osgood's dissertation on Parmouth led him round to
the Church.

'It is quite a recent building. The original fishing
village had no church of its own, forming an outpost of
the parish of Parr Cross, to which we still belong. That
is why we have no rector or vicar, merely a priest in
charge—a perpetual curate, if you will, though how

perpetual he can remain after recent events, I should not care to hazard. I'm afraid Cottle will find he has forfeited the esteem of most of his congregation.'

Mr Osgood's voice had a penetrating note which had silenced what little talk there was at the table. They were all listening to him.

Tom said in his decisive way, 'I think that is an unreasonable view. As far as I know, the Bible does not tell us that the sins of the children will be visited on the fathers.'

Olivia, her uncle and Mr Walker all started to agree with Tom, interrupted each other and broke off. This gave Mr Osgood the chance to go on speaking, sententious and affronted.

'I do not consider this is a time for frivolity. We cannot say how far Cottle is responsible for his son's misconduct. But one thing I can assure you, my dear sir, the young man is not fit to follow his father's profession. Such a lapse in a candidate for Holy Orders is quite disgraceful. I am fairly well acquainted with the Bishop and I flatter myself that Walter Cottle will never receive a curacy in this Diocese.'

Pompous old fool, thought Olivia, wondering why he was so set against the unfortunate Walter. It came to her in a flash that the Osgoods had never considered their son a suitable admirer for their precious daughter, less than ever now, when his troubles seemed to be causing her so much distress. That was probably why her mother had dragged her here this evening, barking up the wrong tree, of course. Madeleine was being forced to demonstrate a proper indifference to Walter's troubles.

At the end of Mr Osgood's denunciation, Bernard made a sharp, clumsy movement and spilt half his wine, while Flora, flushed with indignation, started to say something in Walter's defence. Olivia, catching her eye, mouthed the words, Not now.

Then Madeleine said in a high, clear voice, 'Walter doesn't deserve to be punished. He has done nothing wrong.'

'Mado!' said Bernard urgently. 'I don't think this is the time——'

And Mr Osgood intervened, 'This is foolishness, my dear child. You don't know what you are talking about.'

'Yes, I do, Papa. It wasn't Walter who knocked Mr Chapman into the ditch.'

'Then who was it?' demanded Lion; unwisely misjudging her state of mind, he leant across the table, challenging her.

'It was you!' she replied instantly. 'You knew at the time only you wouldn't stay to find out. You didn't care if you'd hurt him or killed him. You never cared for anyone but yourself.'

'Well, what a fairy-tale!' declared Lion. 'You shouldn't let your spiteful temper lead you into telling fibs. You cannot possibly know what happened unless you were there yourself. Remember that, girl.'

He sounded a little nervous now, though well prepared to defend himself, for he must have calculated all along that the girls could not give him away without revealing their own transgressions, and Bernard would keep quiet for the same reason.

But Madeleine, having taken the plunge, was beyond caution or common sense.

'Of course I was there,' she said dismissively, 'and so were Bernard and Flora. We all know what happened.'

'Madeleine!' exclaimed Mrs Osgood.

She got up and moved along the table to her daughter's chair, gripping her wrist and pulling her to her feet.

'How could you have been at this horrid accident? What have you been doing?'

'Everything you ever told me not to do, Mama.' The words might have sounded defiant, even triumphant, but Madeleine's voice sounded flat, disembodied, as though she had no control over what she was saying. 'I went to Dalney in Lion's curricle and we had dinner there——'

'How could you behave so badly? Not that I believe a word of it. You stupid little fool, don't you see that you will ruin yourself, telling these lies in order to defend that worthless young Cottle?'

'I'm not lying, Mama. I have told lies, but not now.'

Their reluctant audience shifted and murmured and looked away. Only Tom spoke directly to Olivia from the other end of the table.

'You'll have to get them out of here.'

Everything had happened so quickly that she had been temporarily paralysed, but she recognised that Tom's instinct was right. If this scene was going to get worse, it had better do so in private. She too stood up and almost pushed Mrs Osgood and Madeleine out of the dining-room and into the drawing-room next door. There she hovered uncertainly, feeling she ought to go away and leave them, yet hardly liking to. They both looked so strange, standing stiffly a few feet away from each other, the older woman a furious inquisitor, the girl frozen into a sort of trance.

'What did that man do to you? Were you alone with him? Where was Flora? It's all your fault.' Mrs Osgood rounded on Olivia. 'I suppose you knew what was going on. I should never have allowed Madeleine to come to this house. We all know what sort of a reputation your cousin Hetty had before she married.'

Olivia thought this was extremely unjust, but could not protest without drawing attention to the way both Flora and Madeleine had deceived their families, so she merely said, 'I'm very sorry about all this, but from what Flora told me this afternoon I don't believe that she and Mado came to any serious harm.'

Madeleine had begun systematically pulling tiny crystal beads off her white dress.

'Flora was lucky,' she said in a dull voice. 'She was with Bernard.'

'What does that mean?' asked her mother. 'Are you saying Forester made love to you?'

'Oh, yes. If that is what you call it.'

Mrs Osgood drew a deep breath. 'Is it possible that he—that he ravished you?'

'No,' said Madeleine. 'He told me what he wanted and I agreed. After that it was too late.'

She spoke with a dreadful, desolating frankness.

Mrs Osgood began to scream at her daughter.

'You shameless trollop, how could you be so wicked? How could you forget all you have been taught? What is to become of you? Suppose you have a child? You will be disgraced forever! He must be made to marry you.'

'I won't marry him,' said Madeleine. 'I hate him.'

This made Mrs Osgood angrier than ever. In her eyes the only fit penance for a fallen woman was marriage to her seducer, whether she liked him or not. Her abuse became more violent than ever.

'You deserve to be whipped, put in the pillory for everyone to see what you are—vile, depraved—no decent person will ever speak to you again. It is girls like you who are sent on convict ships to Australia.'

The tirade was ridiculous and disgusting. The noise brought Flora and Mrs Walker in with glasses of water and smelling salts. Olivia sent them both away, though she pressed the restoratives on Mrs Osgood and eventually persuaded her to sit down.

Now that the screaming had stopped Madeleine showed signs of coming out of her trance.

She had begun to tremble as she said in an almost natural voice, 'I'm sorry, Mama.'

Mrs Osgood was ravaged and exhausted but her eyes were as hard as flint. She spoke quietly, sounding hoarse after all the screaming.

'Never call me that again. I am not your mother and I thank God for it. No daughter of mine would have acted as you have done. When I think of all the care and attention and high hopes that have been wasted on you! But I might have guessed how it would be—we should never have taken you in. Your natural mother was a woman of loose character, did you never suspect that? Why else do you suppose she was allowed to marry a penniless *émigré* and go to France with him?'

Madeleine's lips moved in some sort of wordless protest.

'Well, at least she expiated her sin and gave you a father. Unlike you, saying you don't want to be married, you indecent little harlot.'

Mrs Osgood's venomous hatred shocked Olivia more than anything else that had happened that day.

'I am sure you will feel differently when you have had time to reflect,' she said, sounding feeble in her own ears, for she was not sure of any such thing. Not that it mattered. Neither Mrs Osgood nor Madeleine was listening to her.

The drawing-room door opened and Mr Osgood appeared, looking harassed.

'The carriage is at the door, my dear,' he announced. 'I sent for it immediately, for I felt sure you would wish to go home. Fenimore quite understands. If you are well enough to make the effort——'

'I am perfectly well.' His wife rose without assistance while he fussed round her chair. 'But that wretched girl is not coming with us. I will not have her in the house.'

'Just as you say, my dear.' Mr Osgood, though still pompous, was a good deal deflated, clearly under the influence of his wife.

Olivia could not believe they meant to walk off, abandoning their adopted daughter.

Speaking softly, she said, 'Will you please tell me, sir, what arrangements you wish to make for Madeleine? Surely you cannot mean to disown her?'

Mr Osgood had not looked at Madeleine. He said heavily, 'My sole duty is towards my wife. You cannot expect me to concern myself with that ungrateful young person who has cruelly deceived her and broken her heart.'

Olivia did not think Mrs Osgood had a heart to break. She saw Bernard in the hall, apparently waiting to show the Osgoods to their carriage. She turned back to Madeleine, still standing in the middle of the room, looking curiously insubstantial: thin and light without much colour. Her beauty had always seemed like an essence, a transparency, which surrounded her with magic. Now it had gone and she stood there, her arms like sticks, her face as blank as though she had been drugged.

'Come and sit by the fire, my love,' said Olivia gently. 'There's no need to look so tragic. Everything will seem better in the morning.'

'No, it won't,' said Madeleine with extraordinary composure. 'They won't change their minds. They've thrown me out, like a piece of broken china.'

Olivia stared at her.

'She does that, you know,' Madeleine continued. 'Mama. I mean Mrs Osgood. If one of her porcelain figures has the smallest chip or crack, she throws it away. Even the most elaborate piece of Meissen. She cannot bear to own anything that is not perfect.'

And Madeleine, of course, was perfect no longer.

Horrified, Olivia was about to say that of course the outcast must stay here, when it crossed her mind that her uncle might not agree. She had no idea how he would take this development. Promising Madeleine she would be back in a few minutes, she left her sitting over the fire and went into the hall.

All the doors were shut. She had no idea of the time, but it seemed an age since she had shepherded Mrs Osgood and Madeleine out of the dining-room, so surely dinner must be over. She wondered where everyone had gone.

Hearing voices in the morning-room, she opened the door. The only people inside were Tom and Lion, apparently playing a scene of their own, for they too were standing and shouting at each other—could not one quarrel sitting down?

'Don't try and fool me with your slippery justifications.' Tom was icily contemptuous. 'I don't care what she may have said. You seduced her and you should offer to marry her.'

'I don't see why,' retorted Lion. 'You've never married any of your cast-off mistresses.'

Tom knocked him down. His right arm shot out, hand curling into a fist, and Lion went crashing to the floor, bringing a chair over with him and clattering the irons in the grate. He stayed there, moaning.

'Get up!' said Tom, showing no pity.

'You've broken my jaw.'

'I wish I had. Any more insolence from you and I'll break your neck.'

They had neither of them noticed Olivia. As she retreated, the door creaked. Tom swung round. His face when he saw her was a study of the chagrin caused by too many awkward associations. She withdrew hastily, to save him from having to speak. She was grateful to anyone who had knocked Lion Forester down for whatever reason.

She found her uncle still in the dining-room with Flora, Bernard and the Walkers, who might surely have had the delicacy to go away. Perhaps her thoughts were only too visible, for at the sight of her Mr Walker began to say that they ought to leave—their presence must be an imposition, in the circumstances. The Fenimores protested but without conviction. As they were going through this farce, Olivia noticed that during her absence the cloth had been drawn and the dessert set out on the table. Most of the delicious sweet dishes were untouched.

CHAPTER FIFTEEN

MADELEINE spent the night at Marine Cottage, Uncle James raising no objections. She was put to bed in Olivia's room, where she could be quiet and private, and lay perfectly still with her eyes closed, after obediently drinking a glass of hot milk laced with laudanum. She did everything she was told, made no reference to the events of the evening, and never shed a tear. Olivia thought she was still too stunned to feel any rational regrets or fears about the future.

Olivia herself moved into Flora's room, which she had formerly shared with Hetty, and was kept awake half the night by Flora crying and feeling guilty because she had deserted Madeleine in her hour of need.

'If only I had stayed with them in the gatehouse and protected her from that hateful Lion!'

'You couldn't,' said Olivia, though she was feeling guilty for very much the same reason. 'She wanted to be left alone with him.'

'That's what Bernard says. But I shall always blame myself. And poor Bernard is afraid that Mr Walker won't employ him now because we have all been so deceitful.'

'And that is supposed to indicate that Bernard won't make a good architect? Surely the man cannot be such a fool!'

'Well, I hope not. Bernard wondered if Mr Brooke would speak up for him. I think he was very angry but only with Lion.'

'He knocked Lion down in the morning-room,' said Olivia, remembering.

'Did he? I'm so glad. I do like Mr Brooke.'

That's all very well, thought Olivia. He does have some splendid qualities, but it was almost certainly his bad example that had taught Lion to think he could corrupt an innocent girl and then desert her with impunity.

Madeleine slept late next morning, rather to Olivia's relief. She wanted to talk the situation over with her uncle. She went downstairs to breakfast, asking the housemaid to keep an eye on on Miss Madeleine, who might be confused or distressed when she woke.

Breakfast was a silent meal. Mr Fenimore was displeased with his daughter for landing them in such an awkward situation, and refused to discuss it until Olivia sent her off to help put away the good china they had used last night.

Then he said to Olivia, 'What are we to do with that unfortunate child uptairs? Have I to support her for the rest of her natural life?'

'Of course not, sir. Surely the Osgoods will come round in time.'

'I should not count on it,' Uncle James replied grimly.

'If only I'd had the wit to discover what those girls were plotting. I must be very dense. I'm afraid I have failed you and Aunt Hester in not taking proper care of Flora.'

'Nonsense, my dear. Everything would have happened in exactly the same way if your aunt had been here. And Flora will come to no harm—provided the gossips don't associate her too closely with poor Madeleine's fall from grace. I don't mean to cast stones, but I fear we cannot keep her here indefinitely, even supposing we were able to hush up the story of what happened at Dalney—and I don't feel too sure of that; Mrs Walker is not a malicious gossip but she is incurably indiscreet. And even if she kept silent on this occasion, Madeleine's being disowned by the Osgoods will start a crop of rumours which must make it too unpleasant for her to remain in Parmouth for the time being.'

Olivia knew he was right.

'Meanwhile,' said Uncle James, 'I am going to do something that no one else may have thought of. I am going round to the Parsonage and tell the Cottles that Walter was not responsible for running down Peter Chapman. That is a piece of cheerful news, and he owes it to Madeleine, incidentally.'

During the past few hours Olivia had almost forgotten Peter Chapman and Walter Cottle, the two other victims of that disastrous expedition.

When her uncle had gone she went upstairs to see whether Madeleine was awake. Opening the door softly, she had a surprise. The room was empty.

'Hannah,' she called to the housemaid whom she could hear moving about in one of the other rooms, 'where is Miss Madeleine?'

'Hasn't she been with you, miss? She said she was afraid of giving trouble and she wanted to go downstairs. She asked me if I could find something of Miss Flora's for her to wear. Which I did, miss. For it stands to reason she couldn't go about all day in that thin white robe with the beads all torn at the front.'

Olivia ran downstairs again to see if Madeleine had joined Flora, who was gloomily watering the pot-plants in the drawing-room. But Flora had not seen

Madeleine, neither had any of the other servants, and she was nowhere in the house.

Where could she have gone, and why? Not to look for Lion at the Vale, Olivia was certain. And, since that infatuation was over, who else would she turn to? Though she knew so many people in Parmouth, Flora was her greatest friend and Marine Cottage the house where she had always been most sure of a welcome. Having been offered sanctuary here, why should she leave to go anywhere else? Even if she had reached the point of recognising her own ambiguous position, her presence would be just as embarrassing to any of her other friends. Olivia could think of only one place where she might have gone. In spite of what she had said last night, she might be hoping that her adopted parents would forgive her, once the worst shock was over. Of course it would be the best solution, only Olivia could not believe in it. She did not believe Mrs Osgood could overcome her savage hatred and revulsion so quickly, if at all. And how dreadful it would be if Madeleine were rejected again, with further brutal accusations, while there was no one beside her to offer comfort.

I won't let that happen, thought Olivia, dragging on a bonnet and pelisse and almost running from the house in her hurry to reach the Villa Romana.

It was a sunless morning, depressing as grey days by the sea so often were. A strong wind was battling roughly with the breakers of an incoming tide. She crossed the Parade and took the road that ran along the eastern arm of the bay towards the Osgoods' house, cupped in a sheltered niche of the headland.

There was no sign of Madeleine ahead of her. The only person visible was a man coming towards her, and after a moment she saw it was Tom. He always went about on foot in Parmouth, he said it wasn't worth taking out his horses.

Olivia was too worried about Madeleine to feel any of the awkwardness that attacked her now when she met Tom. She knew he must have been to the Villa Romana—there was no other house on this road—so she called out, 'Have you seen Madeleine? Has she gone home?'

'No,' he said. 'She's not there. I thought she was with you.'

They had met by now, and stood together by the roadside, where a grassy bank sloped down towards the beach.

'She went out without telling anyone. I thought she must have come here.' Olivia looked hopefully at Tom. 'You've seen the Osgoods this morning—have they had a change of heart?'

'I'm afraid not. Nor likely to. I can't understand such people. That they should be angry and shocked, that's natural enough. But they want to disown her utterly. They kept insisting that she wasn't their own flesh and blood, as though that were sufficient excuse. Damn it, she's lived with them for ten years. They gave her their surname and taught her to call them Mama and Papa; does that mean nothing?'

Olivia repeated what Madeleine had said about Mrs Osgood throwing away any of her ornaments that had a crack or a chip.

'Just what one might expect,' said Tom. 'Still, if Madeleine said that, she'd hardly come back here, would she? So where would she go? Not to Martha Channing at the Vale, because my miserable godson is still there. Where else? Try to think, Olivia.'

'I have been trying. I know it's all my fault—I should
have stayed upstairs with her this morning instead of
going down to breakfast, only I wanted to consult my
uncle, and I thought she was asleep. I suppose she was
pretending. It was my fault Madeleine and Flora went
to Dalney. You said I should have paid more attention
to what was going on, and you were right.'

'I'm hardly likely to cast it in your teeth, am I,
considering who is chiefly responsible for this whole
wretched business? You've made it plain enough what
you think of me, and, now that I've seen myself
slavishly imitated by Lion, I begin to agree with you.'

He had lost his usual assurance. He sounded pain-
fully humiliated.

'Lion isn't like you.' Olivia spoke impulsively
because she was sorry for him. She heard herself
saying, 'You wouldn't have made Madeleine drunk.'

'Thank you,' said Tom drily.

She flushed, certain in spite of everything that Tom
would not make a woman drunk in order to seduce
her. She did not think he would ever find it necessary—
thank goodness she had not said that. But had she
implied that she thought him capable of all the other
selfish and shabby things Lion had done?

She made another effort to shoulder her share of the
blame.

'I should have paid more attention when you spoke
of interrupting a love-scene.'

'If you didn't, it was my fault,' he said quickly. 'The
flippant, exaggerated way I spoke was enough to make
you think I was simply scoring a point, making a
reference that was in very poor taste. It's true I did not
think Madeleine was in danger of anything worse than
a small disappointment. Even so, I shouldn't have left

the burden of protecting her entirely to you. You can guess why I did.'

She had guessed by now but she made a prosaic excuse for him.

'A girl can be warned and watched over in a way that would be unacceptable to a young man.'

'That is putting is charitably, but you must know why I shirked the duty of telling Lion to behave himself. I wasn't in a position to preach sermons, and he knew it. You heard what he said last night.'

The jeering words echoed in her mind. You've never married any of your cast-off mistresses. She could not look at Tom—anywhere else rather, though she sensed his mortification through every nerve in her body.

She glanced across the beach, bleak and forlorn on such a day. The tide was about halfway in and there were only two people down there: a man in a fisherman's jersey, apparently fixing a loose board in the breakwater, and a woman walking towards the sea. She wore a shawl with a pattern of curiously bright pinks and greens. Flora had one very like it. Surely it couldn't be Flora, whom she had left watering the pot-plants in Marine Cottage? Her heart gave a sudden jerk.

'It's Madeleine,' she said aloud. 'In Flora's clothes.'

'Where?' Tom swung round, took one look and said, 'Oh, my God!'

He started running down the green bank towards the beach. Olivia, catching his alarm, went after him. There was an overpowering instinct to reach Madeleine before it was too late—even though she kept telling herself that this was a nonsensical panic. Anyone might wish to walk by the sea in a melancholy mood. She hurried on, all the same.

Tom had jumped down on to the beach, shouting something to the man beside the breakwater, who looked round, followed his pointing arm, and also set off running towards Madeleine. She was standing perfectly still at the frothing edge of the tide.

Olivia had reached the edge of the grass. It was quite a drop on to the beach but she managed to scramble down, scraping the palms of her hands and tearing her skirt. While this was happening she was unable to watch the scene in front of her.

When she looked again, Madeleine was ankle-deep in swirling water with Tom and the fisherman racing towards her. They did not seem to be gaining much ground and neither did Olivia, struggling through the heavy sand as though her feet were made of lead. It was like one of those nightmares when you ran and ran and got no further.

Madeleine moved implacably on. The water was nearly up to her waist. There was no sense in shouting to her—the wind and the waves swallowed every other sound. But surely no one could drown simply by walking into the sea? It would require too great a strength of will. Unless the sea itself took a hand. All that was visible now was a triangle of pink and green which vanished under the lip of a huge breaker. Either Madeleine had plunged deliberately or she had been knocked off her feet.

Both the men were in the sea, forcing their way towards the place where she had disappeared. Olivia stood breathless on the beach, knowing she could do nothing to help, for an age of horrifying suspense, while they searched for Madeleine through the tumult of shifting water. Then she saw Tom clutching something dark and dripping. He and the fisherman came wading back to the shore carrying Madeleine, inert and senseless between them.

They laid her down on the sand.

'Is she alive?' Olivia hardly dared to ask.

'I don't know,' said Tom.

The fisherman was kneeling beside her, working at her arms and shoulders with a sort of pumping movement. Madeleine lay still, her wet hair streaming round her like seaweed.

Tom said, 'Let me try, Reuben.'

He lay down almost on top of the unconscious girl, pressing his mouth against hers in the most intimate attitude of kissing. Olivia stared at them, uneasy and astonished, and weird fantasies rushed through her mind—as though it were Tom who had been Madeleine's lover, and he was kissing her dead lips for the last time.

Reuben, the fisherman, saw Olivia's puzzled expression and explained.

'Master Tom's putting the breath back in her body, poor maid.'

And so he was. A minute later her eyelids began to flutter. She was still alive. Olivia felt as though she had seen a miracle. She was ashamed of her recent imaginings, which must never be known to anyone, and this was not the time to talk or think, there was too much to do.

They chafed Madeleine's hands and feet to get the blood going, and propped her in a sitting position so that she could choke up mouthfuls of salt-water. The soaking shawl was taken from under her—it had almost been her winding sheet—and Olivia wrapped her in her own pelisse. She was the only person who had a dry garment to offer.

Tom lifted the exhausted girl and carried her up the steps almost opposite Marine Cottage. Reuben went ahead to see that the coast was clear. It was lucky there were so few people about on this dismal morning.

Once they were back indoors Olivia had recovered her wits and was able to take command. Madeleine's bedroom fire was made up with a fresh scuttle of coal, she was quickly undressed and swathed in blankets while she sat with her feet in a scalding mustard bath.

'The water isn't too hot, is it?' Olivia asked her. 'You ought to have it as near the boil as you can bear.'

'It is very comfortable, thank you,' whispered Madeleine. 'You are so kind to me and I have been so wicked.'

For the first time since the scene at the dinner party she burst into a natural flood of tears.

Olivia was greatly relieved. She felt that Madeleine had returned to her true self and was no longer the petrified creature who had reached the end of her endurance and walked into the sea.

Presently she went downstairs to tell Tom, but he was no longer there. Her uncle had given him a large brandy and advised him to go home and change his clothes.

CHAPTER SIXTEEN

THE next day was Sunday but Olivia did not go to Church. She stayed away to keep Madeleine company—just in case. Though she did not believe Madeleine would make any further rash attempt at suicide. She was very subdued, which was understandable, but she gave an impression of natural sadness, not of inhuman despair.

As they sat in the morning-room, listening to the sound of Church bells, she began to talk.

'I have been very foolish. I was so completely taken in—I don't mean that as an excuse for *doing* wrong but for making such mistakes in feeling and believing. But how is one to tell?'

'How indeed?' said Olivia, who understood exactly what she meant. 'That is the great puzzle no one ever explains.'

Encouraged by this response, Madeleine was anxious to discuss her disastrous love-affair. The whole story came tumbling out. She had of course been charmed and dazzled by Lion. That was not so very strange, was it? She soon began to think herself seriously in love, and was overjoyed when he told her that he loved her in return. He spoke of marriage but said they could not be formally engaged until he had come of age. She accepted this and was quite ready to wait. Only Lion was in trouble over the debts he had run up in Oxford and London; he was being sent away to join the Army, perhaps he would be killed. He wanted to make love

213

to her, to enjoy his rights, he called it, before they
were separated. Here Madeleine drew the line. She
trusted him implicitly and longed to give in, but she
thought it would be wrong. Lion ridiculed her scruples,
said she was cowardly and cold-blooded, that she had
simply led him on out of vanity.

This was the state of affairs on the day of the trip to
Dalney. By the end of the morning she was half won
over but not quite. It was while they were dining in the
gatehouse, when she drank a good deal of champagne,
that her apprehension melted. She was carried away
on a tide of romantic fervour and promised to let him
do what he asked.

They climbed the spiral stairs to the room above and
here everything went wrong. From the way she spoke
it was clear to Olivia that Madeleine had not been
nearly as drunk as she supposed. She had simply taken
enough to unbalance her judgement and dull her fears.
The unheated room and Lion's rough approach to
lovemaking served to clear her brain. She said she did
not want to go any further. He became extremely angry
and said that if she changed her mind now she would
be breaking her promise. She knew this was true and
let herself be bullied into submission. He hurt her a
good deal and it was hardly surprising that this first
experience of love was a humiliating failure.

She had cried most of the way home, and Lion,
instead of comforting her, had jeered and criticised,
telling her that such a little whining puritan would
never learn the art of giving pleasure. The final disillusion came when Lion, after coming up against some
object on the road, refused to stop and investigate.
Madeleine had gone home guilty and frightened and
taken to her bed. She had been physically sick half the

night, and when she heard of the accident to Peter
Chapman, and that her old friend Walter was being
blamed for it, she was overcome with remorse. Among
all these dreadful sensations she hardly felt the full
impact of discovering she was no longer in love.

She's got more sense that I have, thought Olivia.
Once she found out what Lion was really like, she was
able to stop loving him. But there was no true comparison. Lion had treated Madeleine abominably, you
wondered that any man could be not only so cruel, but
such a fool. The answer was, of course, that Lion was
leaving Parmouth, the expedition to Dalney was his
last chance of getting what he wanted, and he would
have no further interest in the wretched girl once he
had gone. Olivia's disillusion with Tom had been far
less violent. Tom was a notorious rake, he had hurt
other women, including his former mistress Anne
Laybourne, he had set a pernicious example to Lion
Forester, but he had not behaved badly to Olivia
herself. He had even made her an honourable proposal
of marriage. Better for me if he'd treated me worse,
she thought cynically. I am still plagued with sweet and
piercing memories that no heartless brutality has blot-
ted out. That's the difference.

All this passed through her mind very swiftly while
she poked the fire. She turned to the passive figure of
Madeleine in the wing-chair.

'You are well rid of Lion. If you can already recognise as much, that is greatly to your advantage.'

'Oh, yes, I am well rid of him. And Mr and Mrs
Osgood are well rid of me. I am not the sort of person
they need to lavish their hopes on. Do you think she
was right when she said that my mother did what I

have done and was obliged to marry my father as a consequence?'

'I think she was in such a state that she would have said anything.'

'Well, I don't care. My real parents loved each other. There was more love in our home in Paris than I ever saw at the Villa Romana.'

'Were you not happy there? You always seemed so contented, more so than many girls and their mothers.'

'Yes, I led a very pleasant life. She was kind, she gave me presents, pretty clothes, everything I wanted. She was proud of me, you see. I am not clever as you are, Olivia, but I was able to learn to sing and dance and play and draw and sew and have pleasing manners—all the things Mrs Osgood sets such store by. She would not have been so fond of a plain, awkward girl.'

Olivia was startled by the younger girl's cool, unemotional verdict on the woman who had spoilt and petted her for ten years, and then turned her out the moment she put a foot wrong. Had she always seen her adopted mother in this light?

Olivia thought about Mrs Osgood, the poised and exquisite leader of Parmouth society, so fastidious in her person and her ideas, so much younger-looking than Aunt Hester or Mrs Channing, probably because she had never borne children. Instead she had taken possession of the eight-year-old Madeleine, already past the tiresome, uncivilised phase of childhood and promising to become a beauty. Just what the adopting mother required. Behind an agreeable surface, there had always been a self-gratifying egotist with a will of iron who regarded other people as objects created for her own convenience. Lovely, sweet-tempered, docile

Madeleine had fitted admirably into the life of the Villa Romana. Now she had proved unworthy—and well out of such a home, Olivia considered. Only what was to become of her?

Madeleine was staring into the fire. As though the question had been asked aloud, she said, 'I think I should like to go to the French Convent. It is not very far from Brantisford so I could get there quite easily.'

'Go into a Convent?' echoed Olivia, who found this suggestion particularly disagreeable, though she could not immediately think why, apart from the fact that it sounded alien to her Protestant ears. 'My dear, you cannot wish to become a nun. You are only eighteen and your life is not over, whatever you may think at the moment.'

'I am not good enough to be a nun. But they would give me sanctuary, I am sure of that, for I heard quite lately of a lady who took refuge with a community of sisters after she had been ruined by a scandal. It was— Lion who told us about her.' She stumbled a little over the name. 'And, now I think of it, you were there too. Do you remember?'

'I remember,' said Olivia, with a dull recognition of the dismay she had felt when she first heard of Anne Laybourne's flight into the Convent after Tom had deserted her.

'Of course it wasn't the same Convent,' Madeleine was saying. 'That happened in quite another part of England. But I think they were French nuns too. Well, I suppose all the nuns we hear about are French, because English people are not supposed to be Catholics, are they? It's against the law.'

It was true, while English Catholics were still denied their full rights as citizens, persecuted monks and nuns from across the Channel had been allowed to set up houses in England and treated with great kindness and generosity. Victims of persecution always excited the chivalry of the English. It was probably this, and the affecting story of Lady Laybourne, which had started Madeleine thinking about Convents. Another romantic illusion, Olivia decided, and was promptly jolted out of her complacency by what Madeleine said next.

'If I went to the nuns, I should be able to see a priest. I could make my confession and be reconciled to the Church.'

Olivia looked at her in astonishment.

'Surely you are not a Roman Catholic, Madeleine?'

'I was baptised and brought up in the Catholic faith, did you not know? When I went to live with the Osgoods, I had to become English and go to the Parish Church. I was too young to understand or to resist, so I don't think it was so very wicked. Only I have done such bad things since. Not only what happened with Lion, but trying to drown myself. That is a mortal sin too, worse than the other. How could I have done anything so terrible?'

'You were not in full command of your reason,' said Olivia soothingly, for she saw that Madeleine was working herself into a fit of remorse. She hunted for a distraction.

'I had quite forgotten that your father was French. And you remember living over there?'

'Yes, very well. That is another reason I should like to talk to the nuns. And I have just thought, Olivia. I am not Miss Osgood any more, so I can be called Madeleine de Cressy again, which is a far nicer name, though I suppose it is frivolous to care about such things.'

When Flora and her father came back from Morning Service, she was able to tell Madeleine that Walter had been there, and it was now generally known that he was not responsible for Peter Chapman's accident. Flora had told him that it was Madeleine who had revealed the truth, and he sent her his undying gratitude for her sacrifice. They had prayed for Peter Chapman, who was making a very good recovery.

Olivia did not know what to think about Madeleine's wish to visit the nearby Convent. There were so many aspects to consider. She did not think either her uncle or Flora was the right person to consult, so in the early afternoon she went to call on Mrs Channing.

She walked through the quiet melancholy of Parmouth out of season, so unlike the vivid, echoing liveliness of July, and felt that she herself was sadly altered from the heartwhole, confident girl who had come here in the summer, looking for fun and flirtation and eager to captivate the fascinating stranger who had accosted her at the posting-inn. She had come by a great deal of experience in the last few months which she had rather have done without. In a literal sense she had come off lightly, but the anguish of other women acted as a commentary on her own unhappiness.

She took the road that led to the Vale, ignoring the wooded seclusion of Rosamond's Bower as it towered above her.

When she reached the front door of the Vale and pulled the bell, she saw out of the tail of her eye someone turn the corner of the house and stop still. He then beat a hasty retreat, but not before she had recognised the dashing good looks and slim figure of Lion Forester. He was frightened to meet her—and so he should be, she thought grimly.

She was shown into the library, where the master of the house was sitting companionably with Mrs Channing, who was hemming shirts for the poor, the only work she would do on a Sunday.

Olivia answered all their enquiries, and was able to give Tom a rather incoherent message from Madeleine to thank him for saving her life.

He was dismissive. 'There was nothing very heroic about wading ten yards into the sea. I spoilt an old coat I was attached to, but I don't expect Madeleine to set much store by that.'

'You can never bear to be thanked, can you?' said Mrs Channing, re-threading her needle.

'The poor girl may not have much reason for gratitude. What is to be done with her now?'

This was Olivia's, cue, but she hesitated, realising that any mention of a betrayed female wishing to hide her shame in a Convent would sound very embarrassing in front of Tom.

After a momentary pause he started talking about Lion.

'I am thankful to say he is leaving Parmouth tomorrow. My friend Durnford is still away from home, but he has arranged for Lion to hold a commission in his regiment, now stationed at Gibraltar. He is to sail with the next draft. By good fortune another of the officers is passing through from Cornwall. He is to call for Lion and they will travel to Portsmouth together.'

'Is Lion willing to go?' asked Olivia.

'Oh, yes. He knows he can't draw another penny of his allowance unless he does what he's told. And besides, he has made this place too hot to hold him and is anxious to escape.'

Olivia reflected that Lion might have thought he

could shrug off the seduction of a girl whose moral frailty would act as his excuse, but to run down a local citizen in his curricle and then keep quiet and let another man take the blame—that was beyond the pale.

'We shall all feel more comfortable when Lion has gone,' said Mrs Channing. 'But it doesn't solve the problem of Madeleine. Your uncle has been exceedingly kind, Olivia, but it really is not fitting for Madeleine to remain in Parmouth now the Osgoods have turned her out. Everyone must be speculating as to the reason, even if they have not guessed the truth.'

'They won't have to guess much, thanks to Margaret Walker!' commented Tom. 'I gather she has been spreading the story far and wide, with many expressions of pity and indignation. She is not an ill-natured woman but she simply cannot hold her tongue.'

There was a depressing silence, and as Tom showed no sign of going away Olivia decided that she would have to come out with Madeleine's own solution. As she expected, she was interrupted almost immediately.

'Go into a Convent?' they both exclaimed, just as she had done.

'Not *into* a Convent, not forever, at least I don't think so. But she has given me some good reasons, I don't think this is a mere whim.'

And she repeated a good deal of what Madeleine had said that morning. Mrs Channing looked doubtful. Perhaps it seemed to her that anyone who had been rescued from the Catholic Church in infancy should not run the risk of being converted. Olivia did not agree. She felt that Madeleine wanted to return to the Church of her childhood, and that if she was denied the opportunity this would add one more load of guilt to her conscience.

Tom got up and walked over to the window, where he stood with his back to them, facing out. They both waited curiously to hear his opinion. Perhaps he was having a pang of conscience on his own account, connected with Anne Laybourne. But when he turned round he was entirely practical.

'I think she should pay the nuns a visit, if that is what she wants. By washing their hands of her, the Osgoods have done their best to cancel her existence—the only existence she has had since she was brought to this country: an English girl, Madeleine Osgood, their daughter. It is worth trying whether the French sisters can restore the faith and hope of Madeleine de Cressy. And I don't think they will wall her up alive or do any of the things you are wondering about, my dear Martha.'

'Of course I wasn't thinking any such thing,' said Mrs Channing indignantly. 'And, now I come to consider, the company of some of those French ladies may do just what you suggest—beside making it plain to Selina Osgood that no one is going to beg *her* to take any further interest in Madeleine, which I am sure is what she expects.'

'That will put her in her place, won't it?' said Tom smoothly. 'A very Christian achievement. So who is going to take Madeleine to the Convent and explain matters? Clearly, I can't. Will you go with her, Martha?'

But here there was a difficulty.

'Oh, dear,' said Mrs Channing. 'I don't see how I can. You know how John would take it, and I cannot argue with him in his present state of health.'

'No, of course not. I was a fool not to think about John.'

Olivia grasped without needing to be told that Captain Channing really did disapprove of the Catholic Church and all its doings, that he would not wish his wife to escort a young girl into a Convent, and that, because he was a very sick man, neither she nor his close friend and benefactor was prepared to argue with him.

Olivia could see a simple solution.

'I can go with Madeleine to the Convent,' she volunteered.

They both turned towards her.

'No!' exclaimed Tom. 'That won't do. You are the very last person.'

Olivia winced at the expression in his voice, even though she didn't quite understand it. His blue glance seemed to travel over and through her, and she found herself trembling from the sense of humiliation, which was absurd. Mrs Channing did not understand him either.

She said, 'I cannot see that there is any very strong objection.'

'She is much too young and herself ummarried.' Tom was recovering his manners and floundering in the process. 'My dear Miss Olivia, I did not mean to sound so—so——'

'Hostile?' suggested Olivia in a small voice.

'Certainly not hostile. Uncivil. But I am sure you ought not to be involved in such a delicate affair. Your uncle and aunt would not approve. And Lizzie Wakelin certainly wouldn't.'

This conclusion, coming down to earth with a bump, would have made Olivia laugh if she had not been feeling so diminished by his obviously poor opinion. It was unreasonable to set such a high value on his judgement when she thought so badly of his character, but she could not help herself. She bit her lip and said nothing.

'It seems to me very odd,' said Mrs Channing, 'considering how deeply involved Olivia is already in this delicate affair—as you call it. Why should she not accompany Madeleine to the Convent? Unless you think the nuns would find it improper? If that is what is troubling you, I tell you what I'll do, Tom. I'll write a letter to the Mother Superior explaining the whole situation. This won't involve arguing with John or lying to him because he'll never know. I'll explain that I cannot leave my sick husband and that the letter is brought by Miss Fenimore, a young lady of the highest character. All Olivia need do is to go with Madeleine in the carriage, hand over the letter, and wait until it is certain that Madeleine can stay with the nuns. Or, of course, bring her back if they refuse to keep her. What harm can there be in that?'

Olivia would not reply until she heard what Tom had to say.

'It sounds an excellent plan. Unanswerable.' He spoke very quietly. 'If you are still prepared to go, Miss Olivia?'

'Yes, Mr Brooke.'

The Convent was only an hour's drive, they told her, and it was decided that the girls should go tomorrow. There was no point in delay. Tom would lend them his carriage and they would start first thing in the morning—provided Mr Fenimore agreed, they all said as a matter of form. Olivia knew he would.

When she rose to leave, she half hoped that Tom

would offer to walk home with her. Instead he said an abrupt goodbye and turned away, directing his attention to some papers on his desk. She thought he must blame her for letting Madeleine become fascinated by Lion and all that had led to. Indeed she blamed herself. But yesterday, when they met on the road to the Villa Romana, he had seemed kind and friendly, anxious to shoulder his own share of responsibility. Today she was in his black books again, and she had no idea why.

CHAPTER SEVENTEEN

TOM'S comfortable travelling carriage arrived at ten o'clock, and the girls were seen off by Uncle James and a tearful Flora, who obviously thought she was never going to see her dear friend again.

Olivia was afraid she might start Madeleine off crying, but Madeleine was calm, only afraid she had not thanked Mr Fenimore enough for his great kindness. She knew she had not deserved the kindness everyone had shown her.

'Not forgetting Mr Brooke,' said Olivia, determined to be commonplace and jolly. 'I must say it is considerate of him to own such a luxurious carriage when he never drives anywhere except in his curricle. These rugs are so soft, and hot bricks for our feet too! We are in clover.'

The weather had cleared, the sun was shining, and after they left the Brantisford road the way was new to Olivia. She looked out of the window, admiring the scenery and persuading Madeleine to take an interest in their surroundings and if possible stop brooding on the ordeal ahead.

For it would be an ordeal, and as they neared the end of their journey she became extremely nervous, communicating her nervousness to Olivia.

Suppose the nuns refused to take her in? Olivia thought. Poor little Madeleine, she is not fit to stand another rejection. It would have been wiser for Mrs Channing to write in advance, asking for advice. The sisters might not be censorious, but they would be superstitious, probably ill-educated. Olivia had known good, charitable nuns in Ireland, working among the poor. She could not imagine dear old Sister Bridget knowing quite what to say to Madeleine in her present confusion.

Olivia knew that she herself was too impulsive, but it did seem odd that Tom and Mrs Channing, once they accepted the idea of the Convent, had been in such a hurry to send Madeleine there without making enquiries.

Madeleine said with a quavering smile, 'I shall find it very strange at first.'

'You needn't stay if you don't like it,' said Olivia, taking her hand. 'You can come back with me to Marine Cottage. You have only to say.'

She was so concerned for Madeleine that she hardly noticed when they passed through a gateway, being only dimly aware of high walls on either side of them. The approach to the Convent was quite short. The carriage stopped. She looked out of the window at a fine Elizabethan building, and got the shock of her life.

'This is Maygrove Manor!'

'Yes,' said Madeleine, as though it was a matter of course. 'The nuns came to the house about three years ago, I think. I have never been here before.'

But I have, thought Olivia, remembering that awkward occasion on Hetty and Alfred's wedding tour, when silly Hetty had manoeuvred them into the village to gape at the home of Tom's ancestors, and Alfred had been so hurt and angry.

If this house really belonged to Tom, how could it possibly contain a community of nuns? The woman at the inn had said he kept his mistresses here. That was

more like it. But why had he sent her and Madeleine
to such a place in his carriage? Could it be a joke? A
very sinister joke, if so, and in the worst possible taste.
While she was struggling with her incredulity, the
footman got down from the box and asked for instructions. She handed Mrs Channing's letter to him, like
an automaton. He knocked on the front door. Shortly
afterwards a panel slid back and someone looked at
him through a grille.

The door was opened and the letter was taken in by
a woman wearing a costume Olivia had never actually
seen before, though she knew from pictures that it was
the habit of a religious order. The nun disappeared
with the letter, the girls remained in the carriage.

They were kept waiting a little while, though not
long enough for Olivia, who had to come to terms with
her first brief suspicion, quite as disgraceful as the
fantasy which had shot through her mind when Tom
lay down by Madeleine on the beach and brought her
back to life by breathing into her mouth. It really was
too shaming, these images that kept assaulting her
mind. But then, to think of Tom filling his house with
Roman Catholic nuns—surely that could not be true?

It must be, however. The door had opened again
and another nun appeared and spoke to them in perfect
English with the faintest trace of an accent.

'Miss Fenimore, Mademoiselle de Cressy, do come
indoors. I am Sister Thérèse, and I am sorry you have
been kept waiting in the cold.'

She was a tall woman, probably in her early forties,
though her smooth oval face, enclosed in its white
wimple, looked younger.

She ushered them into a plain stone hall and said to

Madeleine, 'Reverend Mother would like to talk to you, my dear child. Alone, if you please.'

Madeleine looked frightened for an instant, and Olivia was prepared to make a stand and insist on going with her to face the dragon.

The nun said gently, 'It is always easier, do you not think, to talk privately if there is no one else listening? Even an audience of one can be a little daunting. Reverend Mother will be glad to meet you afterwards, Miss Fenimore, and of course nothing wil be arranged without your knowledge.'

Olivia had the sense to realise that the Mother Superior wanted to make certain that Madeleine had come here of her own free will, and was not being thrust into obscurity by people who had been embarrassed or disgusted by the scandal she had created.

She allowed herself to be shown into a parlour leading off the hall, while Madeleine and Sister Thérèse went off together, chatting to each other in French.

Olivia sat down and looked around her. She was in a low panelled room, very simply furnished and almost empty. There was a carved crucifix on one wall and a picture of the Holy Family over the empty fireplace. The floor was uncarpeted. Outside the window she could see the enclosed garden that she and Hetty and Alfred had peered at through the gates four months ago.

She tried to make sense out of her memories of that day. How could they have imagined that Tom kept his mistresses in this house? The innkeeper's wife had made it sound almost like a brothel. What could she have said to give them that impression? Something about whores of Babylon and why did the Parson allow it? That was the answer, of course. The cross woman at the inn had been not a moralist but a narrow-minded bigot. What she objected to so strongly was a houseful of Roman Catholic nuns. What a ludicrous misunderstanding, and thank heaven Tom did not know about it. She hoped the village people were not unpleasant to their unusual neighbours; perhaps it was just that one woman. And, while on the subject of prejudice, she reminded herself that she had expected these French sisters to be as ignorant as the nuns she had known in Ireland, forgetting that most Irish Catholics were peasants—the English would not let them be anything else. Sister Thérèse was a lady of gentle, probably noble birth.

The door opened and a black-robed figure paused on the threshold. Another of the nuns, thought Olivia. She then found herself being addressed by a perfectly English voice.

'You are Miss Fenimore, I think.'

Looking more closely, she saw that the lady was not wearing the habit of a religious, but was dressed in deep mourning with a widow's cap.

Getting up, she said, 'Yes, ma'am. I am Olivia Fenimore.'

'And I am Anne Laybourne. I have been so curious to meet you, and you are even more charming than I expected.'

Olivia gazed at her in dumb astonishment. More surprising even than finding Maygrove Manor a nunnery was finding Tom's former mistress inside. Faced by a person who had become an almost mythical figure in her imagination, she saw that Anne Laybourne was not so tall as herself, with a fair skin and light brown hair. She had beautiful features, though these were at present much too thin, and soft, luminous grey eyes.

Smiling very sweetly at Olivia, she said, 'Shall we sit down? I am sorry there is no fire. The sisters are very hardy and I am afraid very poor. It is a great convenience for them to find a mortification that is also an economy.'

Olivia pulled herself together. 'I beg your pardon, you must find me very stupid. But who can have described me, or said that I was charming?'

'An old friend of mine. I was also told something else—I hope you will not mind my mentioning it: that you were on the point of becoming engaged to Tom Brooke. I do hope that it is not on my account that the match has been broken off.'

Olivia found herself turning brick-red. The old friend was probably Louisa Woodvile—but why had she found it necessary to pass on such a piece of news to this poor woman who must be so desperately jealous of her?

'Forgive me if I am impertinent,' said Lady Laybourne. 'I only raised the matter in order to set your mind at rest. If you were told that I have recently received an offer of marriage from Tom, I can understand your reluctance to listen to any proposals addressed to yourself. You must have thought him so inconstant that his admiration was an insult. But I assure you that the case is not quite what it seems.' She had been looking directly at Olivia, now she looked away, twisting her long white fingers in her lap as she continued.

'I am sure you have heard my story—how I was married young and not very happily and how I betrayed my husband for love of Tom Brooke. At the height of our forbidden passion Tom swore he would marry me if ever I was free. We were thinking then not of

Martin's death, but of his divorcing me for adultery. However, he didn't divorce me, though he was intensely jealous, and eventually I told Tom I could not continue our guilty association and our secret meetings must end. That was six years ago. Since then nothing wrong has ever taken place between us. We took care never to be alone together, though since we moved in the same circle we met continually in public and I'm afraid my husband went on suffering all the miseries of suspicion. When he became ill and we retired to the country, it even disturbed him to know that Tom was living five miles away, and once Tom understood this he went into a kind of voluntary exile and seldom came to Cassondon. I believe this self-denying generosity actually drew attention to our situation, and many of our friends believed that we were still lovers and only kept apart by fear of Martin's retribution. Luckily Martin himself never understood this, and I only mention it now in order to explain that any recent gossip you have heard about us is long out of date.

'When Martin died in September, Tom appeared on my doorstep, reminded me of his promise, and said he would marry me whenever I chose. He came in great haste because he knew that Martin's brother John had succeeded to the baronetcy and John has always disliked me on account of my being such a bad wife. It was generally thought that John would turn me out of doors.'

Olivia had begun to feel very odd, as though the room were spinning round her.

She said, 'May I interrupt you, Lady Laybourne? Have I understood you right? Are you telling me that

Mr Brooke made you an offer of marriage after your husband's death?'

'You didn't know!' Anne Laybourne's dismay was almost comic. She hastened to repair the damage she thought she had done. 'This is what comes of meddling. I meant well, and that is always fatal. Forget everything I said, except that I can assure you he only asked me because of his old promise, and because he was afraid I might be disowned by Martin's family and left without a penny. In this he was mistaken. Martin told John he had forgiven me, and John has made no attempt to withhold my settlement. But Tom wasn't to know that, and he acted purely out of chivalry. That is the kind of man he is, as I dare say you know.'

Anne stopped speaking and looked curiously at Olivia, who was now speechless.

There was a short silence, then Anne began again.

'Did Tom make you an offer? I beg your pardon—I shouldn't ask, should I?'

'I don't mind,' whispered Olivia. 'Yes, he did, and I refused him.'

'I am very sorry, because I believe you and he would be well suited. He has so many good qualities, and I feel he deserves to be happy, though of course I know that what he and I did was very wrong. But he, after all, was free and unmarried at the time. I was the one who broke a solemn vow. You cannot think how deeply I regret the past. I was married at seventeen to a man I did not love. He was clever, cold, and austere, and I was afraid of him. He seemed to me more like an unusually stern father than anything else. I thought his jealousy was founded on outraged virtue and wounded pride. It was only when he became ill and dependent that I realised he had always loved me without being able to show it. During those last years we grew closer together. We were almost happy, even though we both knew he was dying. Now he has gone, I am haunted by guilt, regret for a past that might have been so different. When I heard you were here at Maygrove, I wanted to plead Tom's cause with you because I feel I have done him a great injury too. But I must make it clear that I am not personally concerned. I doubt if I shall ever marry again but, if I did, the one man I could never marry is Tom. Do you understand?'

'Yes. I am grateful to you for telling me so much. It is quite true that I have been mistaken about Tom's attachment to you, Lady Laybourne, though not in the way you supposed. I was told that, having placed you in a most vulnerable situation, he wouldn't put matters right when the opportunity came.'

'Good heavens, who told you that?' asked Anne, opening her eyes very wide. 'Are people saying that he deserted me? That is most unjust. Do tell me what you have heard and from whom.'

By now Olivia was too confused to remember the names of the women who had written to Louisa and to Lizzie. In any case she thought they were related to Anne, and there was no point in making mischief. So she said that a certain amount of gossip had reached Parmouth through the post.

'I understood you had left your own home and gone straight to Tom's house after your husband's death. And a few days later I heard you had entered a Convent.'

'Well, I did both those things. I came here. This house belongs to Tom, did you not know?'

'Oh,' said Olivia, nonplussed. 'How stupid of me. I should have realised directly you spoke to me. But some of your friends must have been wrongly informed. They implied you had gone to Cassondon.'

Anne said philosophically, 'I expect it was more interesting for them to think that. Someone jumped to the wrong conclusion. The fact is, I planned to come here as soon as my husband's suffering ended, for I had about a month's warning. The sisters here are friends of mine. The older members of the community fled to England at the time of the Terror, and my husband lent them a house on his estate. After my marriage I came to know them well. After a few years they came down here.'

Her explanations became specious. Considering her remarkable frankness up to now, Olivia guessed what it was she did not want to say: that Sir Martin, in his state of bitter resentment, had turned against the nuns, perhaps because they had tried to befriend his wife. This seemed all the more likely when Anne added that Tom, hearing they had nowhere to go, had offered them Maygrove Manor.

'So I asked if they would take me in,' she went on placidly. 'It is quite usual on the Continent, you know, for Convents to accept solitary female boarders. My family are in an uproar. They are afraid that I shall "go over to Rome", as they put it, and take the veil. Perhaps I may; the right path is not clear to me yet. My decision will have no effect on anyone else. I have no great wealth to pass on, no children to influence against the wishes of their other relations. I am looking for peace of mind and conscience, and here I believe I shall find it.'

Olivia felt she was right. The atmosphere of the quiet house seemed to be charged with a life-giving spirit, a timeless calm. She felt a strong liking for Anne but not the slightest sense of pity or rivalry. Anne had out-grown the violence of passion. Her long-standing affection for Tom was muted now, its keenest element was probably a sense of responsibility. Each had done the other a good deal of harm.

'I hope,' she said to Olivia, 'that what I have told you will not harden your heart against Tom. His great kindness and generosity outweigh all his faults, and I am sure he would make a faithful husband if he was living with a wife and family in his own home. One reason for his rake's progress in the last few years has been his constant, restless moving about among people who have drawn him into stupid freaks because he had nothing better to do. He loves Cassondon but he has hardly been there since he realised that his presence in the neighbourhood was threatening my marriage. I hope you have not absolutely refused him.'

Olivia said miserably, 'I have refused him. You see, I made a terrible mistake, listening to all those false rumours. I told him I could never accept a man who could behave so barbarously to—to the lady he ought to have married.'

'*Well*,' said Anne Laybourne after a pause of pure astonishment. 'That is a reason for refusing an offer which I have never come across before. Very few people are truly disinterested. We are all apt to think that devotion to ourselves is the only thing that counts. What did Tom say?'

'He was very angry, and I don't wonder. I wasn't trying to be noble. I wanted him to know that I should never marry a man I did not trust. But why didn't he explain?' asked Olivia, almost in tears.

'My dear, how could he? How could he say, "I did ask my former mistress to marry me two days ago, but

she turned me down, so will you take me instead?"'
Unexpectedly Anne laughed, showing how enchanting
she could be when not overshadowed by grief and
remorse. 'I cannot help being diverted, though I ought
not to be. Poor Tom, the invincible bachelor whom
everyone has tried to catch—fancy his proposing to us
both, one after the other, and receiving two refusals. I
dare say it will have done him no harm.'

Olivia did try to laugh, but it was a poor effort.

Sister Thérèse came in with Madeleine, and Anne
tactfully faded away before Olivia had a chance to say
goodbye to her. Madeleine was no longer looking
frightened, and said she was sure she would like to stay
at the Convent for the time being. She would be able
to study French history and literature, do her share in
the kitchen and garden, and help the nuns with the fine
needlework which they sold in order to augment their
small income.

'That will exactly suit you.' Olivia turned to Sister
Thérèse. 'Madeleine won't have told you so herself,
but she is an exceptionally gifted embroideress.'

'Then we shall be able to make very good use of
her,' said Sister Thérèse, smiling. 'And now, if you
please, Miss Fenimore, Reverend Mother would be
glad to see you.'

Reverend Mother was a formidable French lady who
might have been a duchess if she had not set her mind
on higher things. But she was kind and sensible.

'That poor child is in need of a great deal of care and
guidance. I am very glad you have brought her to us.
There is a true desire for goodness there, I am sure. I
have written to Mrs Channing to assure her and Mr
Brooke that we are prepared to care for Madeleine in
any contingency.'

Reverend Mother handed a letter to Olivia, who now realised that, though she had brought Madeleine to Maygrove without any prior arrangement, Mrs Channing and Tom had known she would not be turned away. The nuns would do anything in their power for Tom, who was, surprisingly, their benefactor.

Olivia's mind was now in such a state of confusion that she was hardly able to take in everything Reverend Mother said. It was not until some time later that she understood what was meant by 'any contingency'. If Madeleine turned out to be pregnant, the nuns would cope with that situation too. At the moment it was simply a matter of saying goodbye to Madeleine, who hugged her gratefully and said she would write.

Olivia got into the carriage and was driven away.

CHAPTER EIGHTEEN

FOR the first few minutes Olivia sorted out her impressions of the Convent, thought of Madeleine in her new surroundings, of the unexpected meeting with Anne Laybourne, what a delightful and interesting creature she was, and how odd it seemed that she and Madeleine would be living under the same roof. Probably each would gain from the other's company.

But, when all these things had been considered rather incoherently, Olivia was forced to think about Tom. How could she have misread his character so completely? Yet how could she have done anything else?

He had been a rake in his younger days, for he had tempted Anne Laybourne to be unfaithful to her husband, put her marriage in jeopardy, and made her the centre of a half-hidden scandal that was still vividly remembered by those who knew of it. Painful though it was, Olivia had found no great difficulty in believing the story Louisa Woodvile had told her as they sat on a grassy bank among the ruins of Dalney Castle. Where she had gone wrong was in accepting the second report, which had come in a letter to her cousin Lizzie. How could she have been taken in by that? Considering what she knew of Tom's great kindness and generosity to so many different people, why hadn't her instinct told her that the heartless desertion of Anne Laybourne would have been totally alien to his character?

239

It was the old battle of the sexes, she supposed. The difficulty of men and women understanding each other's values. Men believed that when a pretty woman did not discourage them she was fair game, available for flirtation or dalliance. In revenge, women believed that when a man set out to charm them without serious intentions he was by definition a monster, capable of every other sort of villainy.

But I shouldn't have fallen into that trap, she thought despairingly, as she remembered long, unconventional talks with Tom, outside the narrow limits set by society for unmarried ladies and gentlemen who were not related to them. I suppose in spite of everything I never really learnt to trust him or myself. Such a degree of fascination always held a hint of danger.

So she had spoilt everything, and now it was all over, the hope and the hating, she ached with longing for what she had lost, and knew how passionately she could have loved Tom and how happy she could have been with him. She stared through the carriage window at the sad monochrome of the November land and sky. There was nothing to look forward to any more, but she did wish she could have told Tom how much she had come to value and admire him as a man, independent of all the deceptive charms of love and dalliance.

Could she write him a brief note to say she was sorry she had done him such an injustice, or would he misunderstand her motives and despise her like all the other girls who ran after him? Well, it hardly mattered, for he would soon be out of reach. He was only waiting to see the last of the wretched Lion, who was due to leave Parmouth today. So if she wrote her letter and sent it to the Vale at the latest possible moment, surely he would accept it as a straightforward apology, nothing more.

She spent the rest of the journey composing in her mind an awkward epistle which began stiffly, 'Dear Mr Brooke. . .' and then fell apart in disjointed phrases, which were either too formal, too servile, too full of excuses, or in most cases too lovesick and too revealing.

They had made the journey to Maygrove with one pair of horses, which had been rested during the hour she spent at the Convent. Coming home, the coachman had told her they would have to change at the Golden Fleece in Brantisford. She had not argued, knowing that the stage from Brantisford to Parmouth, though short, was thought to be a hard one on account of the hills. She did not want to stop at the Golden Fleece, which held a far too vivid memory of last summer and her first sight of Tom.

She went into the inn, however, passing under the board with its rather bucolic sheep coloured a bright cornfield-yellow. She was quite glad to drink a bowl of hot soup in a private parlour.

Five minutes later she had just stepped back into the carriage when a curricle came smartly round the corner from the direction of Parmouth, and she recognised Tom with his servant beside him and his groom perched up at the back and a good deal of baggage strapped on—plainly he was on his way to London, or to Cassondon, it didn't matter where. She would never see him again.

Tom of course recognised his own travelling chaise. His attention was fixed as though he was trying to see inside.

At that moment a child ran out from a doorway, a

woman screamed. Tom looked back at the road just in time and had to rein in sharply. The nearside leader reared, unbalancing the light body of the curricle violently sideways, and Tom was flung out on to the cobbles.

He lay there for a moment quite still. Then people began to shout and run about. The ostlers came out in a bunch to help Tom's groom control the frightened horses, the bawling child was picked up unhurt by his distracted mother, and Olivia stepped out of the carriage and reached Tom before anyone else.

His eyes were closed and for a dreadful moment she thought he was dead. Then she stooped and felt for his wrist, and the pulse was strong.

'We'll get him indoors, miss,' said the innkeeper, coming up beside her.

'Yes, and send for Dr Prowse, if you please.'

She knew this was the name of the leading physician in Brantisford, someone who knew more than a mere surgeon or apothecary.

The innkeeper and one of his servants carried Tom into the parlour where Olivia had drunk her soup, and laid him on a large settee. Tom's valet followed them in, badly shaken.

'My poor master, whatever shall we do?' he moaned.

'Fetch me a large glass of brandy,' said Tom loudly. He opened his eyes and his very blue gaze lighted on Olivia. 'What are you doing here?'

'I happened to be passing,' she said absurdly.

She felt somehow responsible for the accident, for she was sure Tom's attention had been distracted by the sight of the carriage. Perhaps he had been trying to see whether or not Madeleine had remained at the Convent.

He was frowning, trying to sort out recent events in his memory.

'I didn't hit that child, did I?'

No, they assured him, Mrs Larkin's young George was safe and sound.

'Good. Where's that brandy?'

'I don't think you ought to drink spirits, Mr Brooke,' said Olivia, rather primly. 'Not after a blow on the head.'

'Nonsense. I wasn't out above a minute.'

Tom pulled himself upwards on the settee and tried to get to his feet. He sat down again hastily.

'Devil take it, I think I've broken my ankle.'

The innkeeper had already sent someone for Dr Prowse, and the valet suggested that his master's boot should be cut off.

'Don't be a fool, I'm damned if I'll let anyone ruin these boots.'

Olivia said to the landlord, 'That was a very good strengthening bowl of broth I had just now. If there is any left, I think Mr Brooke might like it while we are waiting for the doctor.'

'I don't need a doctor!' exclaimed Tom, very much displeased. 'Have you all gone mad?'

'Someone will have to set your leg if you have really broken it,' Olivia pointed out, though in fact she was more anxious about the risk of a head injury. Tom did not answer, and when the reviving broth was carried in he consented to drink it and pronounced it tolerable.

'Though I don't require an audience,' he added, spoon in hand, as he gazed at the large number of people who had come to see how he was.

Taking the hint, they began to remove themselves. Olivia stayed behind. She had forgotten her recent heart-searching and her plunge into despair in her determination to hear what the doctor had to say, and if possible prevent Tom from getting hold of any brandy.

'I hope that delicate hint wasn't directed at me,' she said.

'Certainly not. I want to talk to you. I see no sign of Madeleine, so can I conclude that all was satisfactory at Maygrove?'

'Yes indeed. They were very kind and understanding, and I am sure they will take good care of her. She seemed quite happy to stay.'

'That's good. And you went into the house yourself? Who did you see?'

Olivia described her conversations with Sister Thérèse and Reverend Mother rather absently, for she was wondering how to approach the subject that overshadowed everything else. In the end she came straight out with it.

'I also met Lady Laybourne—I expect that is what you wanted to know. She came and talked to me.'

'I was afraid she would.'

'I don't know why you should be. She spoke of you in glowing terms.'

'I dare say. But I can guess what you made of her story, which must have sounded pretty disgraceful, however she glossed it over.'

'Oh, no!' exclaimed Olivia, surprised into glancing directly at him. He was staring straight ahead, his face set in rigid lines.

After a moment she said, 'It did not seem to me at all disgraceful. At least—I mean—I know that your connection with Lady Laybourne was wrong, but that happened a long time ago and it is not for me to judge.

Besides, I knew about it already. The only new thing I learnt today was that you did ask her to marry you after Sir Martin's death. And I am so very sorry that I did not understand before, and that I was so extremely disagreeable the day you came to—the day you called at Marine Cottage. I should never have believed those horrible things Lizzie was saying about you.'

'And you wanted me to marry Anne.'

Olivia could not think how to explain her contradictory feelings, so she said nothing.

'They told you how badly I treated her. Oh, yes, I did, even if I tried to make amends later. I seduced her when she was nineteen, not much older than Madeleine, and though she was a married woman I came between her and poor Laybourne, ruined their lives you might say, for they could have been happy together—though I only discovered that when I saw her in September. It came as a great shock. But none of this is any real excuse for the way I treated you. What can you have thought of me on the night of the concert? What game did you think I was playing? After all those weeks of advancing so carefully, trying to establish a real understanding between us, avoiding the artificial rigmarole that so often passes for courtship at a watering-place. Surely you must have known that I was on the point of asking you to marry me?'

'Yes. I did think that.'

'I see,' he said enigmatically, and then fell silent.

She was not at all sure what he saw.

'I treated you abominably,' he continued, 'rushing off without a word of explanation. It was a dastardly way to behave. Everything happened so quickly. Lion arrived to tell me that Martin Laybourne was dead, that he had disinherited Anne, and that her brother-in-

law was going to turn her out of the house without a
penny to live on. I had not even known that
Laybourne's illness was mortal. I had come to think of
him as one of those invalids who might live another
twenty years, like Frank Channing. I was horrified. If
Anne was in such deep trouble I knew I was responsible, and I knew what I ought to do.

'I had made her a kind of promise years ago—a
conditional promise, and she wouldn't have held me to
it. In the very last letter she wrote to me, when we
agreed to part, she said she hoped I should soon find a
wife I could be happy with. If I'd been already married,
or even engaged, two months ago, I could have done
nothing to protect her. It seemed an ominous stroke of
fate that Laybourne should die at that precise moment,
while I was still free to discharge what I regarded as a
moral obligation. I ought to have come and told you
the whole story then, but I hadn't the courage. I was
afraid my resolution would weaken. So I travelled
north with a heavy heart, only to find I was the last
person Anne wanted to see. A very unwelcome ghost
from the past. She seemed a good deal concerned in
case she had hurt my feelings, so I told her about you
and she wished me joy, which was a trifle premature. I
came back to Parmouth hoping to put things right, and
found I had walked into a hornets' nest. Well, it was
no more than I deserved.'

He stopped abruptly, and Olivia could not think of
anything to say. The room seemed cold, in spite of the
log fire glowing in its ashes. It was the cold of desolation. She looked at him but he would not look at her,
and she had no clue to what he was thinking. She
remembered how angry and resentful he had been
when she accused him of deserting Anne. Having

discovered her mistake, she felt he had been justified, but he was not angry now, or only with himself, poor Tom. She longed to help him but sensed that he did not want her help. Why not? If he still loved her——— But perhaps he had been disillusioned and disenchanted by her lack of faith, even if he did not blame her for it. Love was not ruled by logic.

He made a restless movement and she saw that he must be very uncomfortable, trying to find a position that suited his injured leg. She got up and fetched a cushion to prop under his knee.

'Is that better?'

'Yes, thank you,' he said distantly, as though she were a stranger. 'There is no need for you to stay here if you want to get home. You have seen how many people there are anxious to take care of me.'

Olivia winced inwardly. 'I am sorry if you find my presence disagreeable———'

'Disagreeable? Good God, no!' This had made him look at her. 'I am always delighted to have your company, my dear Olivia. There is no reason we should not go on being friends, as we were before. Just tell me this. Did you always mean to refuse me, even before you knew about Anne?'

Olivia could hardly believe her ears.

'I—I don't understand,' she faltered. 'Why should you think—how *could* you think———? You never asked me—that is, before you went away. . .'

'No,' he agreed, 'though I was conceited enough to imagine I could guess your answer. But when it turned out that you wanted me to marry Anne, what was I to conclude, except that I had joined the long line of your unsuccessful suitors?'

He tried to speak lightly, though it was not a great success.

'I didn't want you to marry her,' she protested, now thoroughly confused, 'or only because I felt you ought, and if you wouldn't—oh, dear, it is so difficult to explain.'

Tom, like Anne herself, seemed to find Olivia's attitude incomprehensible unless it was seen as some heroic act of renunciation. This upset Olivia, because she did not feel noble or self-sacrificing; she had seen the situation entirely in the terms of her own personal love.

'When I first heard about Anne,' she tried again, 'I took it for granted you were bound to marry her, and though that made me very unhappy I could not see you acting differently. It was only when I was told you had rejected her that I began to feel I had indeed lost you—that I had been breaking my heart over a man who never existed. In that sense I suppose I wanted you to marry her, more than I wanted you to leave her destitute and friendless. But I was stupid to doubt you, for I have come to understand how kind and generous you are, in spite of a few irregularities.'

'Is that how you describe my former way of life? A few irregularities! My dear girl, have you had a knock on the head too?'

'Don't laugh at me, Tom.' Her throat was choked with tears, which left her defenceless.

'I'm not laughing, love. Far from it.'

He reached out towards her. She was sitting on a low chair, quite close to the settee. She gripped his hand convulsively.

'Now we have sorted out the past,' he said, 'we can start again, but before I do, are you sure you will be able to trust me? I will promise to be faithful to you and do my best to make you happy, but there is no particular reason that I can see why you should believe me after such an exhibition of double-dealing and folly. But I still hope you can.'

She must have made some sort of assent, for his hand tightened over hers and she slid out of the chair and ended half sitting, half kneeling on the floor close against the settee with his arm around her. She felt him wince as he tried to heave himself up.

'Your poor ankle.'

'Never mind my ankle.' He kissed her, gently at first, and then long and hard. 'So will you marry me, my lovely Olivia?'

'Oh, Tom!'

'I hope, "Oh, Tom!" means yes, because I love you desperately and I don't think I can exist without you. My life has become a desert.'

'So has mine.'

They began to kiss again, breaking off every now and then to gaze and gaze in wonder and amazement. Scraps of conversation punctuated the kissing and the gazing.

'I made a terrible hash of my last proposal, didn't I? I know I sounded arrogant and patronising, any woman of sense must have refused me. I was in such a ferment. I knew I ought to tell you about Anne and that I ought to tell you first, but I thought I would soften your heart by making my intentions plain at the outset. So I walked into a trap of my own making, for of course you thought I never meant to tell you at all.'

'Poor Tom, what a hard time you had, trying to get yourself a wife and finding that no one would take you. That's what comes of leaving things so late.'

'Spitfire,' said her aged suitor amiably. I shall be thirty-three next birthday, in case you didn't know, and, in view of the ten years' difference between us, I hope to be treated with proper respect.'

'Very well, Mr Brooke.'

When he reverted to his unfortunate proposal, he was serious again.

'I was too mortified to speak to you the next time we met. Do you remember that rainy Sunday and all those umbrellas?'

'Yes, and that awful subscription ball. You stood about looking grand and then marched off to the card-room.'

'That was because I knew you wouldn't dance with me. You pretended you'd hurt your foot.'

'Only because there weren't enough men to go round before you arrived. So I thought I might as well sit down.'

'And let the other girls have all the partners. That was so like you, my darling.'

Tom was in the mood to see perfection even where it didn't exist. Very gratifying in a newly engaged man.

'It was that evening Lion first set eyes on Madeleine,' he added, frowning. 'Do you think, when he carried out his heartless campaign on her innocence, he thought he was following my example—that any man of the world would have done the same? It was what he implied, and I can't get the idea out of my head.'

'He's not such a fool,' she said briskly. 'We all know you have been a tremendous flirt, but you haven't left a trail of wronged maidens behind you wherever you went. Someone would have noticed. My aunt Hester hasn't accused you of that.'

Tom laughed. 'She's not going to like our engagement, is she? I hope I am in better standing with your uncle. I never could make out why they were convinced I was going to marry Hetty.'

Because Hetty herself was bewitched by her romantic illusions, thought Olivia, watching her dear love and deciding not to tell him the full scope of Hetty's infatuation—the boasting to her friends and the pathetic trip to Maygrove.

Tom's conscience had been sufficiently lacerated in the last few days, and with all his charm and guile there was an endearing absence of vanity.

She was curious enough to ask, 'What did you do to fascinate Hetty? Did you ever kiss her?'

'Certainly not. I make a point of never kissing unattached young ladies.'

'You kissed me. I don't mean the time on the beach. You were on the point of making me an offer and, owing to your lack of experience, you put the cart before the horse. I mean at Rosamond's Bower the day I turned the fountain on.'

'That was different. You weren't a sentimental goose like the others and you were on your mettle, daring me to try.'

Olivia was about to contradict him when it struck her that he was probably right, even though she had not realised it at the time. 'And besides,' he added, 'I was more than half in love with you already. I think I knew in my bones how it would end.'

'No, you didn't. You thought I was a hussy.'

'You are a hussy, my love. Look at the dance you led those Irish earls through their potato patches.'

'There was only one earl,' she protested.

'Only one? How paltry. I have been deceived.'

He had taken off her bonnet and was unwinding the

knot of smooth dark hair so that it fell over her
shoulders.

'I've always wanted to do that,' he remarked with
satisfaction.

'Now which of your bones have you broken this
time?' boomed the loud voice of the doctor as he flung
open the door.

Olivia scrambled to her feet. The doctor surveyed
them both with disapproval and addressed his patient.

'I was told you were on your deathbed, my dear sir,
but I see it's no such thing. Can you forgo your
favourite pastime long enough to let me examine you?'

'Oh, there you are, Doctor,' said Tom, trying to
appear nonchalant and dignified. 'This is Dr Prowse,
my dear, who has known me since I had the measles in
my grandmother's house at Maygrove when I was seven
years old. Miss Olivia Fenimore and I have just become
engaged.'

'And high time, I should think,' observed the doctor.
'Now what about this fall you've had?'

Olivia retired into the background and tried to put
up her hair without a comb or a looking-glass, while at
the same time carefully observing Dr Prowse, who
asked Tom a good many questions, felt the bruise on
his temple, and tested the sight first of one eye and
then the other. He seemed to her reassuringly
competent.

'Not much wrong there,' he said eventually. 'You've
been lucky. Now we'd better have that boot off.'

He produced a serviceable razor and paid no attention when Tom said it was criminal to spoil a good pair
of boots. Having slit the leather neatly down the seam,
the doctor decided the ankle was sprained, not broken,
and applied a cold compress to reduce the swelling.

'Where were you going when the accident happened—London? You won't want to make a long journey over bad roads at present, and you can hardly wish to stay here.'

'Of course not. I shall return to Parmouth.'

'Won't that be a trifle awkward?'

'Why should it be?' asked Tom, surprised.

Olivia realised what the doctor was thinking.

'Mr Brooke and I were not travelling together, sir,' she said demurely.

'Oh. Glad to hear it. I thought I'd stumbled on an elopement.'

'Nothing of the kind!' said Tom indignantly. 'Miss Fenimore just happened to be passing when I was stupid enough to fall out of my curricle.'

'He had to stop very suddenly when a child ran in front of his horses,' translated Olivia.

'And as for eloping,' added Tom, 'I should not dream of starting my married life in such an improper fashion. What do you take me for? No, on second thoughts, you had better not answer.'

The doctor begged pardon, glancing from one to the other. Then, as though taking in Olivia's name for the first time, he exclaimed, 'Fenimore! Good God, you must be James's niece. So you are going to take on this unmanageable fellow. I hope you may be happy.'

'He needn't have sounded so doubtful,' complained Tom, when the doctor had gone. They both began to laugh. 'I suppose it will take some time to convince everyone that I am a reformed character.'

'You've convinced me, and that is all that matters,' Olivia insisted.

'I'm glad to hear it, my love, for it so happens that

I'm just about to ask you to do something very shocking.'

'What can you mean?'

'I've smashed up my curricle and, since we shall be travelling in the same direction, it seems reasonable that we should both make use of the chaise—provided you are willing to drive to Parmouth with me, unchaperoned, in a closed carriage?'

He challenged her with a glance full of mockery and delight, for he already knew how willing she would be.

They had come full circle to the place where they had first met, only five months ago, yet they felt as though they had packed into it a lifetime of experience.

The horses were ordered round, and Tom assisted the short distance to the front door, grumbling at his own incompetence.

He and Olivia were shut into the well-sprung carriage, with a stool and two pillows to support his injured leg. The world outside was cold and drear, a poor exchange for the brilliance of midsummer, but they did not notice or care. They did not even look out of the windows.